Morel Of The Story

ᴬ Tiger Lily's Café® Mystery

By Kathleen Thompson

Kathleen Thompson

Morel Of The Story

Volume 11

ᴬ Tiger Lily's Café® Mystery

By Kathleen Thompson

ISBN-13: 978-1-7320166-0-6

ISBN-10: 1-7320166-0-7

© Registration # TX 8-648-752

Library of Congress Control Number: 2018910785

Kathleen Thompson

A List of Tiger Lily's Café® Mystery Series Books:

This cozy mystery series has everything you seek: an eclectic cast of characters, a mystery or two, and diligent detectives on duty. The detectives just happen to be feline.

Tiger Lily's Café is set in a Midwestern town nestled into the coast of a Great Lake. The setting itself acts as a character, bringing the reader into the sights, sounds and smells of the small resort community of Chelsea.

Read the series in order, or read any book alone. While characters grown and change, each volume stands alone with a clear beginning and a clear end.

- Turtle Soup (2014)
- Boo! (2015)
- Phishing (2015)
- Holiday (2016)
- A Rock And A Hard Place (2016)
- Splash (2016)
- Chasing A Butterfly (2017)
- Pumpkin Squash (2017)
- Snowblind (2017)
- Hearts On Fire (2018)
- Morel Of The Story (2018)
- Dragon Fire (2019)
- Beach Bunnies (2020)
- Shipwreck (2020)

Kathleen Thompson

Cast of Characters

Humans

Annie Mack, with the help of her "kids" and a talented staff, owns and manages a bed and breakfast, a cafe and other businesses on the south side of The Avenue. She has lived in Chelsea for only a few years, but her ancestral roots to the town date to the Civil War era.

Annie's SASHET Rainbow: (sa SHAY) a model that assigns color to each core feeling. **S**adness is blue; **A**nger red; **S**care green; **H**appiness yellow; **E**xcitement orange; and **T**enderness purple.

For more information, visit Liberation Psychotherapy: www.libpsych.com/articles/sashet/sashet.html.

Austin and Angela live in another state. They are the parents of Chris and have not been supportive of his career in the Coast Guard or his choice of a woman. Annie.

Ben and JoJo are college students. They work part-time all over town, including most of Annie's businesses.

Boone is the person to call if you need anything: mowing, snow removal, landscaping, maintenance, preventative maintenance, and just about anything else. He is married to **Harriet (Hilly),** who provides business cleaning services. His sons **Daryl** and **Donny** work for him. Their roots are in rural Appalachia, and they are so much more than people think.

Brian and Janet Thomas own the Chateau Simon Winery in rural Chelsea. Their biggest competition is the Blue Bottle Winery. Jesus and Minnie are their silent partners.

Candice is the head waitress at Mo's Tap. A native of Chelsea, her long, thick, dark hair is the envy of most women who meet her. She is married to George.

Carlos is the manager and baker at Mr. Bean's Confectionary. He is a citizen of the US but was originally from Mexico. He supports his mother and younger sisters, who still live there. He is married to Isabel.

Cheryl inherited The Marina from her parents. It's a small deep water marina with basic amenities. Cheryl is married to Ray. She has known Annie since they were children.

Chris is Annie's special friend. They have committed to a permanent relationship that doesn't necessarily include marriage. He is the Officer in Charge of the Coast Guard Station. His stress relieving hobby is art. His watercolors and sketches – in charcoal, pencil and pastel – are sold for charity.

Clara owns the flower and gift shop, Bloomin' Crazy. She is a citizen of the US, originally from Haiti, and has an ebullient personality. She keeps The Avenue decorated with fresh and silk flowers year-round.

Collette is Henrie's special friend. She is a civil attorney in a small city a short distance from Chelsea.

Daniela is a former professional baker from Mexico. She has been a mother figure to Isabel, who is married to Carlos. She and her adult daughters, **Rosa** and **Valeria**, now live in Chelsea

Diana is the chief instructor at L'Socks' Virasana (Veer AHS ana). She is Mem's daughter. Diana left home right after high school and did not speak to her mother until her return ten years later. Their relationship, while tenuous, continues to grow stronger.

Felicity is the chef at Tiger Lily's Café. She is young, perky and extremely talented in the kitchen. She manages the Café, the upstairs catering facility and outside catering operations.

Frank owns an antique shop, Antiques On Main. He and Mem are in a relationship.

Gema owns Gema's Creations. She makes and sells unique jewelry pieces from a space in the front corner of Antiques On Main.

George is the bartender and manager of Mo's Tap. He is a top-notch bartender and can be counted on to keep confidences. He is a volunteer with the local Coast Guard and is married to Candice.

Georgia is the head cook at Mo's Tap. Her father, **Fred Calendar**, comes to town on occasion to see her and her daughter Frederica **(Little Fred)**.

Geraldine has turned a corner and is no longer a thorn in Annie's side. She has developed community spirit. Somehow. It's a mystery…. **Everett** is her on-again-off-again husband.

Ginger is the daughter of Pete, the Chief of Police, and Janet. She works part-time at L'Socks' Virasana. Because she moved to town as a teen (when her father retired from the Marine Corps), and because she is one of the few African American teens in town, she sometimes feels like an outsider.

Greg is a progressive realtor in Chelsea. His goal is to get the right property to the right owner, always moving Chelsea forward.

Gwen is Annie's accountant. A motherly figure, her financial acumen is hidden from all but those lucky enough to have her in their corner.

Hank is a former member of the Town Council. He opposes Annie in every way.

Harry is the regular driver for the rental company used almost exclusively by folks on The Avenue.

Henrie manages the KaliKo Inn in an elegant manner. He does not invite confidences and speaks little about himself. Always formal in tone, people have difficulty pegging his accent. Is it French? Cameroon? Rwandan?

Holly and Jolly, twins, own DoubleGood, an electronics and hardware store. Holly lives in a wheelchair. Natives of Chelsea, they used to hate the names given them by their parents. Now, they enjoy the novelty of it.

Ian is a childhood friend of George. He coordinates local sporting and community events. He is light-hearted and fancy-free, especially for a loan officer at a local bank.

Isabel is married to Carlos. She is attending classes to become a citizen. She works in the kitchen at Mo's Tap.

Janet is Pete's wife. She spent twenty years as a Marine officer's wife. She traveled the world and is now living in Chelsea. She is an outsider, not having grown up here like Pete. She is the ultimate community volunteer.

Jennifer and Marie, sisters and nurse practitioners, own The Drug Store and The Clinic. Folks call the sisters before calling nine-one-one. Chelsea natives, they know everyone. And their secrets.

Jenny is an attorney who focuses on family law. She enjoys taking on cases that will right an injustice. She is always ready to engage in battle with those who don't believe a woman, much less a woman of color, can dance with the big boys.

Jerry learned how to make candy in a minimum security federal prison. He was not an employee. Jerry works hard to overcome his shyness, particularly around women.

Jet is from Puerto Rico. He moved in with Holly and Jolly, taking up residence with Holly. He works at Sassy P's Wine & Cheese.

Jerry is the candy maker at Mr. Bean's Confectionary. He learned how to make candy in a minimum security federal prison. He was not an employee.

Jesus manages Sassy P's Wine & Cheese and also selects the wines. His family, famous vintners in the Napa Valley, owned, farmed and made wine for generations before California became a part of the United States.

Joan is a member of the Town Council. She opposes Hank in every way. Clara's pet name for her is "Joan of Chelsea."

Juanita is a reporter for the local newspaper. As every reporter on every small town paper, she also sells ads, develops and places the ads, does photography and…reports.

Justin is a former bully boy who now works for Boone. Justin is making a break from his former bad partners and misplaced energy. He attends community college part-time.

Laila owns Babar Foods. A traditional Pakistani, she is raising her children without the assistance of a husband. Her children are **James, Ava** and **Carl**, who lives with Autism.

Marco is a police officer in Chelsea. He is "second in command" because he was the only officer that didn't go off-kilter during a hostage situation. Marco prides himself on being one-hundred-percent-Italian-American.

Martha used to own a bed and breakfast. The cottage was renovated to add an apartment suite, now occupied by Georgia and Little Fred. Martha is retired and enjoys spending time at the Inn.

Mem owns the health food store and cyber café, CyberHealth. Her wisdom is reassuring to everyone, including her daughter, Diana. She teaches the safe use of social media to all ages and has equipment and technology that is helpful to the small-town police department.

Minnie chooses perfect cheeses to accompany the rotating wine selections at Sassy P's Wine & Cheese. She comes from several generations of cheese makers in Wisconsin.

Nancy and Sam are Annie's mother and step-father. They have been married since Annie was a child. They moved to Chelsea to be closer to Annie.

Pete is a native of Chelsea. He retired from the Marine Corps and is now the Chief of Police. Like Annie, his ancestors arrived in the Civil War era. His, however, came up via the Underground Railroad. He and his wife Janet have three children, the eldest of whom is Ginger. Clarice and Tamara are in high school and junior high.

Ramon is Clara's boyfriend. A Jamaican by ancestry, he plays saxophone with a jazz fusion band called Bergamasco (after the breed of his dog). He and Clara work hard to maintain their mostly long-distance relationship.

Ray owns and operates The Escape, a yacht fashioned into a cruiser for fishing, diving and pleasure. He is married to Cheryl; Chris is his best friend.

Teresa is a newcomer to the area. She came to this community to serve. She pastors a small church, Soul's Harbor, and pastors the community through her outreach.

Terrence and Jerald Timmer-Schmidt are recent arrivals to Chelsea. Terrence is a heart surgeon; Jerald is a psychiatrist. They opened a medical office building in town.

Trudie is the barista at Tiger Lily's Café. She is from Jamaica and ended up in Chelsea when a former boyfriend dumped her at the campground. Felicity saved her, and they have been the best of friends ever since.

WQVX Channel Two. "The Lake Region's good news station." The "ace onsite reporter" is **Dan Tapper**. **Felix** does weather.

Annie's Cats

Annie has seven cats. Most people would call them "rescue kitties." From Annie's perspective, each of them rescued her.

Tiger Lily is a beautiful tabby cat with soft green eyes. She is the titular manager of Tiger Lily's Café, the main gathering place for Chelsea. She is generally calm and logical.

Little Socks is a bright-eyed black cat with white socks. She has a commanding personality and is small and sneaky enough to serve as a cat burglar. She spends time at the yoga studio, L'Socks' Virasana (Veer AHS ana).

Kali, Ko and Mo are litter mates. They shared a secret language as kittens; Kali and Ko now speak "cat," but Mo still speaks "secret." Kali and Ko can be found at the KaliKo Inn, a lakeside bed and breakfast. Mo spends time at Mo's Tap, an upscale blues bar.

Sassy Pants is aptly named; it's difficult to keep this little girl's attention. She is overly sensitive and will react out of emotion instead of reason. She entertains at Sassy P's Wine & Cheese.

Mr. Bean is the baby of the family and is mostly gray with traces of tiger. He has two speeds: fast and love me.

Other Companions

Brown Mousie lives in the long building and roams from the Café to the Wine & Cheese shop. He stays primarily at Sassy P's.

Claire is a blue point Himalayan cat whose human is Frank. She's beautiful and loves people. She is stand-offish with other cats.

Cyril is an English setter whose human is Pete, the Chief of Police. Cyril is friendly and calm. He is an excellent hunter.

Daryll is a multi-colored tabby cat with an air of perpetual confusion. His original human was the manager of the state park. Following his untimely death, Daryll was rescued by Tiger Lily and eventually went to live with Martha.

Fiamma is a Bergamasco. Dreadlocks cover her face. In fact, her entire body is covered with a combination of long dreadlocks and mats of hair. She is an outrageous flirt. Her human is Ramon.

Honey Bear is a large, golden, long-haired mutt of a cat who believes it is his perfect right to be anywhere. Other cats hate him. His human is Annie's mother, Nancy.

Jock is a Portuguese water dog whose human is Ray, the captain of The Escape. Jock is spirited and affectionate; he loves children.

Moriah is a dilute calico cat with long hair and a lioness mane. She is "fluffy" all over, with a sexy little waddle. Clara is her fur-ever human.

Oscar McMurphy was a stray, named Scaredy Cat by Annie's cats. Despite the name, she is a girl who now lives with Holly and Jolly. She claims Holly as her very own. She is often in and out of the Inn and other places on The Avenue with her brother, Simon Finnegan.

Simon Finnegan was a stray, named Fat Cat by Annie's cats, who now lives with Holly and Jolly. He claims Jolly to be his mom. He is often in and out of the Inn and other places on The Avenue with his sister, Oscar McMurphy.

Simon is a famous local winery cat. He lives at Chateau Simon Winery. His humans are Brian and Janet Thomas. He is a tuxedo cat with a wicked white stripe from his nose to the middle of his eyes.

Sis is a dark gray giant schnauzer. Tiger Lily rescued her during a snow storm. Together, the kids introduced her to Chris, who is now her human.

Speckles is a tortoise shell cat, named for her orange speckles. She belongs to Georgia and is Little Fred's chief nanny.

Tillie came to live on The Avenue with her dreadful family from England. She is a Jack Russell Terrier and now lives with Carlos and Isabel above the Confectionary. She has free run of The Avenue, including the Inn. She is small enough to squeeze in and out of the cat doors.

Guests at the Inn

Guests from Perdition: Jim and **Connie** and their children, **Clarke** aged seventeen, **Brooke** aged sixteen, **Marty**, aged fourteen, and, **Cassie** aged eleven. Jim and Connie have come for a break, and have let their children roam all of Chelsea without supervision.

Mitch and **Livia** are newlyweds on their honeymoon.

Louis (LOO ee) is visiting from Paris. He is scouting lakefront property for an upscale resort.

Lavender Lake

Dennis is the grounds manager of the campground where Annie and Chris are vacationing, Lavender Lake.

Kyle and **Dani** are millennials, moving from one region of the country to another as they make a living online.

John and **Lucy Hunt** are an older couple, retired, vacationing from the east coast.

Sondra Tate is the Sheriff who covers Lavender Lake.

Stan Graff is the Chief Deputy of Lavender Lake. He wants to be the Sheriff.

Christine Himes is a detective with the Sheriff's Department of Lavender Lake.

Jay Kranski is an attorney in Lavender Lake and an associate of Annie's attorney, Jenny.

Cameroon

Maria Masilla, or **Grand-mère**, is Henrie's maternal grandmother.

Bertrand drives a taxi and is connected to Boco Haram.

Yannick is the manager of the hotel in Maroua, Cameroon, where Henrie and Collette have been staying.

Mr. Jones. "You may call me Mr. Jones." He works for the United States Embassy in Cameroon.

1: Chelsea

George turned off the alarm with a groan. With one eye open, he looked at the time. Five a.m. He groaned again, then remembered his promise to Candice. He would not wake her this morning. Not as he had for the last three.

He took a deep breath and rolled out of bed as quietly as he could. Standing in the shower, he tried to think. What day was this? Sunday? No. Monday. If he could get through this day, there were only three more. Then life would return to normal.

As if.

He had often envied Henrie and the position he assumed had been much easier than his own. As manager and bartender of Mo's Tap, George had long days, starting around ten in the morning and ending sometime after midnight, later on weekends.

He had to admit that as the years rolled on, he delegated closing duties to others more often than not, but his days were still long. He had assumed Henrie, the manager of the Inn, started at breakfast and was relieved of his duties by mid-afternoon.

When Annie, who owned the Inn, the bar, and every other business on this side of The Avenue, had asked George to cover for Henrie, he had quickly agreed.

Too quickly.

Henrie would return from his two-week vacation on Thursday. The first week – for George – had been fairly simple. He went to the Inn a few times to assist Annie and learn the routine. Unfortunately, Annie had been gone since last Thursday, and George was on his own.

Almost.

JoJo, a college student who worked for several of Annie's businesses part-time, slept in and was onsite for overnight emergencies. She was up early in the morning to start breakfast. She left during the day to attend classes and returned in the evening.

Hilly, who kept the Inn sparkling, was there every weekday. To help George, she made sure the guests had an afternoon snack before leaving. She indicated a willingness to come during the weekend if he needed her, but George told her not to worry.

What a mistake.

George didn't want to admit defeat and refused to call her back this past weekend.

Well, it was Monday now. He had made it through the weekend – barely – but certainly they were on the downhill slide now.

At least the guests-from-perdition would leave Wednesday. He and Hilly could straighten the Inn before Henrie returned, and maybe they could pretend everything had gone smoothly.

George thought through the last three days, trying to sharpen the blurry edges. The guests-from-perdition arrived Friday evening, early enough to order dinner-to-go from the winery, charged, of course, to their Inn reservation. George left, believing things to be well in hand. Then JoJo called.

The other guests had complained about loud music coming from the second floor, and she had been unable to get the youth of the family to cooperate. The parents had been uncooperative as well. George assured JoJo he would take care of the issue first thing Saturday morning.

On Saturday, George walked through the Inn picking up books, magazines, movies, video games, remote controls, dishes, half-filled glasses, food dropped on the floor, and clothes. He stood still more than once, so as not to be run over, as the teen and pre-teen demons raced into and out of the Inn.

He tried to talk to the parents about menial issues, such as asking their kids to use coasters on the wooden furniture, to pick up after themselves, to turn down the music in their bedrooms at night. The parents zoned out.

At one point, he corralled the youth long enough to lecture them about Inn policies and courtesy to other guests. In response, he received blank looks, eye rolls, muffled curses and shrugged shoulders.

Saturday night, JoJo called again. George stormed over and up to the second floor. He pounded on doors and demanded the music be turned down. When it was not, he pounded on the door of the parents and demanded they do something about it. The father had come into the hallway and yelled, "No allowance for a month if you don't turn it down!"

The volume – music from three different genres from three different rooms, each turned up to drown out the others – went down a bit. George stared at the father for a while until the father knocked on each door. George heard,

"Your allowance is docked for one week. Turn it down and keep it down or it's gone for a month."

Eventually, the hallway quieted to a low rumble.

George repeated the same steps Sunday. He also took phone calls and emails from shop owners across The Avenue. Each had a list of items pilfered from their places of business the day before.

Clara, from the flower and gift shop, was the last to call. George had a special affinity for Clara. She had the same devil-may-care attitude as he, but she also had insight into the human soul. She realized his frustration. She came to the Inn and walked him through Henrie's solution to that kind of problem. She called it "that Henrie thing."

George also had to spend quality time with JoJo. The demons were rude at the breakfast buffet. They were sloppy, greedy and ungrateful. JoJo took it personally. Well, she was young. George did what he could to prop her up.

He realized the water had gone cold. How long had he been standing here? He jumped out of the shower, looking at the clock as he dried off. It was nearly five thirty. So much for that run on the beach. It would have to wait.

The problem was that Annie had planned a vacation without speaking to Henrie. Actually, it was Annie's friend, Chris, who put a deposit on a hard-to-rent cabin. When Henrie mentioned his desire to go to Africa, Chris was unable to change the dates. Annie and Henrie decided that certainly, they could find someone to cover.

They found their sucker in George.

Never again.

This was Chelsea, a small resort town on the sunset side of a Great Lake. Sunset Avenue, known as The Avenue by locals, was a long city block, starting at the town circle and ending at an expanse of sand and public parking on the edge of the lake.

The KaliKo Inn, the largest and most popular bed and breakfast in town, sat at the corner of The Avenue and the lake. Annie, who owned the Inn, also owned the two story brick building that ran from the Inn to the town circle. That building housed several business, all named for Annie's cats.

The cats went to "work" every day. They were as well known around town as the humans who lived and worked there. While each business had human managers and staff, the cats took management of their respective places seriously.

The Inn was named for Kali and Ko, dilute calico cats. They were big girls, pretty, soft, and scared of almost everything. They weren't scared of their guests, though. They took their responsibilities for the comfort of each and every guest seriously. Unless they were in the carriage house. They didn't go into the carriage house unless they had to. That was too far from their safety zone.

In the main house, they performed admirably. They assisted as each guest was welcomed, followed or led Henrie as he gave the initial guest tour, sniffed and left love hairs on every piece of luggage, and jumped onto furniture as Henrie described the amenities of the room.

They followed Hilly into the rooms to assure she had cleaned them properly. They checked the truffles left on the bedside every afternoon. If any were in question, they took extra time to taste them. Just to check. One couldn't be too careful.

The first business in the two-story building, starting from the Inn, was Sassy P's Wine & Cheese. Sassy Pants, the business namesake, was as scattered of mind as she was of color. Her eyes, generally unfocused, tried to catch everything going on around her. Sometimes, she succeeded. She had a good friend at Sassy P's, Brown Mousie. Brown Mousie appeared one rainy day and had turned out to be a useful spy.

When not visiting with her friend, Sassy Pants chased corks tossed on the floor, or she jumped to the bar or to a table to present her tummy for rubs. Her manager, Jesus, and his helper, Minnie, did little to reign her in.

The next business was Mr. Bean's Confectionary, a bakery and chocolate shop. Mr. Bean was the youngest of Annie's family. He was a strong gray kitten with two speeds: fast and love me.

His favorite thing in the whole world was to dance in the window to bring customers into the Confectionary. Recently, he had to share that honor with a Jack Russell terrier, Tillie, who now lived with Carlos, the manager, and his wife Isabel. After a tumultuous start, Mr. Bean and Tillie figured out how to share the duty.

Mr. Bean had another favorite thing in the whole world. He loved to dance for Carlos, particularly when Carlos would stop and hold his hands to whirl him around the room in a tango or a minuet.

Mr. Bean was the master truffle taster. Truth be known, he passed his wisdom to Kali and Ko, assisting often in the evening duties of truffle testing at the Inn. Jerry, the candy maker, was known to make kitty-sized truffles made of cat friendly substances, like carob instead of chocolate. Jerry was generally quick to point out that Mr. Bean was not spoiled. No, he was not. Never. Not ever.

The next business was Mo's Tap, a blues bar, named for the long-haired litter mate of Kali and Ko. Mo was a beautiful cat who used his sexiness to great advantage.

Mo helped George at the bar by supervising the cleanliness of the glasses. Sometimes, he sat at the computer to help with inventory. He loved the online manager meetings Annie held once a week. That gave him the opportunity to sit in front of the monitor – typically in front of George's face – and show his beautiful self to all the managers on The Avenue.

He could be found in the arms of any human in the bar, male or female. He had two particular skills. One was to calm the overt urges of lovers. If one's hands were busy with Mo, then one would not act in an unseemly manner in public with another human. Another skill was to sooth the broken hearted. Again, if one's hands were busy with Mo, then how could one miss a lost lover?

Mo loved to dance around the candles that were lit every evening on the tables. For this reason, Candice, George's wife and the floor manager, made sure Mo left for home before they were lit. Or she grabbed him and stamped out smoke or flames emanating from his handsome butt, then sent him home.

Little Socks, Annie's alpha cat, was also the smallest. A tuxedo, she spent her days at L'Socks' Virasana, a yoga studio. She could generally be found napping on one of the black cushions in the windows, curled so that none of her white spots were visible.

Other times, she could be found on the floor, performing yoga exercises with her guests. On occasion, she would deign to exhibit her signature yoga move, the Lessiver Mon Derriere, or for those who can't handle a foreign language, the Wash My Behind. It was a move few humans could duplicate.

Little Socks did not engage in frivolities with the customers like her siblings. Her queenly bearing – some people said she was aloof – kept most humans in their place. She had special feelings for some, like Clara, who allowed her to pick out a special flower on occasion, and Ray, who saved her after she had been kidnapped. Otherwise, she had little need for human affection.

Last but not least, the business at the corner of Sunset Avenue and Main Street, Tiger Lily's Café, was the gathering place for locals and tourists alike. Here, gossip could be found and the problems of the world solved, all monitored by the gray and brown tabby who sat at the hostess stand.

Tiger Lily greeted customers both upon entering and leaving. She visited at table with her friends and with tourists. Each table was fitted with platforms that could allow her access to the table without getting on top of it. She was often seen on a platform, particularly at the table of tourists, pointing out menu items they might enjoy.

More often than not, the tourists agreed with her selections and left satisfied.

Tiger Lily managed Felicity, the chef, and Trudie, the barista, as well as all of the servers. She made sure the catering business flourished by checking out meals as they were packaged, and helped taste test the day's specials.

Tiger Lily appreciated Felicity. Certainly, Felicity's vibrant, eclectic menu had something to do with the Café's success, but Tiger Lily was sure people came to see her.

Because this was the town's best place for gossip, Tiger Lily was the best informed cat in all of Chelsea. She relished her role and sometimes had to hold herself back from lording it over her siblings.

This was Annie's world. But Annie was on vacation.

Not George. He was here. In Perdition.

George finished dressing, leaned over Candice to kiss her on the forehead, and left for the Inn.

Ray's yacht-for-hire, The Escape, was almost ready to go. The boating season in the Great Lakes was short. Mid-April was the cusp of the season. His calendar was nearly filled starting next week, but this week, he had only one customer.

One man, in town from France, wanted to tour the coastline, both up and down, for two or three days. The trips would be unscripted. He had a few planned stops, but otherwise, the man would tell Ray where to pull in so he could have a closer look.

The man was a scout for a French real estate developer. They planned to build an upscale resort that would be large enough for an eighteen-hole golf course, an Olympic-sized swimming pool, tennis, pickle ball and racquetball courts, a high-rise hotel, an area for private cabins, and two or three restaurants.

Ray did not want to see this kind of growth come to the small resort town he had come to love. He met Cheryl, a Chelsea native and now his wife, and moved to town when he retired from the Navy. He bought and renovated The Escape and docked it at The Marina, which belonged to Cheryl.

Even given the prospect of the hated resort, Ray was anxious to get on the water. He loved the water. Didn't know what he would do if he couldn't be on big water. Hated the long months of relative inactivity when it came to hiring out The Escape.

As he walked down the dock, he spoke to Jock, a black Portuguese water dog and Ray's best friend and constant companion. "I hope he finds something a few hours away."

Jock yipped in approval.

"A resort would change everything here. We're big enough as it is."

Jock yipped, again in approval.

"I'll have to ask George about this guy. He's staying at the Inn. Maybe George is growing a sixth sense like Henrie. Do you think?"

Jock yipped, this time in disapproval. Ray sensed the difference.

"Nah, I don't think so, either. But I can always ask. No harm getting as much information as possible, especially if someone is going to come in and junk up the coastline."

Jock didn't have time to answer. He jumped onto The Escape and looked back, as if to say, *"Come on. Day's a-wastin'!"*

Jim and Connie looked at one another across the small table. They had the front room of the KaliKo Inn, the room facing The Avenue. They made a habit of rising early to make coffee in the room. They sat on the deck, enjoyed their coffee at the small deck set, and watched the resort town of Chelsea come to life. Cars filled the street, and foot traffic streamed in and out of the bakery and the café up the street. The tea shop across The Avenue also had early morning customers. Walkers moved from the shopping district down to the beach and out to the lighthouse.

Men, women and children with fishing gear were already on the jetty long before Jim and Connie were out. Some were already on their way back, headed to work or school or…whatever.

Jim and Connie were on vacation. They enjoyed their long mornings on the deck, all thoughts of work and family forgotten. They could even pretend their four obnoxious children were not sleeping in other rooms in this very Inn.

They took a vacation once a year. Their typical destination was a smaller town with a bed and breakfast to handle their room requirements. They wanted a B&B for the inclusive breakfast and to add a measure of safety for the children. The generally unsupervised children.

An added bonus for this B&B was that as long as they stayed on The Avenue, the children could charge meals and other incidentals. Jim and Connie did not have to be disturbed for any reason.

Generally, the family required all of the rooms. The KaliKo Inn was larger than most, but still, only one additional room was in the house proper. Another room in the carriage house was being used as well. With only two other reservations, the children were in a relatively safe environment.

The family never returned to the same B&B. They never returned to the same town. They were discouraged from doing so.

One week with this family was one week too many.

They knew it. But they loved being able to take one week every year – just one week – to pretend their lifestyle was something other than what it was.

They saw a water balloon fly from the lake side of the Inn to the median of The Avenue. It landed on the head of a woman carrying a rod and a tackle box.

With pride, Jim said, "That Clarke sure has an arm. He'll get a baseball scholarship for sure."

JoJo pulled the breakfast skillet out of the oven. It had asparagus, onions, cremini mushrooms and new potatoes, and it smelled like heaven. She turned back to deal with the French toast casserole, fragrant with cinnamon, honey and peaches. She was learning to cook by watching Henrie; his vacation allowed her to go solo for the first time.

JoJo thought she might like running an Inn of her own someday, but not now. Now, she missed Henrie. Henrie would have put this family in its place days ago. JoJo didn't know how to do that. Neither did George.

Speaking of the devil, in he walked.

"Morning, JoJo. Sorry I'm late. I fell asleep in the shower."

JoJo thought about that for a few seconds before she answered. "Um, okay. Can you help with the bacon?"

"Sure."

George pulled bacon, ham and link sausage from the refrigerator and carried it to the stove. JoJo had already pulled out a large skillet and serving platters. Actually, she had pre-cooked the meats the night before, too. George had only to heat and serve them.

They talked, she at the large ovens on one side of the kitchen and he at the range on the other, backs to one another. George said, "I'm pretty sure Henrie doesn't have to pre-cook anything, but it's sure easier when you do that. Thanks. What do I need to do today?"

JoJo took time to pour a cup of coffee for George before she answered. As she went to another oven to remove fresh breads, she said, "I think we're set. The newlyweds want to use the car today."

George pulled the faces of the newlyweds from his memory banks before answering. "They seemed nice when they checked in. Nice, but, you know. Newlyweds. Nervous, kind of. Did they say where they were going?"

"No, just touring the coastline, doing some shopping. He asked for suggestions for a five-star restaurant."

George stopped what he was doing and turned to JoJo. Her back was still to him. "Does he seem like the kind of guy that can afford a five-star meal?"

JoJo turned to look at George. "No, but she seems like a five-star kind of woman."

George nodded, pensive. He turned back to the bacon. "They're going to have a hard time staying out of debt."

Someone banged on the kitchen door. George sighed, and his chin dropped to his chest. "How much do you want to bet this is another complaint?"

"No bet." JoJo opened the door to an irate woman holding a fishing rod in one hand and a busted balloon in the other. Her head was wet, and she sported a bright red "O" on her forehead.

2: Lavender Lake

Annie sat on the front porch of the cabin, her hands wrapped around a cup of steaming tea. She breathed in the fresh, country air as she looked over the lake. A small lake. She could see the other side, unlike the lake she saw every other day of her life, where all she could see on the other side was the horizon.

A mist rose, blurring – ever so briefly – the glow from the rising sun. It was a cool April day, temperature in the mid-sixties and a little cloudy.

Spring was her second favorite season, behind fall. She liked snow in winter and heat in summer, but she loved the cool, fresh air of fall and spring.

She sipped ginger peach tea and turned her head to the right and toward the woods. The cats were just this side of the thick trees. Seven cats, all in hunter stance. Tails twitched in unison. They had something in their sights.

Tiger Lily seemed to sense Annie's gaze. She broke her stare into the trees to look back, blinked once, and resumed the hunt.

Behind her, Annie could hear Chris in the cabin's kitchen. She heard the tea kettle whistle, stop. Dishes clattered, and she wondered what he would make for breakfast.

They had been together – alone, except for the cats and Sis, the giant schnauzer – for several days. Since Thursday. Briefly, Annie wondered what day it was, but she realized she didn't have to care.

Chris had set his phone alarm to alert them the day before they had to leave. That would give them time to take a final boat ride around the lake, go for a long walk around the grounds, pack their bags, and decide what to do for their last supper. Until then, she didn't have to know what day it was.

Until then, she could continue to enjoy meals prepared by Chris. She hadn't known what a creative genius he was in the kitchen. No wonder Sis loved her new home.

Speaking of Sis, she wondered where the big dog was. Maybe she was inside with Chris. Hearing another sound, she looked further to her right. A man walked slowly in the direction of the cabin. On the edge of the woods, he peered into the bushes and brambles as he walked. Every now and then, he set a small post into the ground, the kind of post used by utility companies to mark buried lines. Sis followed him, sniffing at the ground wherever a post went in.

The man stopped when he reached the cats. They now looked at him instead of their invisible prey. Sis wandered to the edge of the group and sat next to Little Socks.

The man looked around, saw Annie and waved.

She hated to break the silence of the morning, so she stood and walked over to him. She whispered, "Morning, Dennis. What's up?"

Dennis whispered back. "It's spring. Time for babies. I'm marking likely places for rabbit warrens so I won't mow close to them."

"Is that what the cats are stalking?"

"That, or just about anything. There's at least one litter of fox cubs in there, and I've seen two young raccoons. Probably baby opossums, too."

Annie continued to whisper, "Last night, I saw three young deer. It's that time of year. I love seeing the babies."

Dennis nodded. "This is the best time of year. The hummingbirds and orioles will be here by next week, and their babies will be coming on."

Annie and Chris met Dennis their first day at the small campground. He managed the grounds for the owner, which meant that he did everything from landscape architecture to dock and boat repair.

The campground, Lavender Lake, was situated around a man-made lake and consisted of several upscale cabins, each with a private dock and a small fishing boat with an outboard motor and oars. Wooded areas wound around the grounds, maintaining the privacy of each cabin.

Annie had given her cats strict instructions to stay out of the woods and within eyesight of the cabin. At night, with the danger of predatory animals, the doors, screened, were firmly latched. Annie's cats were urban. They wouldn't be safe in the woods at night with natural predators so close at hand.

In a normal voice, Dennis said, "I need to finish this. By the way, tonight is the new moon. The clouds are supposed to clear up by this evening. You should see a million stars."

"Thanks. This might be a good night for a campfire, s'mores, hot chocolate and ghost stories."

Dennis laughed. "Maybe I'll drop by."

"Do that! Come to think of it, Chris and I met two couples yesterday. I'll walk over and invite them to come, too."

"Which couples did you meet?"

"Um, excuse me, I'm really bad with names, the young folks, the ones that work online from wherever they happen to be…"

"Kyle and Dani."

"Yeah, them. And the older couple from somewhere on the east coast."

"John and Lucy. They're from the area where I grew up. The lakes region of upstate New York."

"Huh. If they're from a lakes region, why would they come here? To a lake?"

"Dunno. The boss seemed to think they wanted a change of scenery. And really, that region is fairly touristy. This area isn't."

"You're right about that. So, we'll expect you around dusk?"

"Sure thing. I'll bring sticks for the marshmallows."

Annie returned to the front porch, poured ginger peach tea from a thermos, and sat. Once again, she looked over the lake.

Sis, Tiger Lily and Little Socks walked slowly and quietly to get out of Annie's field of vision. Sis said, *"I smell lots of things in there. Do you want to go in and take a look?"*

Little Socks jumped up to go, but Tiger Lily stopped her. *"We can't. Mommy won't let us come outside if we don't follow the rules."*

"That's not fair. She brought us here, to the country, and now we can't enjoy it?"

"We could get eaten by a big meat-eating animal."

"What are you talking about? I didn't hear anything that Mommy and Dennis talked about that sounded like a meat-eater."

Tiger Lily said, *"Foxes. They eat meat."*

Sis said, *"Raccoons eat meat, and they aren't nice. They would hurt you even if they aren't hungry."*

"And opossums," said Tiger Lily. *They like meat."*

"We like meat, too," huffed Little Socks. *"That doesn't mean we'd eat them. Why do we have to assume they'd eat us?"*

"Good question," said Tiger Lily. She turned to Sis. *"What do you think?"*

Sis looked at her feet. She was by far the largest of all of them, being a giant schnauzer. Unfortunately, she was more timid than most of the cats. Initially, she liked the idea of going into the woods, but talk of meat-eaters made her rethink her position. *"I think we should wait. Annie and Chris always take a walk, and they always take us. Maybe today they'll take us into the woods. We'll be able to look around, but we'll be safer."*

3: Cameroon

On the other side of the world, Henrie and Collette rose from a late breakfast. They had eaten at an internet café in the tourist section. In this part of town, they rarely saw the local militia. Intermittent sounds of gunfire were far away, toward the mountains or north of town. Here, they felt safe during the day.

In Cameroon, two entities were known to be dangerous. The one familiar to the world was the rebel group, Boko Haram. The other was the local militia.

Henrie's grandmother had made comments in the past about the militia, but Henrie, fed a media diet, thought she exaggerated. He put her concerns into a category of those belonging to someone who did not care for the police. That was a sizeable part of any country's population.

Now that he was here, he was cautious around anyone carrying a weapon, even those wearing a uniform.

Henrie, the chief cook, toilet bowl cleaner and bottle washer of the KaliKo Inn, was home. Kind of. He held few memories of the town or the country as a child, but he lived here until he was old enough to go to school. His parents, eager to find work and to give Henrie a western education, moved to London in time to enroll him in an English school.

Henrie was an only child. His hard-working parents were able to provide an excellent education for him from the earliest grades through an advanced degree.

Both worked at a major hotel in London, his father as a concierge and his mother as a chef. He planned to join them in what he considered to be the family business, but on the management end.

Before he graduated from Oxford School of Hospitality Management, his parents died in a traffic accident. Henrie, having no ties, moved to New York following graduation and took a position as a lower level manager in a five-star hotel. Before long, he advanced to upper management. He excelled in everything he touched, but he was not happy.

He had literally hundreds of acquaintances, but he was alone. No parents, no siblings, no close ties. He enjoyed a long-distance relationship with his maternal grandmother in Cameroon, but he was not anxious to return to his native country.

One day, as he chatted with guests at his luxury hotel, he met Victor Mack, a third-generation owner of a medium-sized bed and breakfast in the Midwest.

Victor painted a glorious picture of life in a resort community on a Great Lake. He mentioned updating the inn so that he would be able to hand it over to his daughter. The tourist trade was just beginning to pick up in their town, and with the right management, they could tip the scales for the business and for the community.

As they talked, Victor mentioned that a man such as Henrie could be a great benefit to the inn.

As they talked, Henrie also believed that a man such as himself could be a great benefit to the inn, and further, that perhaps a small resort town and a large lake might be just the thing for him.

When he left the bustle of the city and entered the slower pace of Chelsea, he found true happiness.

Recently, he added a new layer of happiness.

He met Collette, an attorney, and they had progressed to sharing life stories. Henrie shared his desire to meet his grandmother in person before it was too late.

He was aware Cameroon had been at war with Boko Haram for the past four years. He was aware of the atrocities committed by the group. The media – certainly media graphics – focused on violence in tribal villages. Henrie believed if they stayed in the center city area, they would not be in danger.

Collette shared his desire and insisted on making the trip, regardless of travel warnings. After all, his grandmother was a resident and Henrie was a native.

Thus, they travelled to Maroua, the major city in the Far North region of Cameroon.

Maroua stretched along the banks of two major rivers in the foothills of the Mandara Mountains. A classic combination of modern and tribal Africa, huts and native farmlands appeared to be suburbs of town. The region survived mainly on agriculture, tourism and contraband. Criminals and tribal chiefs were more influential than any government agency.

Over two hundred languages were spoken in the country. Most natives in the far north spoke English as a second language, but French influence was prominent. This was the accent Henrie's friends in Chelsea noted whenever he spoke.

The town was one hundred fifty miles from Maiduguri, Nigeria, the birthplace of Boko Haram. Every year, thousands of refugees streamed across the border into Maroua. Boko Haram followed.

Henrie and Collette had been shocked to find the level of ongoing violence in Maroua. They did not witness open revolts or large-scale conflict, but every day they saw or heard evidence of open fighting. The native population took it in stride. They seemed to know which streets to avoid on a given day or how to navigate from home to work and back in safety.

They had not visited areas of town that Henrie wanted to see, but with his grandmother in tow, they had gone once to his home village, now essentially a suburb of Maroua. There, Henrie met extended family members and a few people who remembered his parents.

Henrie and Collette settled into a daily routine. They slept in, had breakfast at an internet café near the hotel – there were two – and went each day to visit Henrie's grandmother. They stayed in well-traveled areas and were sure to be inside the hotel by late afternoon.

The night before, gunfire erupted near the center of downtown and too close to the hotel for comfort. Henrie and Collette locked themselves into the bathroom and prayed the hotel would remain unscathed. It had, and life seemed to return to normal by morning.

As they finished breakfast, Collette said, "Let us try one more time, Henrie."

Henrie nodded. "A computer is free in the corner. If there has been even one cancellation, you are leaving early."

"If there has been only one cancellation, I will wait with you."

As they settled at the computer, Henrie said, "I wish Grand-mère would come with us."

Collette shook her head sadly. "She is old. She is ready to die. She does not care if it is from old age or a stray bullet. In truth, neither Boko Haram nor the militia will bother with a woman of her age. If anything, they will spit on her and pass her by."

With each day that passed, they became more anxious to leave. Henrie had resisted at first, but even his grandmother had insisted they take the earliest possible flight.

They were due to fly out on Wednesday, leaving from the regional airport south of town and connecting with a flight from the international airport in Yaoundé. Due to the ongoing violence, almost every flight out was overbooked.

Henrie had tried daily for the past five days to find early tickets. Today, he still doubted tickets would come available before Wednesday. Even then, with tickets purchased months before, they might be placed on stand-by.

It would be a two-pronged process. In the unlikely event earlier tickets could be had at Yaoundé, they still had to procure tickets from Maroua.

In Cameroon, travel by rail did not extend to the Far North region. Travel by car from Maroua to Yaoundé was a twenty hour trip, if they could make it at all with uncertain roads and poorly maintained vehicles.

If they could not make connections from Maroua for the next day, Tuesday, the only option was to wait until Wednesday and hope they were able board the plane as ticketed.

Henrie did not have to log onto the Maroua airport ticket site. None were available at Yaoundé.

At the hotel, Yannick, the elderly manager, greeted them. "Mr. Henrie, Miss Collette, your dear grandmamá has called to ask that you try one more time to leave the country early. I must admit, I agree."

Henrie smiled at the elderly man. "Thank you, Yannick. We tried just now. We will have to wait until Wednesday. Do not worry. All will be well."

4: Chelsea

George finished serving breakfast in time for Louis to emerge from the back room. Louis arrived Sunday and made quick time in finding what he needed.

A boat.

To be specific, a boat that could motor up and down the coast, ferrying him to a variety of ports that could hold potential investment sites.

George was happy to direct him toward Ray and The Escape. He was not happy to aid in the potential development of another lakeside resort. He kept those thoughts to himself.

"Morning, Louis. Coffee?"

"Please. Thank you. And how are you this morning?"

George poured coffee and set it on the table while Louis helped his plate from the buffet. Louis spoke in a lilting accent, French, more French than Henrie's accent. Still, it gave George a small amount of comfort to hear it. He missed Henrie. Had it only been twelve days?

He answered. "Great, thanks. What time are you taking off?"

"I just have time to partake of this wonderful meal. Thank you for the referral. The gentleman is quite capable, and the marina is so close. It will be a pleasant walk."

"It will. It might be raining by the time you get back, though. Call from The Marina. Someone will pick you up."

"Thank you."

Further conversation was interrupted by pounding footsteps from the second floor. George was certain horses were galloping down the stairs at breakneck speed. He took a deep breath and backed out of the way.

Four youth, paying no heed to the man helping himself to breakfast, barreled into the room, grabbed plates, and heaped most of the food from the buffet onto them. They slammed the plates onto the table and jostled one another at the drinks bar, spilling more juice and milk on the floor than into their glasses.

Once they were seated and shoveling food into their mouths, George spoke.

"A woman came to the door today. She was injured by a water balloon thrown, I'm assuming, from your balcony, Clarke."

Clarke, a large boy, aged seventeen, said, "I'm gonna get a baseball scholarship. Need practice."

"Not on humans, Clarke. I'm going to have to tell someone about this."

"Go ahead."

George shook his head, both at the comment, and at Louis, who walked out, handing George his half-filled plate on the way.

George heard the kitchen door open and then he heard another woman's voice.

Cripes. He had forgotten about Georgia and Little Fred.

His head cook would bring her daughter here every day this week. Her daycare operator was taking a break for oral surgery. Little Fred was too much for Martha to handle. Martha, Georgia's landlord, could handle several things, but an active two-year-old all day for several days in a row wasn't on the menu. JoJo had permission to be absent from class this week to tend to Little Fred.

Two small cats wandered in from the kitchen. They looked up at George, then, eyes widening, took in the four hooligans. They turned and sprinted back to the kitchen, tails between their legs.

George followed them. Bravely, he managed to keep his tail from going between his legs.

Georgia looked up and said, "I hope you don't mind that I brought Speckles and Daryll. They stood at the door and ran out as soon as I opened it."

"I don't mind. Did you tell them all of their friends are gone for the week?"

"I did. They wanted to come anyway."

George bent down to say hello to the precocious child standing at the kitchen island. "Good morning, Little Fred. Are you going to entertain JoJo today?"

She gave a solemn nod and dropped to her seat. Still wearing a diaper, the sound was more of a plop than a thud. The two cats ran to her and gathered around her, settling quietly as she grabbed a tail in each hand.

George sighed. If only he could sit and hold onto the tails of two cats. But no. He heard "the parents" come downstairs. He sighed again and rose to go into the dining room. It was time for "the talk" with "the parents" about "the behavior" of "the children."

He liked dealing with the adults that came into Mo's Tap. The occasional drunk was easier to deal with than this pack of juveniles and their parents.

Never again.

Jim and Connie left the dining room and followed the noise. The over-loud sound of a video game at top volume led them to the library. The boys were in front of the large screen television with a game of some sort; the girls had every magazine from the shelves and racks spread over the floor.

Connie had no idea why they threw magazines around like they did. They lay on the two decorative rugs, noses buried in their cell phones.

Connie said, "Kids, we have to talk."

No one moved or acknowledged her presence.

Jim said, "Kids, pay attention to your mother."

No one moved or acknowledged his presence.

Jim walked to the television set and turned it off, to loud groans from the boys and a few curse words from Clarke. He continued to stand in front of it, hands on hips.

Connie turned to the girls. Brooke, aged sixteen, and Cassie, aged eleven, stayed in the same room upstairs. The girls got along, generally, and Connie had enough parental ethics – even on vacation – to realize an eleven-year-old could not be left completely to her own devices.

Connie told Brooke at the beginning of the week that if Cassie was well-supervised, she would receive an additional five hundred dollars in her wardrobe budget next fall. Every now and then, she flashed five fingers at Brooke as incentive.

The good news was that their spring break was off-schedule from most schools. There were no boys in town during the day to take Brooke's interest.

Connie told the girls to pick up the magazines and put them away. They glared and turned back to their phones.

Jim took a hand from his hip and shook a finger at Clarke. He yelled, "Do you know what you did? Do you?"

Marty, aged fourteen, sniggered. Jim, by now, was truly angry. He yelled, "Shut up! I'm not talkin' to you!"

Marty rolled his eyes and sat back, arms going wide.

Jim spat, "You're more like your brother every day. No respect."

Marty shook his head and tuned out. Jim turned on Clarke. "What was that stunt this morning, with the water balloon?"

"You told me to keep my arm in shape. I was doing that. Needed a moving target for practice, is all."

"You coulda hurt that woman. If she hasn't already gone to the police, that George guy is going to."

"The police? What are you talkin' about? It was only a water balloon!"

"Whatever. You have to cut that out."

Jim had run out of steam. He was ready to pretend he was on vacation again, happy and childless.

Connie still had a thing or two to say. At least the girls had looked up during their father's conversation with the boys. Connie took advantage. "Girls, I don't want to hear of anything like that from you, do you hear me?"

Brooke rolled her eyes. "Geez, Mom. We don't do that stuff."

"Make sure you don't."

Maternal instincts again kicking in, she asked, "Are you kids finding enough to eat? Things to do?"

The four of them murmured assent.

Jim and Connie looked at one another, shrugged their shoulders, and left. They planned to spend the rest of the morning doing absolutely nothing. Coffee on the deck, maybe a book, maybe a nap. Lunch would be at Sassy P's Wine & Cheese. Lunch would start around eleven and end around four. Or five. Or six. Maybe later. Then, well, maybe they would have energy to do something. Or not. As long as the kids didn't interfere, they'd be fine.

When their parents were gone, Brooke asked the boys, "What are you doin' today?"

Clarke answered for them. "Saturday, we saw the new God of War game at that hardware store, Double something."

Marty added, "They have the standard edition, but also the deluxe and the stonecutters. I want the stonecutters."

Cassie asked, "Are you gonna open it here, or wait 'til we get home?"

Marty and Clarke looked at each other. Clarke answered. "I think we need to take it home. George or that girl might know they don't have the game here. They might start askin' questions. What about you?"

Cassie said, "I saw some jewelry at that flower and gift shop. We didn't have a chance to pick it up Saturday. Maybe we can get it today."

Clarke said, "Yesterday, me and Marty walked up Main Street. Did you see that antique store?"

Brooke shook her head. "Saw it. Didn't pay it no mind."

"Well, there's a jewelry store inside. You think you found nice stuff at that flower place, this place has expensive stuff."

"Were they open yesterday?"

"Nah. We saw it through the window."

Brooke looked at Cassie then back at the boys. "Something like that would take some planning. Why don't we all meet there after lunch, case it. If we see anything interesting, we can plan something for tomorrow."

Marty nodded. "That's our last day here. We could get something really nice, then we're outta here."

Clarke added, "If we're lucky, we'll get something worth big dough. Uncle Charlie could fence it for us."

Brooke said, "He'll tell Mom."

"He won't tell Mom anything. If he tells, it'll be worse for him than it is for us. Mom doesn't know what he does on the side."

Mitch and Livia were in the Inn's vehicle, the one guests were allowed to use. They were headed toward Marsh Haven, a town a little larger than Chelsea.

They were on their honeymoon, and for now, they had exhausted their communication.

Mitch was grateful for that. He needed to think, and silence would help. He was in trouble. Real trouble.

Mitch could have had the world on a string. His parents could have given him anything. Instead, they spent their time and money buying his way out of trouble.

As a pre-teen and a teen, he was arrested several times for theft. Silly stuff. A candy bar from the corner drug store. A carton of cigarettes from the grocery store. Money from purses at school.

The thefts grew in daring and in amounts as he aged, and his parents grew increasingly alarmed. They didn't know how to stop it but hoped he would eventually grow out of it. In the meantime, they made donations here and under-the-table payments there. Mitch generally left juvenile court with a slap on the wrist.

The problems increased as he received his driver license. Following the gift of a car, he planned and executed a series of house burglaries with a group of friends. He was arrested as he tried to fence a few pieces of expensive jewelry.

The court system would no longer look the other way. He spent two years in a juvenile facility and received his high school equivalency degree from the state.

Luckily, his record as a juvenile was a secret, long ago and now far away.

With the help of his parents, he enrolled in a college that didn't look too closely at his school record. He kept his grades up and transferred to a major university in his junior year. Now he held a position with a medium-sized brokerage firm in a medium-sized city that allowed him to blend in.

His good looks brought him into contact with Livia, the boss's daughter and now his wife.

His natural inclination to take chances and a personality that came close to that of a sociopath would allow him to become rich, eventually. If he didn't have to file for bankruptcy first.

He and Livia, a woman raised in privilege, had a traditional wedding. Mitch, who sadly informed anyone who asked that his parents had died in a tragic accident when he was but a youth, insisted on paying for the rehearsal dinner.

They would have wanted to do it, he said.

They would have loved his beautiful bride, he said.

They would have wanted the best, he said.

They had dreamed of this day, he said.

The cost of the rehearsal dinner – held in one of the best venues in town – went on one of Mitch's credit cards. That card was now maxed out.

Two other cards were maxed out as well, cards used during the year that Mitch and Livia dated. Luckily for Mitch, Livia had not asked to be taken anywhere on vacation. Well, besides that trip to Europe. He was able to get out of that because a co-worker had a heart attack. Mitch had to stay home to cover for him. Mitch didn't disclose that he had paid the man to fake the attack. It was less expensive than the trip would have been.

By shaving a little here and a little there from client accounts, he had managed to keep up with minimum credit card payments. It didn't put him ahead, but it kept him out of hock. Luckily, his new father-in-law would hand over several additional clients when he returned from the honeymoon.

Another piece of luck was that Livia's parents purchased a fully furnished house for them. Thank goodness. No mortgage, only taxes, utilities, insurance and incidentals. Those expenses would start next month.

Livia had jumped at the "opportunity" to take a low-key honeymoon. Mitch, thinking of the money he would save, convinced her they would be on the fast track as soon as they got home. Doing something slow would be a much-needed respite between the wedding and real life.

The reservation at the KaliKo Inn was on the last card he had with any juice. He hoped it would get them through the week. One more card had a couple hundred dollars left. He would use that for today's trip. If he was lucky – really lucky – Livia wouldn't find anything that she absolutely had to have in the small town they were headed toward.

And if his luck held, the five-star restaurant where they would enjoy a late lunch would have two-star prices.

5: Lavender Lake

Annie went inside the cabin for breakfast. Chris once again astonished her. She took in a deep breath. The ginger was pungent.

Chris placed a bowl in front of her and said, "This is breakfast miso. You can smell the ginger, and it has snow peas, soy sauce, boiled eggs, pumpkin and tofu. Everything your body needs to start the day."

"And bread?"

"Oh. Yes. We need bread for breakfast."

Chris went to the small oven, opened it, and Annie smelled even more ginger. "What is it?"

"Lemon ginger fruit bread."

"Yum."

Sis came into the house, stepping over the rock that propped open the screen door.

Chris reached into his pocket for a dog treat and said, "You know we'll get mosquitos with that door open."

"It's too early in the season for mosquitos."

"Flies, then."

"I can't lock them in. Well, I can, at night. Too many predators out there. But during the day, I want them to have free run of the place."

"Yeah. You give that little lecture about not going into the woods every morning. How long do you think they'll listen to you?"

"Tiger Lily will keep them in line. We have an understanding."

Chris laughed.

Sis, apparently realizing that one treat was all she would get, turned to go outside again. She stopped at the door when Chris and Annie spoke again.

In between sips of miso, Annie said, "I invited Dennis to dinner tonight. Told him we could have s'mores and hot chocolate. Tell ghost stories. He said he'd bring the sticks."

"Great. I was going to make shrimp fettucine Alfredo. I have enough to feed at least six, maybe eight. Should we invite those folks we met yesterday?"

"I was thinking the same thing. Why don't we wander over while we hunt for mushrooms in the woods?"

"Is that what we're doing today?"

Annie laughed. "Yes. It's morel time. If we don't find a lot, we don't have to share them. We can wait until it's just the two of us again."

Sis left to tell the cats what the plans for the day would be. She trotted to the group and once again sat by Little Socks, her favorite.

Little Socks basked in the glow of being someone's favorite. This was unusual. In her opinion, this was because her wit was sharper than most, leading to jealousy. In truth, it was unusual because Little Socks could be demanding and petulant much of the time.

Sis liked her for other reasons. When the cats rescued her from a fierce snowstorm, and when they learned her human was abusive, Little Socks talked her through some of the finer points of adopting Chris to be her human. Little Socks also accompanied Sis on her first trip to the condominium where she now lived, helping to keep her calm.

Sis now said, *"We're having company for dinner, and we're going to have s'mores. What are s'mores?"*

Tiger Lily answered, *"Stuff we can't have, because it's chocolate."*

"Then what will we eat?"

"They'll have something for us. Plus, if they're having s'mores, we'll be outside. At night! That will be fun."

Sassy Pants, whose command of the English language was tenuous at best, said, *"What we do outside at night? Dere's aminals dat will eats us."*

Mr. Bean, the youngest and strongest of the group, said, *"I'll protect you. They'll have to go through me to get to you."*

Kali and Ko, the largest of the crew and the resident scaredy cats, spoke at the same time. *"I'm going to stay inside!" "I won't be anybody's dinner!"*

Mo trilled. A littermate with his dilute calico sisters – the names Kali, Ko and Mo had come to Annie in an instant – Mo had never progressed beyond speaking their secret kitten language. Kali and Ko stood as translators. So, inexplicably, did Sassy Pants, who could read minds.

Sassy Pants answered for him, because Kali and Ko still quivered and hid their heads. *"He say dere's a pretty bunny out dere dat he want to meet."*

Little Socks spat out a laugh. *"He can't love up a bunny! He's a cat!"*

Mo trilled again. Sassy Pants said, *"He know dat. He tink da bunny pretty, an he want to meets her."*

Tiger Lily decided to end the bunny talk. She looked at Sis. *"Is that all you heard?"*

Sis shook her head. *"There's more. We're going into the woods today, and we'll hunt for mushrooms. What are they? Do they bite?"*

Little Socks laughed again, this time in a more polite manner. This was Sis, after all. And to be honest, she wasn't sure what a mushroom was in the wild. She didn't know if it was a plant or an animal. *"We have to get you to the Café more often. Mushrooms taste really good, and I've never seen any teeth on them."*

Mr. Bean said, *"You mean we're gonna hunt for food?"*

Kali and Ko said together, *"They're nasty." "You can have mine."*

Then they looked at one another and said, again together, *"Do they bite?" "Are they mean?"*

Tiger Lily looked at the ground and shook her head. There was no training this bunch. Then she looked into the trees. Without turning to Sis, she said, *"Don't worry about those mushrooms. They won't hurt us, but they're important enough to Mommy that she'll let us go into the woods. We'll be with her. We'll be safe."*

Sis and the cats turned to look into the trees. Varying degrees of happiness and scare settled in.

6: Cameroon

Henrie and Collette freshened themselves in the room. As they left the hotel, Yannick looked up to nod good-bye. Henrie nearly said to Collette, "Let us stay here this afternoon," but Grand-mère waited.

On the curb, Henrie led Collette to a lone bright yellow taxicab with the same driver they had used the past three days. Henrie gave the address. As they seated themselves in the back seat, Henrie realized that had this been the Maroua of his childhood, this kind of transportation would not have been available to him.

The cab was a wreck by US standards. Dents and scrapes could be seen from every angle. The front and back bumpers sagged in opposite directions, and one tire was larger than the others. The cab had an odd backfire that seemed to occur every ten or twelve seconds, no matter what it was doing. Forward, pop pop, ten seconds, pop pop, ten seconds pop pop. Idle, pop pop, ten seconds, pop pop. He did not recall observing the taxi going in reverse, but assumed it would do the same.

He glanced at the driver who was, at that moment, looking at him through the rearview mirror. Henrie nodded.

In broken English, the driver asked, "You here several days. You tourist?"

"Yes. No. I was born here, outside Maroua."

"This address I take you again, is it family?"

"Yes. We visit my grandmother."

"But she not live outside town. This almost modern apartment."

"She has lived in town for a long time."

"You remember your home? Your first home?"

"Barely. I was quite young."

"But you live outside town?"

"It was outside town then. It appears the village is now a suburb of Maroua."

"Close to the mountains?"

"Yes."

"You come up in world."

"I am not certain that is the case. I visited the village. The residents have all they need and want."

"All they need, yes, but no one afford extras, you know, like to travel. Like you."

"I have been lucky in life."

"Yes. That is apparent."

The hair on the back of Henrie's neck stood up.

The driver, winding through the narrow streets, continued to talk. "You know about the troubles?"

Henrie locked eyes with the driver in the mirror. "Do you refer to the gunshots we hear?"

"Yes, the troubles."

"I know there are issues, and we have kept a respectful distance from the fighting. Has your business been affected?"

"Oh, yes. My business. My family. You probably not know what they shooting at."

"No. I must confess, I am not aware."

"They shooting at family. They – the militia – every day they kill someone's family."

"No. Why would they do that?"

"They think kill the mother and the babies and the rebels go away."

"Rebels?"

"You know Boko Haram?"

"Yes. No. I have heard of them, but I am not educated about the group or their issues."

"You come home to Maroua and you not know?"

"I know what the media tells us, and while the reporting is most likely factual, many of the details are missing."

"Details, like?"

"The daily violence, how close to Maroua the incursions have come. Perhaps we would have visited another time."

"And you think the 'incursions' Boko Haram?"

Alarms went off in Henrie's head, and he noticed the driver had passed the turn to his grandmother's home. "Excuse me, our turn was just there."

"One minute. You think violence the fault of Boko Haram?"

Collette took hold of Henrie's hand and gave it a squeeze. Henrie responded in kind and said, "I am sure I do not know who is doing what to whom."

The driver looked through the mirror, once again locking eyes with Henrie. "Perhaps we teach you."

For the first time, Henrie noticed the interior door handles had been removed. There would be no escape. At least, not from this car.

7: Chelsea

Clara left her flower and gift shop to walk across the street. Moriah, her new kitty, saved by Annie, of course, trotted in front. She knew they were going to Tiger Lily's Café, and she looked forward to the treats that staff and customers would "accidentally" drop to the floor.

Annie found Moriah under a bush during a late winter rainstorm. The kitten was soaked, cold and scared, but she went to Annie and held on for dear life. She had dilute coloring a couple of shades lighter than Kali and Ko and long hair like Mo. And she was a cat. Annie couldn't resist.

She took Moriah home, made sure she was healthy with a couple of trips to Dr. Ralph, and looked for a fur-ever home. Clara came to mind immediately. The beautiful Haitian with black hair slicked back from her face and the light-colored cat with a fluffy lion mane now fit together like Mutt and Jeff.

As they entered the Café, Moriah spied one of her best friends on the floor under a table. She ran to the table and jumped onto Cyril's side, kneading her way onto his soft, brown and white fur. Cyril was an English setter with classic colors, and he loved the neighborhood cats.

Cyril particularly liked this new kitty. She was soft, she gave good nuzzle, and, being stout in the mid-section, she had a sexy little waddle. He enjoyed watching as she groomed herself. When she lifted her leg and bent to clean the back of it, she would almost roll over in the effort.

Clara invited herself to sit at the table of Cyril's human, Pete, the Chief of Police. She was always in search of gossip and he was generally a good source. She dived in.

"Did I see George go to the police station today? What's up?"

Pete laughed. "I think he wants me to arrest that family of guests."

Clara said, "You have my vote. They're a pack of thieves."

"George told me he's doing what he called 'that Henrie thing' for everyone on The Avenue."

"He is. Every day at closing, we send him an email of the items the kids lifted and the retail price. So far, the total is covered by the amount he pre-charged their card."

Pete said, "That's something I still don't understand."

"It's the Henrie thing. The contract is written so they can pre-charge the card for more than the reservation price of the Inn. Guests charge meals and things at all of Annie's places. Henrie wanted to make sure they have enough to cover. Once or twice, it has helped us. You know, when their guests have a light touch."

"It's a good thing George knew about it."

Clara laughed. "He didn't. I told him, so he read the contract and charged the card enough to cover. At least, we all hope it will cover."

Hearing a crash from a nearby table, Clara and Pete turned to look. Clara said, "Someone got excited over there. They need to stop talking with their hands."

Pete laughed at the mess, then turned sober. "I should talk to you and every other owner in town. Do you want to press charges?"

"Not if I get paid."

"What are those kids learning, though? That theft has no consequences?"

"Trust me," said Clara, "when the parents have to pay for it, they'll learn something about consequences."

"They'll learn a little about that this afternoon. I'm going over to talk to them about a water balloon assault."

"I heard about that. Joyce Harrold went fishing before work and ended up with a knot on her head. So you're charging the parents?"

"I'm going to threaten to charge them. She'll be happy with cash to cover the doctor's expenses, and maybe a little extra."

"Good luck. So, other than that, is George hanging in there?"

"He appears to be. He seemed tired today. He said something about this guy that has Henrie's accent, was kind of talking in circles."

Their attention was drawn again to the sound of a crash. This time, a server dropped a tray filled with plates and bowls. They looked underneath the table. Several angelic cats gazed back. Cyril hid behind his paws.

Simon Finnegan and Oscar McMurphy trotted into the Café, followed by Speckles and Daryll. Moriah sat up. *"What are you guys doing here?"* She was speaking to Speckles and Daryll.

Simon Finnegan and Oscar McMurphy, large cats, siblings, lived next door to Moriah and above the hardware store. The two little ones lived in a residential neighborhood and did not come to The Avenue without being driven by their human.

Daryll, always hesitant, sat down in front of Moriah. *"Hi? I'm Daryll?"*

"I know. We've met before. How did you get here?"

"We came with Simon Finnegan? And Oscar McMurphy?"

"I mean, how did you get to The Avenue?"

"Georgia brought us? With Little Fred?"

"Really? How long are you staying?"

Speckles jumped in, wanting to speed this thing up. *"She's going to bring us every day this week, something about Little Fred's daycare not working."*

"It got broken?"

"I don't know, but it's not working. JoJo is keeping Little Fred at the Inn and Georgia brings us, too."

"Cool."

Simon Finnegan jumped in. *"Yeah. Now we have four detectives. Well, two detectives and two in training. And it's time to train you."*

Cyril yawned, then asked, *"How are you going to train her? Do you have a case?"*

"Yeah," said Oscar McMurphy. *"The kids at the Inn. They're robbing all of us blind."*

Speckles said, *"They were loud."*

Daryll added, *"And obnoxious? Scary?"*

Moriah asked, *"So I can train to be a detective?"*

"Yeah," said Oscar McMurphy. *"We need another cat burglar."*

Cyril sat up quickly, and Moriah landed with four feet on the floor. Cyril said, *"What? How are you going to teach her to do that? None of you are cat burglars. That's Little Socks."*

"What is it?" asked Moriah. *"What's a cat burglar? Do you need a cat to be burgled?"*

Speckles laughed. Then she realized Moriah was serious. *"No, that's not it. A cat burglar is a really good burglar. She – or he – can get into and out of places without being seen or heard, and she can find clues and stuff."*

"Clues? What's that?"

Simon Finnegan said, *"That's stuff that helps Pete arrest people."*

"So who do you want him to arrest?"

"Those kids. They're stealing from everyone on The Avenue."

Cyril huffed. *"Pete was just saying that George has that under control. They're keeping track of everything, and he's going to make the parents pay for all of it."*

Moriah looked thoughtful. *"So...I guess...well, this could be good. You know that it's going to be taken care of, so if I screw up, it won't be so bad. Right? How would you train me?"*

Oscar McMurphy said, *"Well, you could come on over to the agency, and we'll talk about it."*

"But the other cats are gone. The detective agency is at their house."

Simon Finnegan puffed up with pride. *"Tiger Lily left me in charge."*

Oscar McMurphy hissed at Simon Finnegan. *"She left us in charge."* She looked back at Moriah. *"In case Pete needs our help."*

Simon Finnegan said, *"We can go to the Inn and talk about it this afternoon, then get there early tomorrow morning. We can spy on everyone at breakfast, and when they leave, we can start training our newest cat burglar."*

Cyril looked at his small friends. He said, *"That could be a good idea. Pete doesn't need you, but there's no reason you can't practice, since you have semi-criminals at hand. And they're young, so...maybe it will work out okay."*

Moriah sat tall. She said, *"You really think I can be a detective? And a cat burglar? I'm not as skinny as Little Socks."*

Daryll said, *"You're a little fat?"*

Moriah huffed. *"I'm not fat. I'm fluffy!"*

"I didn't mean? Um. You're really pretty? I like you fluffy?"

Moriah stared at Daryll. *"Good, because I'm smart, too."*

Speckles nodded. *"You are smart, and you can learn to be a cat burglar. Besides, you have to have a skill to be a detective."*

"What are your skills?"

Simon Finnegan puffed up. *"Me and Oscar McMurphy are protectors. We help weak humans when bad people try to kill them."*

"Wow. That's impressive," said Moriah.

Speckles said, *"I'm a ninja kitty."*

"What's that?"

Instead of telling her, Speckles demonstrated a ninja move, jumping straight up from the floor and turning one hundred eighty degrees in the air, kicking her feet like a helicopter rotor. Unfortunately, she misjudged the distance to the neighboring table. Two glasses of iced coffee and a salad bowl hit the floor.

Speckles dived underneath the table. *"The secret is to be so fast that humans don't know what happened."*

Cyril shook his head. *"We have to be more careful than that. The humans might kick us out of the Café."*

In fact, a few humans – servers – looked under the table to see if the cats were behaving while they cleaned up the mess.

Moriah watched the excitement around her without a ripple of anxiety. She looked at Daryll, who crouched behind Cyril's hip. *"What's your skill?"*

Tentatively, he said, *"I hide and jump out at people? They get really scared?"*

"That sounds interesting. Can I see?"

Cyril said, *"I don't think…"* but Daryll, anxious to impress, pushed himself away. He walked with purpose toward the kitchen door and crouched low, wiggling his hind quarters in anticipation.

When the right moment came, he startled everyone in the Café. A server balancing a tray laden with meals and sides opened the door. Daryll sprang, the server screamed, and food went everywhere.

Proud of himself, Daryll strolled back to the table.

Pete and Clara leaned down to look at the little devils. They looked back, innocence incarnate. Cyril hid behind his paws.

Ray pulled The Escape out of the harbor. He had recommended against Marsh Haven, but Louis had insisted on seeing the town. He also insisted on going into town by himself, even though Ray was familiar with the layout.

Ray had a conversation with Jock while Louis was in town. It went something like this.

"It's okay that he doesn't want my expertise."

Jock's tongue rolled out and he panted a few times.

"I mean, if he wants to purchase property, it would be stupid to have someone along who might know about the town, right?"

Jock licked his lips, rolled his tongue out again and panted a few more times.

"It's okay. What I really want is for him to find a place hundreds of miles from here."

Jock stood, sat, panted.

In other words, the conversation was fairly one-sided.

Now they were headed to the next town north. With the amount of time Louis spent in the first town, they would see no more than two towns a day. Ray didn't care about that. He would be paid no matter how many towns they hit.

Ray looked from his pilot's post to the deck. Louis was in a deck chair, leaned back, face to the sun. He had a bottle of water in his hand and a look on his face that was somewhere between blissful and pensive. Ray wondered if he should be worried that Louis did not want to share his thoughts about his property research. Probably not. He was probably dealing with proprietary information and was unable to share.

Jock looked into Ray's face with adoring eyes. His tongue rolled out and he panted.

Frank and Gema were on semi-high alert. Of course, they heard about the youthful offenders. Every shop on The Avenue had some kind of loss on Saturday. Today was another day, and they had moved from The Avenue to Main Street.

Frank owned Antiques On Main. He rented the front corner of the shop to Gema's Creations. Gema designed and sold unique pieces of jewelry, all high-end.

Frank noticed Gema would pull out one piece at a time, no more. Even when both girls and the younger boy asked to see something at the same time.

Gema was good. She said, "I'll wait on one person at a time. Who's first?"

When the older sister asked to look at the ring on her finger for a while as Gema waited on the younger one, she replied, "I'll give all my attention to one person at a time."

When the older girl asked to try on another ring, so she could compare the two on her hand, Gema said, "Why don't we take a picture of that ring on your finger, and you can compare the picture to the second ring."

When the girl started to insist, Gema lay down her final tool. Calmly, she said, "In order to bring more than one piece from the case, I'll need a cash or credit card deposit of one thousand dollars. Which method do you prefer?"

The girl took the ring from her finger and wandered into the antiques.

Gema's items were locked into cases; she was able to handle quick hands. Frank wasn't so lucky. He had several small items around the store. His vintage jewelry was in a locked case, but several not-so-cheap trinkets could fit easily into pockets.

Frank stayed on alert until the kids left. He didn't notice that Claire, his blue point Himalayan cat, had been on alert as well.

8: Lavender Lake

Annie sat on the front steps of the cabin, the cats arrayed in a semi-circle on the ground looking up at her. She performed her best impression of Mrs. Josephine Rabbit, giving instructions to John, Flopsy, Mopsy, and Cottontail. And three more. Plus Sis.

"Stay close and stay behind us. Do not stray. Do not go hunting. Do not pass Go. Do not collect two hundred dollars. Do you understand? Do you promise?"

Kali and Ko curled their heads to the ground and, staying low, slinked up the steps and back into the cabin, probably, thought Annie, to hide under a bed.

Tiger Lily held Annie's gaze. She blinked once. Then she looked at the other cats. Silently, she told them to do the same. They did.

Annie took a deep breath. Maybe this would be a huge mistake. She looked up at Chris. He looked at Sis. "Do you understand, Sis?"

Sis slowly worked her way to the ground, and on all fours, she looked up at Chris with her big dog eyes and licked her lips.

Chris closed his eyes, sighed, and said, "I guess that was a yes. Let's go hunt some mushrooms."

Annie got her basket and headed to the woods. "Come on, kids."

Tiger Lily could hardly contain her excitement. For so many days, she had stayed at the edge of the woods, looking in, sniffing. She caught glimpses of exciting plants and animals, especially baby animals. Maybe she could get up close and personal now.

She had not spent time in the woods – ever – nor had her siblings. Nonetheless, their hunter instincts kicked in. They slipped under and through shrubs and bushes, feet missing everything that could make the slightest sound.

They fanned out, again by instinct, protecting one another and looking for prey. They wouldn't kill anything. Unless they found bugs. They would kill bugs. But Annie had made sure to feed them breakfast, and their tummies were full.

Tiger Lily looked. Even Sassy Pants was in hunter mode. Her eyes were clear, her steps were sure. She found the first thing. A nest of baby rabbits.

Through some kind of kitty telepathy, four other cats came quickly and quietly, surrounding the nest. Baby rabbits shivered as they looked at the big animals with huge teeth. They didn't recognize Mo's sexy nature, the authoritarian stare of Little Socks, the motherly gaze of Tiger Lily, the excited glances of Mr. Bean and Sassy Pants. They saw teeth.

Mo looked around until he found her. The pretty one. The mommy. She stood still, several feet away, not knowing what to do.

Mo broke away from the group and walked slowly to the mother rabbit. She allowed him to approach, and she listened as he talked. He trilled. And she understood.

Her babies were not in danger. She was able to relax, and she even flirted a little. Until one of those humans called out.

"Kids! Come on!"

Mo took the time to trill a polite, *"Excuse me. I have to go. May I call on you again?"* The pretty mother bunny's heart fluttered as he sauntered away.

They made several new friends on their trip through the woods. They had time to stop and visit, because Chris and Annie were successful finding mushrooms. While they concentrated on their new friends, all took note that mushrooms were more plant than animal and therefore nothing of which to be afraid.

Before the mushroom hunt was over, the cats and Sis found baby raccoons up a tree, little snakes under a rock, tiny chipmunks under a shrub, and, from a distance, young deer hiding in the bushes.

Sassy Pants found a mother mouse and said, by way of introduction, *"Hi. Ize Sassy Pants. Duz you know Brown Mousie? Brown Mousie is my friend."* She was disappointed to learn that this country mouse did not know her city mouse.

Chris said, "Here. I found more."

Annie brought her basket and knelt on the ground. The basket was already half full. Chris said, "Watch the poison ivy…"

"Ack!"

"Here. I brought some cleanser. Clean your hands and don't touch your pants or shoes until we get back to the cabin. I'll get the 'shrooms."

Annie took care of her hands as she watched Chris. "Why aren't you worried about it?"

"Not allergic. At least, I never have been. I hope I'm not surprised."

Annie said, "Why are you so good at this? I'm looking and looking, and you keep finding them."

"I'm not looking for mushrooms. I'm looking for trees."

"Trees? So you've been doing this the whole time, and you haven't told me? I'm getting cross-eyed from looking at the ground."

"I thought you were watching the cats."

"No…where are they?" She made a half-hearted attempt to get a glimpse of her children. She saw a couple of tails and turned back. "Anyway, what trees?"

"Oak, elm, sycamore, ash."

"You know all those trees?"

"I looked them up before leaving the cabin."

"You have a book?"

"I have the internet."

"Geez, Chris. It's as if we don't talk anymore."

"We talk…I just wanted to show off my mushroom chops."

"You're sure about your mushrooms?"

"I think so. I might ask Dennis to take a look at them tonight."

Eventually, baskets full, Annie and Chris reached the edge of the woods near a cabin similar to their own. Smoke curled from the chimney, evidence that the persons inside were fending off the spring chill. The chill was invigorating to Annie.

An older man answered their knock. Chris said, "John, pardon our intrusion."

"Not a problem, Chris. What can I do for you?"

Tiger Lily, Mr. Bean and Little Socks made their way into the cabin, pushing through the door the man held open. He didn't seem to notice their presence.

Little Socks went to the bedroom area and jumped onto a dresser. She walked the length of the dresser, looking at photographs as she went. One framed picture was out of place and she tripped over it, sending it skittering behind the dresser and to the floor.

She stopped quickly and stood still. This was unusual for her, to actually knock something down. The people didn't seem to notice.

Chris was asking, "Are you able to come over for dinner tonight? Shrimp fettucine, and afterwards, s'mores and hot chocolate, maybe some ghost stories around the fire pit."

John motioned them inside while he turned toward the kitchen to speak to Lucy. "Lucy, these young folks have invited us for dinner, then ghost stories around a fire. Would you like to go?"

Wrapped in an afghan, she looked at Annie and Chris before saying, "Well...I don't know..."

Annie said, "We're going to invite that young couple in the next cabin, and Dennis, the groundskeeper, will be there, too."

John and Lucy looked at one another. John looked back and said, "We'd be delighted. What time?"

As John and Chris made arrangements, Annie showed the basket of mushrooms to Lucy. "Would you like some? We hope to find more on the way to the next cabin."

Lucy reached into the basket and fingered the harvest. "Are you sure? I'd love some."

They walked toward the kitchen counter. "Pick out what you want. Take as many as you want."

Lucy took her time selecting several mushrooms, looking up every now and then to see if John and Chris were still talking. She finished about the time that Chris looked up, motioning to Annie to come on.

Before they walked out, Annie counted kitty heads to make sure they were all there. They were. Plus a dog.

Walking through the woods to the next cabin, Annie found she could pick out the right trees. She still looked down more than Chris, however. She watched for ivy, and every now and then she counted cat tails.

Later, at the cabin of the young couple, a similar scene played out, except the young people were both hard at work on their laptop computers. Kyle and Dani were happy to say yes to the invitation. Kyle looked through the basket and selected mushrooms while Mr. Bean, taking over lead investigative duties from Little Socks, looked for interesting things. He didn't find anything.

Annie and Chris walked along the lakeshore on the way back, giving the cats and Sis another avenue of investigation.

Mr. Bean found a snail. He wasn't sure if it was dead or alive, so he batted it around a bit. Getting no reaction, he left to look for other things.

Sassy Pants introduced herself to some minnows. At the edge of the water, she waded in and laughed as they investigated her legs.

Sis splashed into the water to meet three baby turtles, but they slipped off a log and into the water before she got to them. Sis called out, *"I just wanted to say hello!"* Annie and Chris heard a howl.

Mo ventured to the edge of the dock and looked into the clear water. He saw some kind of fish of a decent size to watch. He got onto his stomach on the deck and hung down just a bit, enough for his two front feet to dabble in the water, which scared the fish away. He trilled softly, sad they had not at least said hello.

Tiger Lily and Little Socks found eggs. They moved in close to sniff but were chased away by the parent swans. When they were well away, Little Socks said, *"They were rude!"*

Annie and Chris walked slowly, letting the "kids" enjoy their afternoon walk. Before they got to their cabin, Dennis came near with the riding mower. He pulled over.

Annie showed him the basket. "Can you tell if we got any mushrooms that are poisonous?"

"Let me see," said Dennis. He riffled through the basket, pulling a few out. "These are bad," he said.

Chris and Annie leaned in. "How can you tell? They look like regular morels."

"Look at the stem. See this? They're solid."

He pulled out a morel and showed them the stem. It was hollow.

"Oh, my! We gave some to both of the couples! I don't know if they got the bad ones or not."

"Don't worry," said Dennis. I'll stop what I'm doing and drive to both cabins. I'll take a look before they cook them. I'll do it right now."

Chris said, "I can add these to the pasta tonight."

"If you do, please leave some without, or maybe make them so they can go on top. I have an allergy to mold."

"No problem. We'll use them another day."

As Dennis took off, Annie's attention was drawn toward the edge of the woods. Sis broke from the tree line and ran quickly toward the house. Annie soon smelled the sickly sweet scent of a skunk.

Dennis started with the furthest cabin, with Kyle and Dani. He knocked on the door and spoke to Dani when she answered it.

"I just met Chris and Annie with the mushrooms. They picked some that were poisonous, and said you might have taken some of them."

"Oh! I guess we don't know how to tell. Can you show me?"

"Sure. Where are they?"

Dani led him to the kitchen area, and Dennis went through the bowl. He picked two out and showed her. "See this? The stems are solid. These are bad."

"And the others are okay?"

"They're good. Great. Morels are the best. Do you know how to cook them?"

"I was going to sauté them in a little butter and garlic, or maybe chop them and cook them in scrambled eggs."

"Either way's a good way to eat them. Well, guess I'll see you tonight."

When Dennis arrived at the cabin of the older couple, he found John in the yard, playing a game of croquet with himself.

"Afternoon, John."

The older man nodded.

"I understand the couple over there left you some mushrooms. Some of them might have been poisonous. Mind if I have a look?"

"I know how to tell the bad 'uns from the good."

"Are you sure? They found some that looked an awful lot like morels."

"I'll take a look later."

Dennis persisted. "The bad ones will have solid stems. The real morels have hollow stems."

John sounded impatient. "Okay, okay. I'll check."

Dennis turned to go but turned back. "Say, John, have we met before? I mean, we come from the same area of New York, and sometimes I think… well… I wonder if we met?"

John looked him straight in the eye. After several seconds, he said, "Nah. You'd of remembered us if you met us before."

Dennis turned again to go, but stopped. That had been a strange way of putting it. He turned around, but John was already opening the door to the cabin. Dennis shook his head and left, wondering what he had done to upset the man.

Sis lay in the sun, soaking in the rays and cleaning out her nostrils. She was surrounded by seven cats, still in throes of laughter.

Mr. Bean stopped laughing long enough to choke out, *"Now you smell like a cookie! It's like I'm back at the bakery!"*

Sis put a leg over her face so she wouldn't have to look at the cats. She was embarrassed, and she was tired of smelling herself.

After the incident with the skunk, Chris drove into town to purchase a large bottle of vanilla extract and dog shampoo. He added the vanilla to warm water, held Sis down in the tub for ten minutes, then gave her a shampoo. It worked. But Sis now smelled like a cookie.

Tiger Lily stopped laughing long enough to say, *"I saw those baby skunks, but I knew better than to go near them."*

Sis huffed. *"You should have told me they were there. I ran over them."*

"You didn't smell them?"

"I was running."

Tiger Lily thought about it for a minute, then she said, *"You can't be blamed. You're not a natural hunter like we are."*

"Am too."

"Are not. You're a show dog. Jock said you're in the same class as him, the working group, at that west show."

Sis corrected her. *"Westminster."*

"*Yeah, that. And Jock said you beat his kind out of the show this year.*"

"*I did. We watched the show at Jock's house.*" Sis was beginning to feel better about herself.

"*Jock said you got all the way to the big dance. What's that?*"

"*The big dance is what he called it. It's the final show, where the winners of the seven groups go head to head and the final winner is chosen. The winner is called the Best of Show.*"

"*And you were in that one?*"

"*Well, my breed was. It was a boy dog named Ty.*"

"*And this year, none of our other friends had a breed in that show, right?*"

Sis puffed up a bit as she answered. "*That's right. My breed was the only one.*"

"*And you came in second, right?*"

"*I did. I'm surprised Jock told you. His breed didn't win anything.*"

"*Well, to be honest, he was teasing Cyril about it, that Cyril didn't win anything again this year, and that's how I heard it.*"

"*He's a real tease, that Jock.*"

"*He is.*" Tiger Lily stopped talking and licked her paw for a while. She was pleased with her performance. Sis was coming out of it and wasn't feeling sorry for herself anymore.

Sis lay back, thinking grand thoughts about being a winner, even if she smelled like a cookie.

9: Cameroon

Maria Masilla would have been pacing her apartment, from door to window to door, if she could walk. At the age of eighty – or thereabouts – she had surpassed her life expectancy by over twenty years. At least by Cameroon standards.

Until two years ago, she had managed to get around on her own. Finally, age, time and infirmity had relegated her to a wheelchair. It was a rickety affair, just a chair with two tall wheels and two small ones. The two small ones in front allowed her to make turns. Sometimes. Other times, she had to force herself up and turn the chair on her own.

That was enough to keep her in one place today. She sat in the middle of the small room, next to an end table that held her telephone. She looked to the window with its blinds pulled back, hoping to see a taxi, to the door, willing it to open, back to the window, back to the door.

Henrie and Collette should have arrived by noon. It was four now, and there had been no word. She had already tried his cellphone, more than once, but she received a standard message that the number was not available.

Perhaps they were able to get an earlier flight. Perhaps Henrie had forgotten to call. Perhaps he tried to call but the inconsistent telephone lines were out of order.

Once again, she picked up the receiver. She heard a dial tone. Today, that was both a blessing and a curse.

Finally, unable to bear it anymore, she wheeled herself into the small kitchen where she started to prepare a meal. Just in case. She had the groceries to make a nice, if simple, meal for three, thanks to Henrie. She smiled, thinking of the staples in boxes in her bedroom and in two closets. There would be food for at least two months, three if she was frugal.

Of course, Henrie had been supplying food and shelter for many years now, in the form of money wired to her bank account every month. She didn't know how she would have lived without it.

But more important than the money was Henrie himself. They had not laid eyes on one another since Henrie was a small boy, age five or six, she couldn't remember. Her daughter, Henrie's mother, stayed in touch with letters and photographs through the years, until she died.

Henrie knew of her through those letters, through stories told by his mother, through photographs that made their way from Cameroon on rare occasions.

Once settled in New York, Henrie took up the correspondence. He began to send money every month, what he could afford. As his personal income increased, his contributions to her welfare did as well. Eventually, he convinced her to move into town.

She located an apartment in what was, to her, a modern building. Her front door opened to a small brick sidewalk just a few feet from the street. With the apartment came other conveniences, including the telephone. She learned the voice of Henrie the man.

She was used to hearing that voice once a week. He tried to call on Sundays, but sometimes he had to keep trying because of the lines. Some weeks, she didn't hear from him until Wednesday.

She also came to know him through photographs. In a box on the end table, she had pictures of him alone, of him with his friends in Chelsea, of the Inn he called home. My, my, she thought. It was a grand house. She even had pictures of each of those cats of whom he was so fond.

She stared often at the pictures of him. He was tall, slim and handsome, the very essence of his mother.

Now that she had seen him in person, had come to know him in person, she grieved for the day he would leave. But leave, he must, and she would not go with him.

What would she do? She was just an old African woman, one who had to learn to live in a "modern" apartment at the ripe age of sixty or seventy something. At the age that most women in this country were passing on, she was learning how to clean linoleum floors and how to cook using an electric range and oven.

In her eighties, she had to admit that perhaps, this was easier than life in the village.

As she chopped tomatoes and added spices to make a fragrant tomato sauce, she thought, yes, this was easier than using a fire to cook. And it was a great convenience to have refrigeration. Of course, her village had updated as well through the years, but her friends still did not have the conveniences she did. Well, she really was talking about the children of her friends. Most of her friends were gone.

She reached into the pantry for rice and moved to the small refrigerator for the beef Henrie brought the day before. She would have made this Jollof rice with the help of Collette. She enjoyed teaching the young woman to cook native Cameroon dishes. But it was getting late and they had to get back to the hotel before dark. Perhaps it would be ready when they arrived.

If they arrived.

Should she call someone? If so, who? The hotel? The police? Not the police. They could not be trusted.

Yannick was ready to go home, but he worried about Henrie and Collette. They had not returned. By now, they should have been back.

Typically, they ate a small meal with Mrs. Masilla, returned before dark, had a drink in the hotel bar, and retired to their room before Yannick left for the day.

Perhaps Mrs. Masilla was not well. Perhaps they had convinced her to leave with them, and they were helping her to pack. Perhaps….

The telephone rang and he answered. It was Henrie's grandmamá.

"I am so sorry to bother you. Was Henrie able to leave today? He may have tried to call me, but…I have not heard from him."

Yannick sighed. "No. He was unable to secure early tickets. He did not arrive?"

"No. And he did not call."

"He left – they left – at the regular time. This is not good. Not good at all."

"What should I do?" asked Mrs. Masilla.

"Stay there. They may come, or they may call. I will make calls to the authorities."

If it was possible, Yannick detected an ever greater not of alarm in her voice. "The police? You will call the police?"

"No. I will call the Embassy. Stay calm. Stay home."

As he placed the telephone in the cradle, he thought about the situation. First, he would take a look at Henrie's room and secure it. Then he would call the Embassy.

As he tended to his duties, he marveled that the birthplace of Boko Haram was one hundred fifty miles away, perhaps three or four hours by car if the roads were not washed away.

Yaoundé, where the Embassy was located, was almost twice as far in terms of miles and, in theory, could be travelled in six to eight hours. That was in theory. In reality, unless the Embassy had a small plane or a helicopter at its disposal, it would be this time tomorrow before anyone could arrive to help.

10: Chelsea

Monday evening, George sat at the bar. Candice cashed out and sat beside him.

"What's new?"

"What's not?"

"Really? Tell me."

George said, "I'll tell you a funny story. The cats today were incredible."

"The cats are camping several hours away."

"The other cats. The ones that belong to Holly and Jolly, Georgia's nanny cats, and that little one of Clara's. They spent the afternoon at the Inn."

"You're kidding."

"Nope. They came to the Inn and gathered under that table in the dining room. You know, the one that has a sign that says it's a detective agency?"

"It must be catching. Pretty soon, you'll believe it too, that they're detectives."

George turned in his seat to look at her. "It was weird! They gathered there, and they seemed to have some kind of conference, and then they went upstairs and checked out all of the rooms."

"You followed them?"

"No, Hilly told me as she was getting ready to leave. They went into every upstairs room, just like Kali and Ko do when they're home."

Candice turned a steady gaze in his direction, almost as if to will him to become sane again. She shook her head and said, "Well, Annie, Henrie, Pete…several people…they seem to think these cats have magical abilities."

George shook his head. "When they talk about magical abilities, they mean Annie's cats. These are the neighborhood cats. Maybe they're magical, too." He shook his head again. "I must be going crazy."

Candice put a hand on his arm. "Knowing is half the battle. Let's talk about something else, before I go crazy, too. How are the guests?"

"Well, the normal ones are fine."

"The normal ones?"

"The couple in the honeymoon suite are fine. They came over for breakfast then spent the rest of the day on their own. And the French guy is fine."

"The French guy? This is the one that's going to make a big resort somewhere? What's fine about that?"

"I don't like that, either, but the guy himself is fine."

Candice nodded. "Comes in for breakfast, then leaves?"

"So far."

"I thought that family had all the rooms. Where is everyone staying?"

"The French guy is in that back room, the one that opens up to the beach. The family has every room on the second floor, and the honeymooners are in the carriage house."

"So tell me about the family. I've seen the parents, but thank goodness, the kids are too young to come in here."

George reached for his second beer. "Thank goodness is right. I had the pleasure this morning of telling them their oldest son assaulted a woman with a water balloon. They didn't even care."

"Really?"

"Really. I had to bring Pete in. He had a more, shall I say, convincing talk with them. They agreed to pay for the doctor bills. Plus a little extra."

"What about all the thefts?"

"While Pete was there, I gave them a copy of my list."

"The list of the stolen stuff? Did you have prices for everything?"

"Yep." George took a long drink from his bottle before finishing the thought. "I showed them the contract they signed, told them how much I had pre-approved on their card, and let them know where we stood."

"How'd they take it?"

"Not well. I added two more meals this afternoon, lunch and dinner today for all six. Man. Those kids order the most expensive things on the menu! And the parents! They probably put a high tab from Sassy P's on it again today."

"Where do the kids eat? The Café closes in the afternoon."

"They get to-go from the Winery."

"Oh. Well, they could get to-go from here, too. Any more thefts today?"

"Yeah. The boys got a computer game from DoubleGood, and the girls got some of that fair trade jewelry from Bloomin' Crazy."

Candice thought about it for a minute. "What if they ratchet up? What if they go beyond the limit you put on the card?"

"I thought about that. And then I thought, W-W-H-D?"

"W-W-H-D?"

"What Would Henrie Do? While Pete was there, I asked for – and got – a second card. I put another thousand on it."

"A thousand?"

"I wanted them to know I meant business."

"How long will they be here?"

"They're leaving Wednesday. We need to get through tomorrow, and we'll be fine."

As George rose to leave the bar, he noticed the honeymoon couple at a table close enough to have heard everything.

Jim and Connie waited in the library until the kids came in. It was already dark. A touch of parental concern kicked in when they realized the kids could not have eaten on The Avenue, unless they went to the bar or the winery, and they were not supposed to go into either place.

Finally, they walked in. Connie pounced.

"Where have you been?"

"Chill, Mom!" said Clarke. "We've been walkin' around."

"Have you eaten?"

"Yeah. We got to-go from next door. We ate on the beach."

Marty added, "Thanks for the concern. Didn't realize you cared."

Jim snapped, "Marty! Don't speak to your mother like that!"

"Right."

"Apologize to her!"

"Right."

"Marty!"

Connie, exasperated, said, "Oh, for goodness sakes, Jim, drop it. Let's get to the reason for this little conference."

Brooke gave "the look" for which most teenaged girls are noted and snarled, "Whatever!"

Jim and Connie gave exasperated sighs, and Jim started. "We had a visit from the police today. It seems that not only did you injure a woman today, Clarke, but all of you have been shoplifting."

Four voices chimed in to a chorus of "What?" "Who said?" "I have not!" and a curse word.

Jim waved his hands to quiet them down. "In front of that policeman, George presented a list of items taken and the cost of everything. The threat, of course, is that you will be charged with theft. Us, too, for allowing you to go around town unsupervised."

Connie took over. "This is what's going to happen. You will put everything on the table in the hallway outside our room tonight. We'll turn it all in tomorrow morning. Your father and I will ask no questions. You will not be punished as long as everything is returned."

The four looked at one another, looked back at their parents, and said nothing.

Connie let the silence linger for a few seconds, then she said, "Okay. That's what we'll do. In the morning, we'll turn everything over. It's late. Go to bed."

Connie and Jim left the kids. No hugs. No good nights. It was eight o'clock in the evening.

Cassie said, "What now?"

Brooke answered. "Let's get the beer and go talk about it."

"In our rooms?"

"No," said Clarke. "Let's go to the beach. We don't want them to hear us."

They walked onto the porch, down the sidewalk, and behind some bushes. They picked up two coolers with beer procured from a ne'er-do-well on the street and snacks they had filched from the grocery store earlier in the day.

Brooke pulled out a backpack with two blankets, all stolen from the box store on the access road leading to the interstate. As she picked up the pack, she said, "I'll bet they don't have records on the stuff from that box store. Let's remember where we got things and only give back what's probably on the list."

As they walked toward the beach, Marty asked, "Do we have to give the game back?"

Clarke said, "We'll talk about it. But one thing's for sure."

"What's that?" asked Brooke.

"We're not going back to that antique store. I thought they were onto us today, and now we can be sure they are. Stealing from them might get us arrested."

Outside of town, Louis sat at a quiet corner of the tasting bar at Chateau Simon. The newest winery in the area – or at least the winery with the newest owners – provided an upscale experience. In years to come, more and more of their wine would be made from grapes grown onsite. For now, many of their wines were made with grapes purchased from others.

Brian and Janet, the owners, were positive about the area surrounding Chelsea. They stopped to chat with Louis as they had time.

Simon, their tuxedo cat with a wicked white stripe up his nose, sat politely at the end of the bar, far enough from Louis to keep cat hairs from floating into his glass, but close enough to hear everything.

While Louis asked about several towns up and down the coast, he seemed to spend a lot of time asking questions about The Avenue. He wove the questions in and around his questions about the other towns. Simon thought that he was perhaps the only one in the room piecing the information together. Particularly since he was staying at the bar, and Brian and Janet talked to him in between other customers, and rarely at the same time.

How long had George been the manager at the KaliKo Inn?

Who owned the building across the street from Annie's places?

Did the state own the campground at the state park, or was a private owner involved?

Did the town own the town park and the beach area, or was it leased?

Did Ray own The Marina?

Where are the closest golf courses? Are any PGA-approved?

Are all of the wineries in the area as good as yours?

All in all, it was a disturbing evening for Simon. He wondered how he could communicate with his detective friends. They would know what to make of this man.

At Mo's Tap, Livia finally asked the burning question. "What was the problem with your card, Mitch?"

"Nothing. A misunderstanding. I cancelled that card a while ago, but forgot to take it out of my wallet. It was embarrassing, though. Sorry you had to see that."

"What's a little embarrassment? Especially when no one knows who we are."

"You're right. Are you happy with the things you bought today?"

"Yes! I think I'll wear that special little number tonight. If you don't mind."

"I can't wait." Mitch waited a beat before saying, "Tomorrow, let's stay in town and check out the local shops. JoJo said the Café is an excellent place for lunch, and she recommended the Winery for dinner."

"That sounds good to me."

Mitch said a silent prayer of thanks. He could charge most of tomorrow to the room. Perhaps no one would catch that he was overextended. At least, not until it was time to leave. By then, maybe he would think of something.

He thought about what George said about the kids and thefts on The Avenue. Perhaps he could do something with that. His former skills might once again serve him well.

In the middle of the night, four youth crept silently back and forth, from their rooms to the door of their parents' room. They returned everything that had come from stores on The Avenue. Everything but the video game. They weren't giving that up. They had decided to try to bluff their way out of that one.

Connie, lying in bed and unable to sleep, heard them come, over and over. She sighed. They needed help. All of them. The kids, she and Jim. Maybe they should try family therapy again.

11: Lavender Lake

Dennis arrived for dinner just before dusk, sticks for roasting marshmallows in hand. He was the last to arrive. Everyone else was in the small kitchen and dining room, sitting at the table or helping to put food out.

"Sorry I'm late. I had to trim these sticks down. Didn't want to be doin' it here. Those cats might swallow a small piece of wood, ya know."

Annie laughed. "Thanks, Dennis. Have a seat. Since you're allergic to mushrooms, we made the Alfredo without."

Dennis, making eye contact with everyone as he sat, noticed that John and Lucy exchanged a glance, then looked back, apparently embarrassed about something. Once again, he had the feeling he should know them.

Chris was saying, "And speaking of mushrooms, did we happen to give poison ones to you guys?"

Dani said, "You sure did. But Dennis took them out of our bowl, so you haven't killed us. Yet."

Neither John nor Lucy responded at first. Annie looked at them. "Did you check yours, Lucy?"

"I did. We didn't get any bad ones. I know what to look for."

Annie, pouring water into glasses, stopped what she was doing and looked at Lucy. "Did you notice we had poisonous ones in the basket?"

Lucy coughed, put her hand to her mouth and reached for her water. It was several seconds before she said, "I only looked at the ones I picked out. I didn't notice if there were others there that weren't, you know, good."

Dennis thought about that for a minute. He wasn't there when Lucy apparently chose her own mushrooms, but he couldn't help but think the older woman was lying. And why? Why would she lie about mushrooms?

Throughout dinner, Annie thought she had to carry the conversation from one sentence to the next, from one person to the next. She had never felt more inept as a hostess. They had managed to talk about Annie's cats, Chris's life with the Coast Guard, the lovely campground, Annie's businesses, and what fish might be biting in the lake.

John and Lucy deflected questions about their home in New York. Kyle and Dani seemed shy around everyone – they were the youngest of the group by far – and Dennis had suddenly grown less talkative than normal.

Finally, blissfully, the meal was finished and the dinner party left the cabin for the screened-in gazebo.

Chris had wood for the fire pit and ingredients for s'mores ready in the gazebo, and Annie carried out a thermos of hot chocolate.

She also herded Sis and the cats, minus Kali and Ko, to the gazebo. The screened-in area would keep them safe, and they could enjoy the night air.

The cats made the most of it. They positioned themselves around the base of the gazebo, looking out into the darkening woods. Chris busied himself making the fire. The pit, with a screened cover for windy nights, was in the center of the gazebo.

Once the humans settled in with cups of hot chocolate, Annie tried one more time to enroll the young couple in a conversation. "Kyle, Dani, what is it that you do?"

Dani finally perked up. Perhaps the hot chocolate had an effect. "We write code for several companies in the healthcare industry. We were lucky to get into the same industry right out of college."

"Several companies? Do you have to travel around, or are they all in your home town?"

Dani laughed. "We don't have a home town. We don't live anywhere. We travel the country, making sure to stay where we can get a good internet connection. We're here now, and we'll go further east this summer. We plan to go to the southwest this winter."

Kyle apparently was perked up by hot chocolate as well. He added, "We might try Canada next year. If we can get a visa, we'll stay for twelve to eighteen months."

"I've never been to Canada. Where are you going? Quebec? Ontario?"

"We've always liked Sault Ste. Marie, you know, in the Upper Peninsula? We would try to stay there for a while, then cross over. That would put us in the state of Ontario, but we were thinking of going further in, toward Hudson Bay."

Annie was amazed. "What a wonderful journey. How can you afford this? Oh, I'm sorry! That was rude!"

Kyle and Dani both laughed. "Don't worry about it. We don't mind sharing our story. We were lucky that both of us wanted to write code, and that we both got positions in healthcare. Between us, we make over two hundred thousand a year."

With the exception of the popping fire, Annie swore she could hear a pin drop. She couldn't find her tongue for several seconds. Then she did. "I'm sorry, but you can't be telling this to perfect strangers! They could be all over you for your money, access to your accounts...."

Quickly, Dani said, "Don't worry. All of our money is direct deposited to a brokerage firm, and most of our money is invested in bitcoin."

Kyle cut in, "It was. Bitcoin is dicey now, and our broker is divesting. It should be nearly gone by now, and invested in a range of stocks and bonds to fit today's market."

Dani added, "But we were in bitcoin long enough to make a killing. We're millionaires a couple of times over."

Annie said, "And yet you prefer to live like vagabonds?"

Together, they said, "Yes!"

Chris asked, "Don't you worry about people finding out? Taking advantage?"

"No. We give ourselves a modest monthly income, direct deposited from the brokerage to a checking account, and we use a debit card for just about everything."

"But you could be held for ransom..."

"No," said Dani. We have no family, and the brokerage firm has specific instructions to give nothing in the event a ransom is requested."

"You thought of that?"

"Yeah. The firm counseled us on it. I mean, given our lifestyle...."

Dennis said, "But still, that sounds so inviting, people might be tempted...."

"It wouldn't work. Too many passcodes and secret sentences."

Annie noticed that Dennis had a faraway look in his eyes. Oh, well. She might have that same look. She said, "I think it's wonderful. You're so young, and the world is at your feet."

Kyle said, "Enough about us. John, what brings you and Lucy to this little campground?"

John looked at Lucy, then gave a tentative answer. "We wanted to get away, and this seemed a nice spot."

"Are you enjoying the lake? Fishing? Going to town for restaurants?"

"Oh, no. We're sticking pretty close to the cabin. We just got here, ya know. And we won't be staying long. We just wanted to get away."

"Where's home?" asked Dani.

John looked at Lucy again, then said, "Oh, we live in New York. Not the city. Upstate, kind of."

Conversation flagged again. Annie roasted a marshmallow and wondered why she had decided to ask these strangers to come over.

Dennis came to the rescue. "We talked about telling ghost stories. I figure we couldn't get a better one than the one about the Lavender Lake Wolf Man."

Chris asked, "That's a real thing, isn't it?"

"It's a long-standing myth, with sightings since the late eighteen hundreds. It could be true. Anyway, this is how

I've always heard it told. I've only lived here nine years, so I don't have personal experience."

Dennis leaned back, settling into the deck chair. As he talked, everyone else leaned forward. He spun a fantastic vision of a half-man, half-beast monster. He had long legs, a human torso, canine shoulders, neck and head, and he stood seven feet tall on his hind legs. He was sometimes said to have blue eyes and sometimes amber.

Humans, cats and a dog were captivated by the tale.

When Dennis described the howl, he screamed like a wolf in severe pain. Sis cowered behind Chris, and Annie suddenly had two cats in her lap and three wrapped around her ankles.

Dennis lowered his voice and leaned in toward the fire pit. Now that the sky had grown dark, his face took on an eerie glow. "According to legend, he appears every ten years. Now, let's see…the last time he was in these parts was just about ten years ago. The year before I came. I imagine we might see him here this spring. Maybe this very week."

Dennis squinted his eyes, lowered his head, and looked into the frightened eyes of five cats and a dog. In the same low voice, he said, "Maybe this very night."

He sat taller and looked around the fire, meeting the eyes of the humans. His voice went even lower. "Thirty years ago, a disc jockey from the local radio station decided to prove the Wolf Man really did exist. He researched all of the sightings, where and when they took place and who reported the sighting. It seems it was time for the wolf man to appear again, and hundreds of people came to the lake, hoping to see him. Wouldn't you know, he didn't come."

Dennis looked around the circle again. "Not that night. No, he came the next night, when only the DJ was here. He was found the next morning, clutching his tape recorder. He got that howl on tape before he, you know, died of fright."

Dennis sat back, his story finished. Annie pressed him. "Really, Dennis? Is this really true?"

Dennis laughed. "They say it is, but I've only been here nine years. This is the tenth year since the last sighting. It could be tonight."

Kyle gave a nervous laugh. Dani said, "Well, hey, since he could come out tonight, we should get on home. Thanks for dinner. Maybe we'll see you before we leave."

John added, "We should go, too. It's dark, and we walk pretty slow."

Dennis said, "Let me take the two of you to your cabin. I've got plenty of room on that ATV, and you might step into a hole or something in the dark."

Kyle and Dani were the first to leave. They went to the lake and followed its contours to their own cabin. It was a longer but easier walk than going through the woods in the dark.

Kyle said, "That guy got a funny look."

Dani replied, "He did. Maybe we should stop talking about our money. People can be crazy."

"Our broker said that. He was right to make us lock it all down, but we should have listened to him."

"Let's be smart about it. Let's ditch our reservation and leave early. I'll get on the internet tonight and make a reservation for tomorrow. Should we go west?"

Kyle shook his head. "Let's head for Canada now."

As the humans cleared out of the gazebo, Annie walked the cats back to the cabin. She closed the door and there they were. Locked in.

Tiger Lily fumed.

Sis was still on the outside. The cats gathered at the screen door to talk to her about their predicament.

Tiger Lily said, *"What if that wolf man comes tonight? We won't be able to get out and save people."*

Little Socks said, *"We couldn't save anyone from that monster. He would eat us!"*

Even Mr. Bean agreed with that assessment. He said, *"I don't want to go outside, not at night. I want to stay here with Mommy."*

Kali and Ko didn't come out from under the furniture, but they wailed their agreement. *"We're staying here!"* *"You can't make me go outside!"*

Sis looked at Tiger Lily. *"I don't know why you want to get out. I can't wait for Chris or Annie to come let me in. I don't want to be anywhere near that monster."*

Sis didn't have to wait long. Chris and Annie came in, remnants of hot chocolate and s'mores in their hands, letting Sis in ahead of them.

It had been a long day, but Chris and Annie weren't finished. Chris found an internet station with music from the nineteen seventies. He turned it up as loud as the speakers could handle.

He shouted, "Come dance with me!"

Annie and Chris danced, the cats hid behind pillows, and Sis stayed at the door.

She heard a long, frightened and painful howl in the middle of the woods. It seemed to go on forever.

Tiger Lily came up behind her. *"Did you hear that?"*

Sis looked at her. *"That wolf man came tonight! Just like Dennis said!"*

Tiger Lily, frightened, shook her head. *"That wasn't a wolf man. That was a real man."*

They huddled closer together and remained alert at the door. They stayed at the door after the music ended and after Chris and Annie went to bed. They woke when the sun rose, still huddled together at the foot of the door.

12: Cameroon

Henrie roused himself and looked at Collette. She was still asleep. As situations went, this was not as bad as it could be. At least, that is what he told himself.

He assumed the time to be somewhere between two and four in the morning. If that were true, it would be between nine and eleven in the evening – the day before – at home. As long as he could remember little things like this, he would be okay.

They were in a hut with dirt floors. It was possible they were in a hut in the village of his childhood. That made no difference, actually. They were not going anywhere.

There was one cot – Collette slept there – and several thin cushions, where Henrie had fallen asleep. Now he was awake. It was time to think.

Bertrand, the taxi driver, had seemed almost apologetic. He was reasonable enough, as kidnappers go. At least he had asked for and had been granted the position of interrogator. He, and he alone, would speak to Henrie and Collette when speaking was necessary.

Bertrand told them about the night the police came to his house. Bertrand was on his way home. He had business across the field, and as he neared his home, he heard loud voices. He stopped and hid behind a bush at the edge of the field across the road from the house.

His children screamed, then he heard shots. His wife cried out. Were the children dead? Then he heard the men. They yelled vile things. They accused her of being Boko Haram. They said if they could rid the country of the women and children, eventually the scourge would be gone. They called her names. They asked where he was. Then more shots. Then flames, and the men – four of them in police uniforms– were out of the house. They jumped into their vehicle and fired shots into the air as they left.

He, Bertrand, stayed behind the bush, terrified and in anguish. He knew everyone inside was dead.

That's what they did. The police. They killed Boko Haram.

So what, if he was Boko Haram? He had a purpose. His mission was pure. Boko Haram would establish a "pure" Islamic state ruled by sharia, unlike the majority of Muslim governments. He and his friends attacked only Christians, the wrong kind of Muslims and government. They didn't kill pure people.

They bombed churches, mosques, schools and police stations. They kidnapped western tourists, like Henrie and Collette, but their mission was pure.

The meaning of the term, boko haram, was "western education is forbidden." They did not participate in any government organizations, because Muslim governments were not based on sharia law. They were based on western law.

Eventually, Henrie had drawn Bertrand back to the point he made about kidnapping western tourists.

To each question, Bertrand responded, "Allah gives us what is needed to survive."

Bertrand finally left them alone. Now Henrie thought about their situation. He had read of kidnappings in Nigeria. He had been stupid to think Boko Haram would recognize borders. Henrie was a quick study. If they did not recognize government, they wouldn't recognize something as nebulous as a line on a piece of paper or a GIS map.

They wanted money. They could make a plea to his grandmother. No. Certainly they knew she had no money.

They would call the Inn. They would call Annie. Annie was not home. They would get George. George would get Pete. Pete would know what to do.

No, that did not make sense. Pete could do nothing.

Someone would call the Embassy. Yes. That is what would happen. The request for money would be trapped in some political loop for years. Before they were released, Collette would be sold as a slave and he would be...well, perhaps he would be sold as a slave as well. That would be the good news. He didn't care to think about the bad.

At all costs, he had to keep them from approaching the Embassy. They had to call Chelsea. That was their only hope.

It was too dark to see anything in the hut, but it was reasonable to assume they left nothing that could be used as a weapon or as an aid in escape.

If only he had heeded the warnings. The State Department had been quite specific. But, he thought, worry about that now would not help. Sleep. He must sleep while he could. He would plan in the light of day.

Mr. Jones arrived at the hotel in Maroua. It was early in the morning. So early the sun would not be up for a few hours. He was tired.

He reached the hotel manager only an hour after the initial telephone call. As it happened, he told Yannick, he was available. As it happened, a helicopter was available as well. He could not tell Yannick that when the helicopter departed Maroua, it would carry him, two hostages and a team that had not yet arrived.

Typically, he would not have been sent to this part of Cameroon because tourists had been kidnapped. The State Department gave warnings to everyone traveling here, particularly to the Far North region. He was sent because an opportunity to reach into one of the newest Boko Haram nests had presented. This was not just a rescue operation. It was an incursion.

The hotel manager said a room would be waiting, and it was. He got a key from the night manager and went upstairs, dropping his jacket and valise on the bed. He loosened his tie and picked up the phone. Dialing in the numbers without looking, he left a simple voice mail. "Arrived. No issues."

He noticed a bulky envelope on the opposite bedside table with his name. He opened it and first removed a sheet of paper. It read, "Mr. Jones, the cell phones enclosed were found by a kind citizen. She had second thoughts about giving them to the police, so she brought them to the only place American tourists might be staying. I believe they belong to our two friends. They were found on a street close to the apartment of Mrs. Masilla. Perhaps they passed that complex and went toward the mountains."

He took the phones from the envelope and opened them. Neither were passcode encrypted. He accessed photos, email, text messages and social media. By the time he put down the second phone, he thought he knew them fairly well.

He would have to call their families. He checked his watch. He should wait until morning on the other side of the world to call the States. That would give him time to get a couple hours of sleep.

13: Chelsea

George arrived at the Inn early. He thought he would get there before Georgia, but he was wrong. Georgia was doing double duty at Mo's Tap and apparently decided to get an early start.

He didn't see Georgia, but he saw a chubby leg sticking out from under the detective table. Leaning down and picking up a corner of the tablecloth, he saw Little Fred napping with her nanny kitties.

He heard voices in the kitchen. Nancy and Sam were back in town following a visit to their daughter, Annie's half-sister. As he walked in, Nancy handed him a cup of coffee.

"I'll be better help to JoJo than you. Sit. Drink. I'll get breakfast for you."

George had to move a large, golden long-haired cat from a chair first. Honey Bear, Nancy's haughty boy, hissed and flipped his tail. He swaggered into the dining room and under the table with Little Fred and the small cats.

Before guests began to come down for breakfast, more cats arrived. George noted Simon Finnegan, Oscar McMurphy and Moriah from across the street. He watched in wonder as they walked in, tails high, and pushed aside the cover to go under the table.

"How do they know to gather? Is it like this all the time?"

Nancy laughed. "I have long given up trying to understand the cats in this community. I can tell you that Honey Bear is a completely different cat. Oh, mind you, he's still aloof and pouty, but he seems to like these cats. He really, really likes them. That would never have happened before."

They heard someone come into the dining room. George rose to start the day. He said, "Good morning, Louis. Coffee?"

"Yes, please. Do you think I have time to eat this morning?"

"Maybe we'll get lucky. Tell you what. If you are interrupted, I'll make a to-go container for you."

"Yes. That would be wonderful." Louis helped his plate as he continued to talk. "George, Ray said this is not your regular job?"

"No. I manage Mo's Tap, the blues bar up the street. Henrie, the manager here, is on vacation."

"And the owner? Annie is her name?"

"Yes. She's on vacation, too."

"They are together?"

George chuckled. "No, it was a mistake. Annie's friend put a deposit on a cabin at a resort, and they couldn't change the reservation. Henrie made plans to visit family in Africa, and he couldn't change his reservations. They decided to bite the bullet, and they asked me to fill in."

"You are good at this, no?"

"You're right. I am good at this. No!"

"You cannot be held responsible for the, shall we say, sins of the children. Especially when the children are not yours."

"That's right. But if Henrie were here, it would be different. Those kids would have misbehaved one time. One time only. You would be looking at angels."

"That is good to know."

"Excuse me?"

"I only meant, it is good to have the information. I appear to have good English, but not always do I translate well."

Louis had nearly finished his breakfast, and George brought out a carrying container with two cups of coffee. He pointed to a dot on top of one. "Give this one to Ray. I made it the way he likes it."

"I thank you. And I am leaving just in time."

Louis waved and left as the youth stampeded into the dining room.

As Louis exited the front door, Mitch and Livia entered. George gave them an apologetic look as he motioned with his head toward the clamor. Mitch shook his head, as if to say, "It's alright."

George went into the kitchen, happy to get away. Nancy could hardly contain herself.

"I've never heard the like! Even my brood of active grandchildren can't compare to this!"

"Do you know how to control them?"

"I wouldn't even attempt it. You have one more morning of this?"

"Yes."

Nancy turned to JoJo. "Tomorrow, they're having hot dogs and cold grits for breakfast. We'll figure out some way to serve them in another room and let the adults eat the good stuff."

George laughed, then he sighed. Thank goodness Nancy was here. It would be okay, after all.

Mitch had practiced this conversation in his head. It would be confusing to Livia, but that couldn't be helped. He needed some shade for what he planned to do.

"Hey, kids, have you been in town for a while?"

Brooke, startled, looked up. "Yeah. Why?"

"Oh, I want to buy something special for my lovely bride, and I don't know where to go."

Marty piped up, "You need to take her to that antique place on Main Street. There's a jewelry store inside, and they have really nice stuff."

"Yeah," said Brooke. "We were there yesterday. But I think you have to have quite a bit of money."

"Would you be willing to walk us down there? Show us where it is?"

The four youth looked at one another. In their silent communication, they said, "If he's in there shopping, we might be able to get away with something."

Brooke looked back at Mitch. "Sure. I wanted to go back anyway. What time are you gonna go?"

"What time do they open?"

"I dunno. Maybe nine?"

"Then nine it is. We'll meet you in the lobby then."

Little Fred had changed tails. She now hung on to Simon Finnegan and Oscar McMurphy. She shifted her little body as the cats sat up to speak to one another.

"See?" said Simon Finnegan. *"I told you if we got here early we'd hear important stuff."*

Speckles asked, *"Is there anything we need to know? Anything important?"*

Oscar McMurphy, in the most pompous voice she could muster – she was a scaredy cat, after all – said, *"It was all important. It's up to us detectives to figure out how to put it all together."*

Moriah was confused. *"So we heard the one guy ask questions about Henrie and stuff. Was that important?"*

"Probably," said Honey Bear. *"From what I've learned of the detective trade, you have to listen to everything. You never know when something might be important. So we have to talk about everything. One thing at a time."*

Simon Finnegan hissed. *"Tiger Lily left me in charge."*

Oscar McMurphy hissed back, *"Us. She left us in charge."*

Honey Bear let the sentences roll over his back. *"As I said, let's take one thing at a time. Moriah, you were right to bring him up first. He was the first person in the room. What did he say?"*

Simon Finnegan and Oscar McMurphy started to protest, but Daryll answered the question. *"He said does he have time to eat?"*

"Yes," said Honey Bear. *"And what else?"*

Speckles almost shouted, *"He asked about Henrie. And Annie."*

Moriah added, *"And he wanted to know if Henrie was a good manager."*

Simon Finnegan looked at Moriah. *"He didn't say anything like that."*

Moriah stood her ground. *"No, he didn't. He asked questions around that. He asked – in a roundabout way – why Henrie left the place alone, and if he would do it on a regular basis, and if he would have managed things better."*

Simon Finnegan started to say something, then stopped. He looked at Oscar McMurphy, then Honey Bear.

Honey Bear said, *"I think our young friend put the hammer to the nail."*

Moriah sat back with a smile. She was going to be good at this.

Speckles asked, *"What about those kids? What did they say that was important?"*

Daryll put a tentative paw up to get the group's attention.

"Yes, Daryll?" asked Honey Bear.

"They already went to the antique place? And they want to go back? Maybe they saw something? To steal?"

Oscar McMurphy put her paw into the middle of the circle. Everyone looked at her. *"I think they didn't decide to go back until that man said something. I think the man might be up to no good."*

Five cats looked at Oscar McMurphy with incredulous eyes. Honey Bear finally said, *"There are times you should let your brother do the speaking for you."*

This time, Oscar McMurphy hissed at Honey Bear.

Honey Bear looked thoughtful. *"I haven't seen the lovely Claire for a while. Perhaps I should go to the antique store to watch the proceedings."*

Claire was a beautiful Himalayan who kept the antique store mouse-free. She didn't leave the building unless her human, Frank, took her. Nonetheless, she and Honey Bear had occasion to get together and had become attracted to one another.

Speckles huffed. *"We're not supposed to leave The Avenue. You know that. They let us roam free, as long as we follow the rules."*

"Who will know?" asked Honey Bear.

Several cats named names at the same time. *"Frank." "Little Fred." "Gema." Everyone at the Café." "George." "JoJo." "Everyone on The Avenue."*

Honey Bear hissed. *"You'll keep naming names as if our mere presence on the street will draw the looks of everyone in a ten mile radius."*

Moriah said, *"We are pretty magnetic."*

Another chorus ensued. *"That's photogenic." "You mean majestic." "Maybe pathetic." "Attention grabbing."*

Honey Bear hissed. *"Quiet!"*

Simon Finnegan said, *"We don't have the same constraints. Holly and Jolly know we roam everywhere, even out in the country. We'll escort you, Honey Bear."*

Honey Bear sent him a withering stare, which made Simon Finnegan add, *"Not that you need it. No. We're just going to give you cover. That's all."*

"Well, okay. But I thought you intended to train Moriah how to be a cat burglar. You can't do both."

Speckles said, *"I know how. I'll teach her."*

Daryll added, *"I'll help?"*

Oscar McMurphy said, *"Then it's settled. Let's leave now. We can be there watching when they come in."*

The three large cats slipped out from under the table and paid no attention when Little Fred crawled out. She stood and walked after them as fast as her little legs would go.

George and Nancy sat down with a cup of coffee. JoJo tried to sit, but she saw Little Fred trot out of the dining room and into the foyer. JoJo caught her in time, just as the tail end of Oscar McMurphy went through the cat door.

She walked back to the kitchen holding Little Fred's hand. Nancy asked, "Where was she going?"

"Oh, those cats that belong to Holly and Jolly were just leaving. She tried to follow them."

Nancy shook her head. "Those cats wander all over town. Even out of town. I hope Honey Bear doesn't take up with them."

They were interrupted by loud footsteps coming into the dining room. And through the dining room into the kitchen.

Connie, shoulders straight, head high and nose in the air, threw a piece of paper at George.

"Your list," she said, and turned on her heel to go.

"Wait!" cried George. He bent to pick it off the floor. "What is this?"

Connie didn't turn around. "Your list. You said they stole these things. You'll find everything upstairs in the hallway. They only borrowed them."

George had followed her through the dining room and into the foyer. Jim waited for his wife, and together they walked swiftly out the door.

George shouted after them, "I have things to add to it! They took more stuff yesterday!"

The door slammed shut.

George sighed. As he mentally added the cost of breakfast to Jim and Connie's bill, probably the most expensive the Café had to offer, he looked at the paper. It was, indeed, the list of items taken from all of the stores on The Avenue before yesterday.

Next on his things-to-do list would have to be checking out the things in the hallway. Maybe he'd get lucky and they would have given back everything. And it would all be in good shape.

Maybe pigs could fly.

George was working himself into a temper when the telephone rang. He grabbed it and, in a less than hospitable tone, he said, "KaliKo Inn. May I help you?"

"Yes," came a soft voice. "I am calling for Annie Mack. Is she available?"

George, still miffed, let it come through his voice again. "No, she's not here at the moment. I'm filling in. May I help you?"

There was silence on the line for a few seconds, then, "You are filling in? May I ask your name, please?"

"You may, but since you're doing the calling, why don't you tell me yours first?"

"Certainly. How rude of me. My name is Mr. Jones. I work for the United States Embassy in Cameroon."

George stopped short. Now concerned, he said, "Cameroon? Is this about Henrie? Is he alright?"

"Please. I must know to whom I am speaking."

"George. I'm George. I work for Annie – Ms. Mack – and I'm taking care of the Inn while she and Henrie are out of town."

"Ms. Mack is the woman with…with Henrie?"

"No. Henrie is with his friend Collette. Annie is on vacation here in the states. What's going on?"

"Yes. That matches the information given to me by the hotel."

"Henrie's hotel?"

"Yes. I am at the hotel now."

"Look. I don't want to talk to you – what did you say your name was?"

"You may call me Mr. Jones."

"I'm going to hang up. I'm going to call the hotel where Henrie is staying, and if they say you're there, I'm going to hang up and figure out how to get in contact with your Embassy."

"I can give you the number…"

"No, thank you. I'll get it myself. If you are who you say you are, hold tight. I'll get back with you."

When George turned around, JoJo was already on the internet, looking up the telephone number for the hotel and the Embassy in Cameroon. Nancy had pulled her cellphone out. She said, "I'm calling Pete."

Moriah whispered, *"Is this what it's like?"*

Speckles and Daryll, shocked, couldn't answer at first, then Speckles said, *"Yes. This is what happens when someone is in bad trouble, and there's nothing we can do to help."*

The three small cats huddled under the detective table, unsure what to do, until Pete and Cyril came through the front door.

14: Lavender Lake

Sis had been pacing for a long time, but something about the fresh air kept the humans asleep. Chris and Annie finally woke to her pacing but remained in bed, enjoying the smell of a spring storm on the way.

Annie said, "Thunder sounds different over a small lake than over our big one."

"You need to hear it when you're on the lake. You'll never be the same."

"How long do you think it will be before it rains?"

"It sounds far away. Hey!"

Sis had taken Chris's hand into her mouth. She didn't bite to break skin, but she had a firm hold.

At last, Chris got out of bed to open the front door. "Okay, girl. You need to go out…" Sis bounded out. Tiger Lily ran between Chris's legs and followed Sis at a dead run into the woods.

"Sis! Tiger Lily! Come back!"

He threw on jeans and a pair of shoes and ran after them. Annie, terrified that Tiger Lily would be lost, counted cat heads before she, too, ran out the door. Without knowing why, she grabbed her cell phone from the table at the door.

She was glad she did. When she finally caught up with him, nearly a football field's length into the woods, Chris stood over a prone Dennis. He was face-down in the weeds near an oak tree. What was he doing in the woods? Sis and Tiger Lily walked all around him, sniffing both Dennis and the ground around him.

Annie whispered, "Is he dead?"

"He looks it, and I didn't feel a pulse. I'll go back and call nine one one."

"I have my phone. I'll call."

As she called, thunder rolled closer, and she saw streaks of lightening in the distance. She hung up and said, "I hope it breaks up or passes north. Anyway, I'll go to the office and lead the rescue folks back here. Keep an eye on Tiger Lily…wait! Where is she? Where'd she go?"

Chris looked around. Sis was still with the body, but Tiger Lily was nowhere to be seen. Sis heard something, though, because she lifted her head and trotted away. He said, "I'll follow her. She may lead me to Tiger Lily. You need to lead the police back here."

Annie didn't know what to do. Should she go or should she stay? Chris took hold of her shoulders and turned her. "Go! I'll find our girls."

When Annie returned with police and rescue workers, Chris was back with the body; Tiger Lily and Sis sat a few feet away, alert but calm. Almost. Every now and then, Tiger Lily cast a startled glance at the sky. The woods had grown visibly darker, and thunder boomed more than it rolled.

A police officer asked Chris for his identification.

"It's in the cabin."

"That's what she said." This was said in an accusatory tone as the officer nodded his head in Annie's direction. "My partner will escort you back to your cabin to get that information. Stay there, and don't come out for any reason. Don't call anyone."

Chris said, "Are we…"

"Just go."

Sis and Tiger Lily didn't hesitate. They took off at a run for the cabin. Chris and Annie walked ahead of their escort. Chris whispered, "We aren't in Chelsea anymore."

Sis and Tiger Lily conferred with the other cats.

Sassy Pants asked, *"Did dat wolf man kill him? Did he bited him up and kill him good?"*

Tiger Lily shook her head. *"The wolf man isn't real. It was a story Dennis made up. A real person killed him."*

Sis said, *"I think he was poisoned. I'm never going to eat a mushroom. That's what he had. I smelled them."*

Tiger Lily added, *"Those two people that he took home were with him in the woods. I followed their smell back to their cabin."*

Sis nodded. *"And I found a second trail. The young couple was there, too. They came in from the lake, and they went back that way, too."*

Mr. Bean asked, *"How did Dennis come in?"*

Sis answered, *"I smelled Dennis on the same trail as the older couple."*

Kali and Ko said together, *"Why did they leave him there?"* *"Why didn't they call a doctor?"*

Little Socks said, *"It's obvious. They killed him."*

"How?" asked Sassy Pants. *"Dey maded him eat a mushroom? And dat kilt him?"*

Mo trilled.

Kali translated. *"It wasn't necessarily the older couple. Both of them were in the same place as Dennis, then they both walked out without him."*

"But why would either couple want to kill him?" asked Mr. Bean.

"That's the question," answered Tiger Lily. *"We'll have to figure it out."*

Sassy Pants added, *"An we has to figure who duz it or if dey duz it togeder."*

Little Socks said, *"Great lot of good that will do. Even if we figure it out, Pete's not here. We'll have a devil of a time talking to the local police."*

Chris dressed – actually, he threw on a shirt to go with the jeans – and made breakfast while they waited. He kept it simple. Orange flavored pancakes with homemade citrus syrup, maple-smoked bacon, and vanilla yogurt with nuts and fresh fruit.

He offered coffee to their officer escort. After the officer declined in a curt fashion, he decided to ignore him. Annie apparently had the same idea. She took a bite of pancake, sighed, leaned in, and whispered, "Do they think we did it?"

"It sure looks that way, and we don't have an alibi."

"We do, too. We were together."

"Exactly. That's not a good one for either one of us."

A knock on the door interrupted the conversation. Chris looked up and saw a woman in uniform on the other side of the screen door. The officer escort had already reached for the door to open it.

Chris said, "Come in," he said. "Pancakes?"

She quickly quashed any thought of a friendly conversation. "I'm not here for pleasantries."

She nodded to the officer and turned back. "I need to keep the two of you separated while I conduct interviews. I'll need you," she nodded to Annie, "to go outside with this officer while I interview him."

Annie looked out the window at the threatening sky. "It's going to rain, and, well, the lightening?"

"You'll be fine. I noticed that covered gazebo out there."

"It won't help if the wind goes sideways."

"Well," said the woman, "we'll cross that bridge if it ever gets here."

Annie looked at Chris, mouthed the words, "We're not in Chelsea anymore," and left the table. She returned to the table, got her cup of ginger peach tea, and went to the gazebo. The officer and four cats followed her.

Sis, Kali, Ko and Mr. Bean sat under the table to listen to the woman and Chris. The woman started.

"I'm Sheriff Tate. I have your registration papers here, but would you verify this information?"

She asked questions about name, address, date of birth. Chris thought to himself that she was trying to catch him in a lie. Oh, well. This wasn't Chelsea and she wasn't Pete.

Eventually, Sheriff Tate got down to business. "Tell me about your contacts with the victim," and Chris told her everything he thought pertinent, from the day they met him as they registered, through the dinner party the night before.

A bright flash of lightening was followed by a loud clap of thunder. Still no rain, but Chris could still smell it approach. Two of the four cats who had followed Annie out appeared like magic at the door. Chris rose and let Sassy Pants and Mo inside.

"And how did you spend the rest of the evening?"

"Annie and I cleaned up and went to bed."

"What time was that?"

Chris thought about it and said, "Well, we were outside until maybe an hour and a half after dark, then they left, and we brought in the dishes. That took maybe ten minutes."

"And you didn't hear anything?"

"No. Well, we put on some music and turned it up loud, danced around the cabin for a while. Then we went to bed."

"How long did that take? The dancing?"

"Um, fifteen minutes? Twenty?"

He almost jumped at the next round of lightning and thunder. It was on top of them now.

"Is there something in particular making you jumpy?"

Chris shook his head. "No. I'm not used to being under the microscope, is all, and I guess that's making me a little nervous."

"If you didn't do anything, there's no need for you to be nervous."

"I just know how these investigations progress. You're going to try to catch me in a lie or something, and, I don't know. It makes me nervous."

"You say that as if you're used to investigations."

"As it happens, yes, I am."

"Murder investigations?"

"A few, yes."

Sheriff Tate leveled her gaze at him. "You've been involved in murder before?"

"Tangentially. Well, now that I think about it, I probably have more experience than is typical. But it only has to do with my relationship with the Chief of Police, and Annie's businesses, and…"

"Her businesses?"

Chris realized he should have kept his mouth shut. "I think I've said enough. Anyway, about Dennis, the last time I saw him, he was taking John and Lucy home."

Sheriff Tate looked him in the eyes for several seconds, until he looked down.

"Why don't you wait right here. I'll send my officer in to stay with you, and I'll interview your friend."

Mr. Bean didn't want to do it, but he followed Sheriff Tate to the gazebo. He flinched at the flash of lightning and rushed in as soon as the sheriff opened the screen door. He trotted to Tiger Lily. *"I don't think this police person likes Chris. And I don't think she's going to be friendly to Mommy. And it's dangerous out here!"*

"I know. Follow that guy back and stay with Chris."

Mr. Bean slipped away with the uniformed officer and rushed to be at the door as soon as it opened.

Sheriff Tate introduced herself and again went through the particulars. She asked Annie to describe her contacts with Dennis.

The conversation was punctuated with bursts of lightning and loud thunder. Rain pelted the top of the gazebo. As the wind picked up, it came in through the west screens. Annie and the sheriff moved to the far east side. Tiger Lily and Little Socks stayed at her ankles.

Over the sounds of rain, thunder and lightning, Annie relayed her first conversation with Dennis the day before. "He said something about the couple being from the same region he was from, the lakes region of upstate New York."

Sheriff Tate shouted, "Did they know one another?"

Annie shouted back. "They didn't appear to. And when we were all together at dinner last night, they didn't seem to know one another aside from here."

"Did they speak often?"

"I don't know. Oh, he went by to check on the poisonous mushrooms."

"What?"

"He went by to check on the mushrooms. Chris and I picked some, and, well, he took the poisonous ones out of our basket and said he'd go check with that couple and the young couple on the other side."

"Why would he do that?"

"Because we gave mushrooms to both of them."

They were still shouting. Annie said, "Can't we go inside?"

"Not yet. Did they have poisonous ones?"

"I'm not sure…No, wait. The young couple said Dennis took out a few poison ones, and the older couple said they didn't find any."

"Do you know how to tell the difference now?"

"Yeah. I only pick ones that look like morels, and if there's a mushroom with a solid stem, that's a bad one. But I doubt I'll go out there again. Poison ivy."

Sheriff Tate looked thoughtful. Annie let the silence linger for several seconds, then asked, "Are we done? Can we go in now?"

"No. Tell me about the young couple. They found bad mushrooms, but the older couple didn't?"

"Right. The rich young couple found a few – maybe a couple – of bad mushrooms. Or Dennis found them, took them out of their bowl."

"Rich?"

"Yeah. They're rich, and they live on the road."

"Was that common knowledge?"

"Not to us. Not until last night."

"They talked about it to strangers?"

"Yeah. That was odd, wasn't it?"

"Yes, it was. And just so I'm clear, Dennis didn't find bad mushrooms with the older couple."

"Right. Wait. Um…he didn't look. He went there, but they checked their own. They seemed to know what was good and what was bad."

A loud crash sounded as lightning seemed to hit a tree in the woods. Thunder was so close on the heels of it,

Annie didn't notice a beat between the two. She yelled, "I don't care what you say, I'm taking my cats inside. Now!"

Annie reached for the cats at her ankles, gathered them as close as she could and ran for the cabin.

The sheriff followed at a sedate pace.

Annie opened the door and dropped Tiger Lily and Little Socks on the floor. She turned to wait under the shelter of the porch for the sheriff. She thought about that last bit. Something about that conversation wasn't right, but she couldn't quite put her finger on it.

15: Cameroon

Bertrand delivered a meal to Henrie and Collette. He sat, waiting for the plates and utensils to be used. Henrie realized he would not make the mistake of leaving anything that could be used as a weapon.

He asked, "Have you made a ransom call?"

"No. We make when we ready."

"Why do you wait? Eventually, someone will look for us, and that could hamper your effort."

"No one look for you."

"How do you know?"

"We keep watch on home of family. No one come or go. No one look for you."

"I understand, but because you see no one does not mean people are not looking. We are supposed to fly out tomorrow. By then, they will look. I could make a call for you, before our people at home become worried."

"Why do that?"

"It might be easier to get funds if they think I am asking for my own benefit."

"What you mean?"

"Well, you see, I could call and say I met new friends, and they are in need of funds. They would wire what I have available."

"How much you have?"

"It may not be nearly so much as you want, but it could be an adequate sum."

"How much?"

"I do not know. I do not look at the statements on a monthly basis."

"We talk about this. This could work, but I do not trust you."

"What can I do or say to ease your concerns?"

Bertrand studied Henrie's face. Finally, he said, "You give me numbers of your people. I talk about this with mine."

As Henrie wrote the numbers, he said, "If we can arrange a transfer of funds, and if you could take us to the airport in your taxi tomorrow morning, no one would be the wiser. You can watch us depart, and you can cover your tracks before we could possibly make contact with anyone."

Mr. Jones was amazed at how quickly George was able to call the hotel and the Embassy to confirm his bona fides. He sat in a private room with Yannick, a conference phone on the table between them.

"May I call you George?"

"Yes, and what should I call you?"

"Mr. Jones."

There was silence on the other end of the line for several seconds. "Okay. Mr. Jones. I called a friend to help with this call. I'm on a speaker phone with the Chelsea Chief of Police."

"Very well. The hotel manager is with me. We will be able to work much more efficiently with all heads together."

Pete took over the Chelsea end of the call. "What can you tell us? Where is Henrie?"

"That is the problem. We do not know where he is. It is approximately two o'clock in the afternoon here. Henrie and his friend have now been missing for twenty-four hours. A report was made to the hotel by his grandmother perhaps six hours after they left the hotel. Immediately, Yannick, the hotel manager, reached out to the Embassy. I arrived in town some hours later. I believe I am up to speed on the situation."

"What could have happened? Is he in a hospital somewhere?"

"We have checked all facilities in the event of an accident. I am afraid they have been kidnapped."

"Kidnapped? Do you have suspects in mind?"

"Unfortunately, we do. We are only one hundred fifty American miles from Maiduguri, Nigeria. That is the birthplace and one of the major centers for Boko Haram. They do not recognize borders, and activity has filtered into Cameroon, particularly into Maroua. Your friends would make valuable captives."

"Will they make a ransom demand?"

"They may make a traditional ransom demand, or they may ask your friends to call and ask that money be wired. Payment for the return of hostages is a major form of income for Boko Haram."

The line went silent. Mr. Jones could imagine what was happening on the other end.

The police officer spoke. "Is there anything we can do from this end?"

"Possibly. Do you have access to money?"

"How much?"

"Lots."

The other end of the line went silent again, until the police officer said, "Define lots."

"I think, probably, in the millions."

"Good grief."

"I take it that is not a possibility."

"It would be a far stretch. But we may have resources."

"While you, on the one hand, seek funds, prepare for a telephone call. Try to record it, or take precise notes. As soon as possible, I will have a hostage negotiator call you from our office in Washington. That person will be able to walk you through various scenarios and how you can respond."

"Mr. Jones, how could this happen?"

"One has to ask instead why these individuals came to the Far North of Cameroon."

"Henrie is visiting family."

"That may be, but the State Department has warned all citizens to avoid travel to this region because of the risk of violent crime. It is very difficult to provide consular services here."

"Would Henrie have known that?"

"Certainly. He would have applied for a visa, and he would have been warned. Nearly forty foreigners have been kidnapped here in the last few years. It is highly unusual that I was granted leave to come here. Your Henrie is responsible for this. He should not have come."

Maria Masilla waited in her apartment for word of Henrie. Oh, if only he had not come. If only he had stayed just a few days. If only.

Intent on her thoughts, she was shocked when her door was kicked in. She could do nothing but stare at the man. He was tall, muscular, and he pointed a rifle at her chest.

She knew this man. He drove a taxi, one of the bright yellow ones. She had seen his face as he dropped Henrie and Collette at her doorstep.

Even though he had kicked in her door, even though he held a rifle to her, his face was not unkind. Stern and purposeful, but not unkind.

He spoke in a native language she did not understand.

"I am so sorry. I did not understand all of that. Do you speak English? Or French?"

He spat on the floor to show his disgust and spoke again in his native tongue.

Maria cringed as she said, "You know there are hundreds of languages in this country." In a native language in which she was fluent, she asked, "Do you speak Fulani?"

He spat again. In broken English, he said "I speak tongue of devil to you. I need telephone of Henrie's people. You give to me."

"Is he alright?"

"For now. You give."

"If he is alright, why do you need me? Oh, my goodness, is he hurt?"

"I no trust him to give me right number. You give."

"You do not trust him? What is happening?"

"Give! Now!"

Maria reached into her box on the table and dug through the photographs until she found a card. On the card were written the telephone numbers for Henrie and for his employer. The number for his place of employment was also on the card.

She thought quickly. She could not turn this over to the man without keeping the numbers for herself. She would never remember them.

She said, "I will write this down for you. Here, on the back of this photograph." She pulled a photograph from the pile, not looking at it.

From her wheelchair, she looked at the man, tears in her eyes. "I want to help. Please, if I help, will he be alright?"

"I no wish to hurt him. Now give, I go."

Maria spoke as she wrote. "This number is for Henrie's friend, his employer. Her name is Annie. And this number is for where he works. Someone should be there, certainly."

The man looked at the numbers, glanced at the numbers on the card in her hand, and seemed content she had given him correct information. He turned the photograph to look at it.

It was Henrie and Annie, chocolate skin against white, tall against short, gleaming bald head against shoulder-length straight dark hair. They stood in front of an elegant house, Henrie's arm around her waist.

"This!" he spat. "This why we fight! Western world not decent. This…this…symbol of greed! He not need palace! He not need white woman! He maybe not be okay!"

Maria shuddered, "But…but that is his boss! And it is not his home. That is where…"

"Silence!" His gun was raised, now pointing to her head. "I did not want to do this! I did not want to be like them! I am better than them!"

Maria quavered in front of him. She screamed, "I am sorry! Please do not hurt me! Please! I will do anything!"

16: Chelsea

Honey Bear and his friends had to wait for a human to leave Antiques On Main before they could enter. Frank didn't have a cat door on the main entry, only on the inside doors.

Once in, Honey Bear made a beeline for the upstairs apartment. His primary goal was to be a detective, but his heart told him to say good morning to the love of his life first. And maybe she could help.

Claire met him midway on the steps between the second and third floors.

"I saw you on the sidewalk," she said. *"I'm glad you're here. We might have trouble."*

"That's why we came. We think someone may try to steal something from you today."

"Those kids. I think they're going to try. I was watching for them, but I saw you first."

The two turned and walked downstairs toward the store. Honey Bear continued, *"What were you going to do if they came?"*

"I don't know. I'm not a detective cat. I don't know what to do. I listen to all of the stories, and I think how brave and smart all of you are, but I'm just..." Claire sighed. *"I'm just a cat."*

Honey Bear couldn't help himself. He was a pompous so-and-so, after all. *"That's right. You're just a cat. But now, I'm here, and I'm a detective cat. I'll figure it out."*

When they got to the store, they sat down with Simon Finnegan and Oscar McMurphy. Oscar McMurphy, only a little jealous of this pretty kitty, said, *"Good morning, Claire. Did Honey Bear tell you why we're here?"*

"Yes. He said you're here to help."

Simon Finnegan said, *"We are. Can you tell us what happened when they were here yesterday?"*

Claire told them the whole story, ending with, *"I was hoping they wouldn't come back, but I was keeping an eye out, just in case. What can you do to help if they come?"*

Everyone looked to Honey Bear. *"Well,"* he said, for once, unsure of himself, *"we'll, uh, we'll watch them. Yes. Watch them. And if they take anything, we'll see what they do with it."*

Oscar McMurphy jumped in. *"Yes. That's what we'll do. Then we'll have to send in our cat burglar to bring it out and give it to Pete."*

Honey Bear took over, now confident in the plan. *"Let's spread out so we can keep an eye on everything. They should be here soon."*

George and Pete got off the telephone and looked at one another. Nancy said, "Sit tight. I've got the cavalry coming."

Hilly had come for the day. She urged JoJo to take Little Fred to the upstairs apartment and helped Nancy get coffee and breakfast plates for everyone else.

Everyone else included Gwen, Annie's accountant, Jenny, her attorney, and Ian, known more for his role as a community volunteer than for his job as a loan officer at the bank.

As the cavalry arrived, Cyril and the cats stayed out from underfoot, just beyond the door of the dining room.

Pete took charge. "Gwen, we know you've had to do this before, decide how much money Annie could come up with quickly. And we know it's probably not enough for what we need."

"You're right. I'm going to guess we need millions, and Annie, one, doesn't have it, and two, doesn't have enough value in her businesses and buildings to come up with that. We could maybe squeeze out seven hundred fifty thousand in a loan, but not right away. What do you think, Ian?"

Ian said, "Just guessing, and without looking at her records, you're probably right. And we would have to have a reason for the loan. Construction or purchase of property…something."

Jenny asked, "Aren't we putting the cart before the horse? Don't we first need to know if Annie will do this?"

George and Nancy answered at the same time. "She'll do it."

George continued, "I'll try to get it touch with her. We know as much as we'll know for a while. Maybe Chris can help."

"He came through before," said Gwen, "but if I remember correctly, he didn't have the amount of money the kidnappers wanted. Well, wait, if I remember correctly, he had it, but he didn't have access to it. He had to lower their expectations."

George shook his head, pulled his cell phone out of his pocket and dialed Annie's number. Chris answered.

What followed was a wide-ranging conversation that, in the end, had everyone even more confused and unsettled.

Before the call ended, Henrie got a call from Gema. He stood up. "Everyone," he said, including Annie, Chris and a police officer on the other end of the line, "I have to go. There's a little problem down the street. George, I may be back to make an arrest. Or four."

Louis had asked Ray to stay close to the coastline today, heading south, so he could take a closer look at beachfront property. He could pretend to look closely and still be within range of cell phone towers.

He looked up. Ray and that ever-present dog of his were in the enclosed helm station and shouldn't be able to hear him over the sound of the engine and the light breeze.

He spoke into the phone. "I was right about this place. It's better than all the others. Have you talked to that state office yet? About the park?"

"Billy made the initial call, and he's pushing them for a quick tour. He's a rich Texan for this one. And about that other thing, Billy's gonna be a corporate realtor. He'll only be on the phone for that. He'll wear an east coast accent and Sheila will be his client. They're gonna work on that marina and yacht-for-hire business. They may make contact today."

"Come to think about it, I'd better clean my accent up. I have to talk like a Frenchie, even when I'm talking to you." He rolled back into a lilting accent. "This man and woman. From where they live?"

The woman on the other end of the line laughed and added what she thought to be an eastern accent. "Bawston."

"Oui. A city I would like to see before I leave America."

The woman on the other end asked, "What about the main place? All of those businesses on that avenue?"

Louis enjoyed using the accent. It allowed him to experiment with words he would rarely otherwise use. He used what he believed to be French pronunciations whenever possible. "So sorry. We must wait for the, uh, the main proprietress to return. We must have agreement from her before we approach the businesses on other side of street."

Louis felt a presence behind and to his left. He lifted his head from the deck chair and turned slightly. That dog was sitting there. Just sitting. And staring. He appeared to have a sixth sense. Whenever Louis tried to call his contact, a woman based in New York, that dog appeared and seemed to listen to the conversation.

Moriah asked, *"What do we do now?"*

Daryll looked at Speckles, as if asking for permission to speak. He then looked at Moriah. *"We can't help Henrie? But we can still practice? Being cat burglars?"*

"How do we do that?"

"We go into rooms? Look at things?"

"But...what do we look for?"

Speckles, being the most experienced kind–of–sort–of detective kitty, said, *"Sometimes Little Socks goes in to look for a clue, but she doesn't know what the clue will be. Not until she finds it."*

Moriah got a puzzled look on her face. *"Then…what does she…um…look for?"*

Both Speckles and Daryll looked at the floor. Darrell finally answered. *"We don't know?"*

Speckles looked up and nodded. *"We don't know. We stay quiet and out of the way until she's done, and then she comes back. Sometimes she has a clue and sometimes she doesn't."*

"So…should I just go and…look?"

Speckles nodded.

Daryll said, *"And try not to lose hairs?"*

"What?"

"You lose hairs everywhere? You can't do that?"

"I can't help it. My hair is fluffy. And it comes off everywhere."

"I thought you were fluffy? Now it's your hair?"

Moriah glared at Daryll. *"I'm fluffy all over."*

"What?"

Speckles said, *"Stop it, Daryll. She can't help it. She really is fluffy all over. And Moriah, if you see your hair on the way out, try to pick it up."*

"Okay." She looked at the floor, then she said, *"Thanks, Daryll, for saying the hard thing."*

"You're welcome?"

After a minute of staring at the floor, Moriah looked up and asked, *"Where do I start?"*

Speckles walked into the foyer and looked up and around. She noticed Hilly had gone to work on the second floor rooms. *"Follow Hilly around. You might find something as she picks up and stuff."*

Daryll added, *"But be cool? If you see something, don't act excited?"*

Speckles walked with Moriah to the bottom of the steps. *"Go on, now, and remember, you're just in training. There aren't any real clues to find up there."*

Moriah walked slowly up the steps, stopping every now and then to look back at the more experienced cats, then up at Hilly as she worked. She took a deep breath and thought, *"I can do this."*

Hilly separated boxes she brought from downstairs. She pushed thoughts of Henrie and Collette out of her mind. There was nothing she or anyone could do, and allowing the worry to keep her from her duties would only make more work for Henrie when he returned.

If he returned.

No. She corrected herself. When he returned.

It wasn't a given that he had been kidnapped. So far, it was just speculation.

She sighed deeply, looked at her list, and began to fill the boxes. She had a box for almost every storefront across The Avenue. There was no need to get a box for the grocery store. No doubt, all the items pilfered from there had been fully or partially eaten.

Sure enough, she spied a box of Oreo Thins that had been half eaten. That went into the trash. She noticed the flavor. Pistachio. She would have to try them sometime.

As she carefully placed a necklace and earring set into the box for Bloomin' Crazy, she noticed Clara's pretty, fluffy cat.

"Hello, Moriah. Are you visiting Speckles and Daryll today? They've got to be around here somewhere."

Moriah looked at her with big, green eyes. She didn't move.

Hilly looked up the hallway. Annie's cats left evidence of their travels throughout the house. Short and long hairs, mostly straight, and mostly in shades of gray, could be found everywhere. When they blew together, they made clumps of straight, wispy gray hair. With the exception of hair from Little Socks, she could not identify the cat or cats who dropped the hair.

Not so with this little one. She saw tufts and swirls of light, fluffy hair. Her hair seemed to stay together in a light, curly lump. If this trip up the hallway was any indication, she would know whenever Moriah spent time at the Inn.

Hilly turned back to her work. When she looked up again, she saw the little cat coming out of one of the rooms, pushing through a cat door and looking left to right as she came. The cat saw Hilly looking, and she stopped mid-stride.

Hilly smiled and turned back to the pile of pilfered goods, the boxes and her list. She figured that, like any cat, Moriah was curious. This was probably the first time she had been able to explore the Inn and its many rooms.

On the way to Antiques On Main, Mitch and Livia stayed behind the teens. Livia leaned in to whisper as they walked. "Tell me again why we needed them to show us this store."

Mitch sighed. "It just seemed they were craving adult attention. Their parents ignore them completely, and I thought we could, you know, be a nice diversion for them. Maybe you can teach the girls something about nice jewelry."

"As if they would ever be able to afford it."

"You never know. They could marry up. Like I did."

Livia squeezed his hand and dropped the subject.

Inside the store, Mitch gave her a meaningful look, and she called to the girls, motioning them to "help" her make a selection.

Mitch walked around the curve of the counter and leaned against it, elbows down and back to the large window looking onto Main Street.

The only person at the jewelry counter went first to Livia and the two girls. Mitch watched as the jeweler skillfully removed one piece at a time, one piece only. Both teens pointed to pieces and asked to try them on.

Livia had gotten into the spirit of the day. She commented on each piece as it came out, allowed the girls to try everything on, and noted how the stone brought out their eyes, or the color of their skin, and wouldn't this look wonderful in gold on you, Brooke. Cassie, I think silver is the best color for you.

The boys split up and wandered the antique store, taking care to look at each small piece. Clarke picked items up, turned them over to look at the price, and, if the price was high enough, regarded it.

Mitch thought that Clarke, in his mind, was measuring the items to the large pockets in his cargo pants. When he put each item down, it was to a slightly different location. A different shelf, or on the right side rather than the left.

Marty carried on the same pattern, but as far from Clarke as he could get.

Mitch saw the owner's sharp eyes on both boys. The owner had a kind but no-nonsense presence. He walked from one boy to the other, then back again. As he approached each boy, he commented on the pieces in their hands. Mitch watched as the owner deftly but pointedly moved pieces back to their original location. By staying in motion, he kept his eyes on everything. Almost.

Mitch watched what must have been an expensive dresser box, rare kelva, painted roses on blue batik, go into a lower pocket in Clarke's pants. The value had to be near two thousand dollars. The owner had been distracted by Marty, who put one piece down – in the wrong place – and immediately picked up a set of brass sleigh bells.

The bells made a gentle ringing sound as the boy asked the owner, "Why are these chained together?"

Mitch almost missed it. He followed the ruse, as had the owner, but realized it for what it was before the owner did. He looked at Clarke the instant the box went into his pocket. Clarke immediately moved a piece to cover the empty space and picked out a piece from another shelf.

When the owner turned and walked to Clarke, he stared at the shelf, but Mitch knew what he thought. Was something else there? I think so, but what was it? Maybe I'm mistaken.

Mitch turned his attention back to the jewelry counter. His moment finally arrived. He moved slowly to come up behind Livia, left arm around her waist, to look at the ruby ring on her finger.

The jeweler had slipped up. A ring set in white gold with an emerald, nearly thirteen carats, surrounded by at least two carats of diamonds, was still on the counter.

Mitch palmed it as he leaned in to kiss Livia on the cheek. The kiss was followed by a sincere look at the jeweler as he asked about the price of the ruby ring, sizing, and how quickly the ring could be made ready for his beloved.

Mitch knew the smell of a sale trumped all other thoughts. The ruby ring, after all, was priced at four thousand and some odd dollars. Mitch ventured a guess that the emerald ring, now in his pocket, was nearly twice the price.

Mitch kissed Livia on the cheek again. "Let's think about it. You saw so many pretty things. We'll have an early lunch at the Café and make a decision this afternoon."

Brooke and Cassie turned away from the jewelry counter, made eye contact with the boys, and they left. On the sidewalk and around the corner from the store, she stopped and wheeled on them all.

"He took it!"

A chorus answered her. "What?" "Took what?" "Who?"

"That guy from the Inn. He took that ring. I saw it yesterday, and I almost had it today. But he palmed it. Man, he's good. He's been doing this a long time."

Cassie's mouth hung open. "I thought you had it. I saw her leave it on the counter, and then it was gone. I thought you had it."

"I was going for it, but he beat me to it."

"That's okay," said Clarke. "I got something."

"Let's see it," said Brooke. "Is it expensive?"

"Twenty five hundred, but let's not look at it here. Let's go back and leave it in the room. Then we can get lunch somewhere."

As Brooke turned to go, Cassie grabbed her arm. "Wait a minute!"

"What?"

"They'll think it was us."

"It was us," said Clarke. "But I covered my tracks. He didn't realize it was missing. We'll be out of town before he figures it out, and then, well, he won't be able to prove it was us."

"No. Not that. The ring. They'll think we took it."

The youth looked at one another, at the sidewalk, at the lake, at the storefronts around them, then back to one another.

Clarke sighed. "We'll have to hide this somewhere, hope it doesn't get broken, and hope we have time to get it before we leave tomorrow. They'll be going through our stuff looking for that ring."

"Where we gonna hide it?" asked Cassie.

Brooke answered. "Where they'll never think to look for it. The Inn is pretty clear of knick knacks, but there are a few nice pieces. On the landing area on the second floor, there's a shelf on the wall with a few pretty things. We'll put it there and hide it in plain sight."

Clarke said, "That's a great idea, but let's duck into the tea shop. Right now."

The others heard the urgency in his voice and they followed. They knew better than to talk about situations around people, so they followed Clarke to one of the tables close to a window without speaking.

As they sat, they watched the Chief of Police and his dog walk quickly up the sidewalk on the other side of the street. At the corner, they crossed and headed toward the antique store.

Marty said, "Let's go hide that thing in plain sight right now."

Gema called Pete's cell phone. "You need to get over here, Pete. Those kids from the Inn got a ring, and it's worth a lot of money." Pete was quick to respond. He and Cyril were there in minutes.

Cyril did what he did. He walked all around the jewelry counter, cataloging the various scents, and walked through the store as well. By the time he sat down next to the cats, he know who had been where, and almost when.

They sat quietly as Gema talked to Pete, and watched as Frank walked through the store. He looked at sheets of paper and occasionally looked at the pieces on display, moving them slightly.

Cyril asked Claire, *"What's he doing?"*

"He has an inventory sheet."

Oscar McMurphy said, *"Holly and Jolly have those, too. It tells what we have and what's no longer there."*

"Right," said Claire. *"He must think something is missing."*

"Something is missing," said Simon Finnegan. *"I saw the older boy, Clarke, put a pretty something-or-other into one of his big pockets."*

"When did that happen?" asked Honey Bear. *"I didn't see it."*

"You were over there with the other boy. Do you remember when he picked up the bells? They made a noise, and he asked Frank about them. That's when Clarke put the thing in his pocket."

Honey Bear sat back, staring at Simon Finnegan in surprise. *"I missed it. Those kids are really good at this."*

"They are. I don't think we can send in a burglar to get this thing, though. It didn't look like something any of us could carry away."

Cyril nodded at the jewelry counter. "We need to pay attention to them and figure out what else was taken."

They turned their attention to Gema and Pete. Gema pulled up a photograph on her phone. "I take pictures of everything I make. This is the ring that's missing, and I know exactly when they took it."

"Tell me," said Pete.

"The woman, Livia, had just tried it on."

"I've met the mother. Her name isn't Livia."

"No, I think, just from listening to them talk, that they're guests at the Inn also."

"Do you think she was involved in the theft?"

Gema thought about it. "No. The girls had that same buggy attitude they had when they were here yesterday, but I didn't get the same feeling from the woman. Or her husband."

"Back up," said Pete. "First of all, the kids were here yesterday?"

By this time, Frank had joined them at the counter. He held an inventory sheet and, with a black marker, he circled an item. He answered Pete. "They were here, the four of them, and we had to keep an eye on everything they did, everywhere they went. We didn't lose anything yesterday, but today we weren't so lucky. One of the boys, the bigger, older one, got an antique dresser box, worth at least two thousand dollars. I had a twenty-five hundred dollar price tag on it."

"Do you have a picture of it?"

"Sure. I'll text it to you. I didn't get hit as hard as Gema, though."

Pete turned back to Gema. "Now tell me about the visit yesterday."

She walked him through the visit as nearly as she could remember, and Frank added thoughts from his perspective.

Pete prompted them to move on. "And today they came in with Livia and…"

"I think his name is Mitch," said Gema. "Honeymooners at the Inn, I think."

"Did it appear they had come in together?"

Gema and Frank looked at one another. After a few seconds, Frank said, "It didn't appear so. They arrived at the same time. The kids came in first, and they were right behind them."

"So, they could have just walked over from the Inn at the same time."

"Possibly," said Gema. "The man seemed to give the woman a look, and she engaged the girls at the counter."

Pete looked at her and said slowly, a bit of space between the words, "Seemed… to give… the woman… a look."

Gema shook her head with a soft laugh. "Pete, you're doing that cop thing to me. That thing where you say something really slow, so it sounds like I'm telling you a lie."

"I am not!"

"Are, too. You did that when you thought I killed that jerk a few years ago."

Pete chuckled. "Okay. You got me. Sometimes it can be used to jog a memory. Did it work?"

"Not really. He gave her a look, she engaged the girls, and I didn't pay any attention to him after that until he came to the counter. But by then, the ring was gone."

"Do you think he was involved in any way?"

"No. The ring was there, the girls were there, he came up to look at another ring with Livia, and the girls were gone."

"Do you have cameras?"

"Outside," said Frank. "When all that vandalism was happening around town, I invested in outdoor cameras, but I didn't cover the interior."

Before Pete left, Cyril remembered something important. He looked closely at Honey Bear. *"You weren't at the Inn this morning."*

Honey Bear thought he was being unfairly chastised. He straightened and looked Cyril in the eyes. *"Yes, I was, but I decided to come here to detect. Simon Finnegan and Oscar McMurphy came along to help."*

Simon Finnegan hissed at Honey Bear. *"Tiger Lily left me in charge."*

Oscar McMurphy hissed at Oscar McMurphy. *"Left us in charge. Us. Not you."*

Cyril closed his eyes and pounded his front paw on the floor. The cats stopped spatting and sat at attention. Cyril told Honey Bear, *"Something bad happened to Henrie. He might have been kidnapped. People were over there trying to figure out if they could get money together to get him back. They called Annie and Chris. There's bad news about them, too. They might be arrested for the murder of some guy found near their cabin."*

"Oh, no!" cried Honey Bear. He wasn't concerned about Henrie, Annie or Chris. Well, perhaps a little, but the next sentence was, *"They always gather the cats together when something bad happens! I have to get home before they know I'm gone! They'll lock me in!"*

17: Lavender Lake

Sheriff Tate stepped into the cabin and brushed water from her short, dark hair. She intended to leave final instructions for this couple. Don't talk to anyone about the case. Don't stray far from the cabin. Don't leave town.

She had to wait. One of the cell phones on the kitchen counter started to buzz. The man, Chris, picked it up and said hello.

He listened for a while, then put the phone on speaker, explaining as he did so. "I'm putting this on speaker. Annie, something's happened to Henrie."

Agitated, the two huddled over the phone at the kitchen table.

Sheriff Tate knew she should leave to continue her investigation, but she wasn't asked to go. The call was intriguing, and she wanted to learn more about these two individuals.

She motioned to her officer to wait at the door. She leaned against the kitchen counter. Chris and Annie seemed oblivious to her presence.

Someone – Annie called him George – explained a serious situation regarding Henrie. Perhaps a brother? A good friend?

There had been a call from Cameroon. That was somewhere in Africa, but she didn't remember her high school geography and didn't know if it was east, west or center.

Someone from the Embassy had called, and a hotel manager. Henrie's grandmother reported Henrie and Collette missing. His grandmother? In Africa?

It was possibly a kidnapping. They were keeping the Inn's telephone line clear for a call from Henrie or the kidnappers.

Several people were there. Sheriff Tate pulled a notebook from her pocket and started to write names as quickly as she could. Gwen, Jenny and Ian were putting financial and other records together. Jenny wanted to hear Annie say she wanted to use her resources to ransom Henrie. Annie said yes. Chris said use mine, too.

Another voice, female, said, "Chris, I don't think between the two of you there will be enough."

Chris said, "Nancy, there will be enough."

Sheriff Tate wrote down that name as well, then the names she hadn't written before. Henrie, George, a woman's name. Was it Coretta? Jeanette? Collette.

Another male voice. Annie said, "Pete, is there anything you can do?"

She wrote this new name and realized, as he answered Annie, that he was a law enforcement officer of some type. Perhaps that Chief of Police to whom Chris had referred.

The male voice, Pete, said, "Annie, do not answer your phone for any reason. If they get the number for the Inn, they'll probably get your number as well. I don't want you bargaining for him. Leave that to us, to George. Promise me."

"But, if they call…"

"No. If they call, you will not be the person coached by the State Department. You won't know what to say."

"If I don't answer…"

"If they call and you don't answer, they will call the Inn. That's where we want the call to come. After this conversation, turn your phone off. We'll call Chris if we need either of you."

"Alright. I'll turn it off. If it's Henrie, if Henrie tries to call, he has Chris's number."

Chris said, "I won't answer if it's Henrie's number or a number I don't know."

A male voice asked Chris how much he could get, in case of a ransom demand. Chris said, "The last time, I didn't have liquid assets. I've changed my situation. While most of it is locked up, I still have access to two and a half, maybe three million."

As the Sheriff wrote that figure down, she realized the telephone conversation had gone silent.

She looked up as Annie said, "That much? You have that much?"

"Liquid. Yes. I'll have to call and find out."

The deep voice, the cop's voice, said, "We'll go with two and a half until you let us know different, and we'll nail down what you can come up with, Annie. When they call, we'll be able to bargain. How much time do you need to get the money, Chris?"

"I don't know. It's liquid. It can probably be sent to the bank today or tomorrow. I'll call as soon as we're finished here."

Annie added, "And then we're coming home. We'll be there before dark."

Sheriff Tate stepped forward. "Excuse me. Excuse me, folks, but you aren't going anywhere."

The line went silent again. The voice identified as Nancy said, "Who are you?"

"I'm Sheriff Sondra Tate, and these two individuals are persons of interest in a murder investigation. They're not leaving my jurisdiction until I say so."

Pandemonium broke out around the imagined table on the other end of the telephone line. A female voice said, "Annie, do you need me? I'll leave right away…"

"No, Jenny. We're fine. Really. A man was found dead a short way from our cabin. We didn't do anything, we just can't leave…"

"Don't you say another word to anyone! I insist! Sheriff – what's your name? Tate? – I am Annie's attorney, and I'll represent Chris too, if he'll have me. I am exercising their rights to say nothing until an attorney is present. Annie, Chris, did you say anything?"

Chris, this time. "It's okay, Jenny. I welcome your representation, but we're fine for now. Apparently, we just can't leave for…," he looked at Sheriff Tate.

She said, "A day, two, maybe more. Depends on the investigation. And of course, if they're charged…"

Jenny's voice was strident. "Say! Nothing!"

Suddenly the cop voice was back on the line, excusing himself. Sheriff Tate took note of his cryptic, "I may be back to make an arrest. Or four."

By now, the conversation on the other end had deteriorated to a point that Chris and Annie had to disconnect. With promises to call as soon as he knew anything, Chris ended with, "We're fine. Really, we're fine. Let's concentrate on Henrie."

Sheriff Tate leaned against the wall, turning toward the door to make sure her officer had heard everything. She watched as he put a notebook and pen into his shirt pocket. Good man, she thought. Good man.

She turned back to Chris and Annie. "I'll be back later. I'm sure you have no reason to leave your cabin for at least a few hours. My officer will be on your front porch, just in case."

She didn't wait for an argument.

Sassy Pants said a very bad word. Tiger Lily's jaw dropped, giving her the appearance of having a permanent o-shaped mouth. When she got hold of her senses, she put on her best no-nonsense face and said, *"You're grounded. You're grounded for a month!"*

Sassy Pants said, *"Ize sorry. I duzn't mean to curse, but you not ground me! You not my mommy!"*

"I'm not your mother, but you are grounded!"

Mr. Bean asked, *"What does that mean? She can't eat treats? She can't go outside? What does that mean?"*

Mo trilled. Kali and Ko jumped in, both to translate for him and to get in their own two cents. *"You can't do that!" "Sassy shouldn't have cursed!" "That's not the point!" "Shut up!" "Fat butt!" "Stinky butt!" "Shut up, fat butt!" "You shut up, stinky butt!"*

Mo bopped both girls on the nose.

A boom of thunder made the cabin shake. Kali and Ko jumped and ran to hide under the bed.

Little Socks, who had rolled in laughter as soon as Sassy Pants uttered the bad word, got herself under control. *"Okay, now. Sassy Pants, you know better. Tiger Lily, so do you. You can't ground her. We have more important things to consider."*

Tiger Lily mumbled something under her breath, then said, *"You're right. We have two big problems. Henrie is in trouble, and this sheriff wants to arrest Mommy and Chris."*

Sis asked, *"Can she do that? They didn't do it."*

Little Socks said, *"If the evidence doesn't point in another direction, they probably can. You said you smelled mushrooms, right? And it sounded like the sheriff wanted to know about mushrooms."*

Tiger Lily said, *"We need to find out who did it, so we can concentrate on getting evidence on the right people."*

A chorus ensued. *"How are we going to do that?"* *"We gonna do what?"* *"We're stuck in here!"*

From under the bed, they heard, *"We have to help Henrie!"* *"Help Henrie first!"*

Little Socks whirled on Kali and Ko. She hissed, *"We can't help him from here! We have to get home first!"*

Sis asked, *"What's wrong with them?"*

Little Socks spat, *"They're what I call cat-a-tonic. They get in the middle of a rumbly storm and they can't think."*

Mr. Bean said, *"They love Henrie."*

Mo trilled for a few seconds.

Sassy Pants interpreted. *"Dey lubs Henrie an dey scairt of loud noises, and you shouldn't be mean to dem."*

Little Socks lay on the floor, covering up all of her white spots, so only her black showed. This was her way of saying *"shut up"* to everyone.

Tiger Lily tried to get control of the group. *"Come on! We have to work through this! If Mommy gets arrested, well, we'd be orphans. And Henrie isn't here to help."*

Sis coughed.

"Yes?"

"I think we can ask our new friends for help."

"What new friends?"

"You know. The animals in the woods. Maybe someone saw something that can narrow it down."

"That's a good idea, but how do we get out there?"

A loud crash of lightning and boom of thunder shook the cabin.

Mr. Bean said, *"Forget how we get out there. Why would we try? We'll get wet, then we'll fry."*

Sassy Pants said, *"We be too wet to fry."*

Little Socks said, *"Water conducts electricity. We'll fry quicker."*

Sis and Tiger Lily looked at one another as the conversation went into the toilet. They walked away, slow and silent, and reached the screen door.

Tiger Lily asked, *"Can you open it?"*

"No," replied Sis. *"But I might be able to rip the screen."*

"Is there another way?"

Sis looked around. Chris and Annie still sat at the table, heads down, hands clasped together. A police officer was on the front porch. She turned back to Tiger Lily and shook her head. *"We'll be in for it, but I don't think we have a choice."*

"*Can you at least be quiet about it?*"

"*I don't think so. I'll have to be quick.*"

Sis considered the claws on her right paw, then her left. "*I'm right-pawed, but I think my left claws are sharper.*"

She closed her eyes, opened them again, looked again at the kitchen table with Chris and Annie, then, with a mighty effort, she ripped the screen door and jumped out. Tiger Lily was dead on her heels, and Little Socks, hearing the noise, got out behind them.

Before anyone else could leave, Annie was in front of the door, shielding it from exit.

18: Cameroon

Mr. Jones took the phone offered by Yannick. "Mr. Jones, here. I understand you have information?"

"Yes, Mr. Jones. My name is Maria Masilla. My grandson, Henrie, is missing."

"Yes, Mrs. Masilla. We are looking for him."

"I know, I know. Please listen to me. A man came…." The line went silent.

Mr. Jones thought he heard the woman sob. He gave her a gentle shove. "A man? Who?"

"He was going to kill me, and he has Henrie!"

Mr. Jones took control of the conversation. "Mrs. Masilla, let's start at the beginning. Tell me about the man. Who is he?"

"He drives that taxi that Henrie brings over here."

"The taxi?"

"A yellow one."

"Most of them are yellow."

"I know, but this is one of the all-yellow ones. No black or white. Even the roof is yellow."

"That helps. Do you know his name?"

"I do not. He did not say."

"Have you seen him before?"

"Only in the taxi, when he brought Henrie."

"What did he want?"

"He wanted telephone numbers. I think he will call Henrie's people and ask for money."

"What numbers did you give him?"

"I gave him the number for the place he works, and for the woman he works for. I think he will ask for money."

Mr. Jones nodded, even though Mrs. Masilla could not see him. "That's good. That's good. Did he give any indication how much he wanted?"

"No. We did not talk about that. I wrote those numbers down. I had to write on something, and I wrote on the picture. And then, he looked at that picture and he got so mad! Now he might hurt Henrie!"

"What was the picture?"

"I do not know for certain. He said something about a fine house and a white woman. That must have been the picture of Henrie and his boss in front of that hotel of hers. Where he works."

Mr. Jones cursed under his breath. "Hold on for a moment, Mrs. Masilla. I will be right back."

He pulled out his cell phone and called the Inn. George answered. "This is Mr. Jones. Contact was made with Mrs. Masilla. They now have the number for the Inn and for Ms. Mack. They also have a photograph that did not go over well, one of the Inn and, perhaps him with Ms. Mack. You have to do what you can to diffuse the situation without letting them know we've talked."

"How?"

"I don't know, but if the conversation starts to go sideways, that might be the reason. You'll have to think on your feet."

Mr. Jones disconnected the call and returned to the hotel phone. "Mrs. Masilla, we will do everything we can to get your grandson to safety."

"Yes, I know. I…just take him home, please."

"That's the plan. Will you be alright?"

"Yes. I am an old woman. They do not want me. They want Henrie for the money they think he has."

"Yes." Mr. Jones sighed. "You understand…"

"Of course I do. Do your job, Mr. Jones. Tell Henrie I did what I could to help."

"You will be alright?"

"I will be fine. I have no intention of leaving my home. No matter what happens, I have met my Henrie, and that is enough."

Henrie heard the taxi pull into the village. Pop pop, every ten seconds. A car door slammed. Bertrand's angry voice, speaking in a language Henrie did not understand, punched through the air.

Collette moved from the cot to sit beside him. "What is he saying?"

"I do not know. There are hundreds of languages and dialects in this part of the world. My guess is that he is speaking a language native to Nigeria."

Collette, perhaps wanting to lighten the mood, perhaps wanting to forget her circumstance, asked, "What language did you speak. You know. Growing up."

"My parents spoke English. There are times one needs to know French as well. Mother taught me basic words and phrases in Fulani, but she did not want me to speak it at home. Grand-mère, also, prefers that I refrain. I have not spoken that language for years, but I would know it if I heard it. That is not Fulani."

Collette said, "I wonder if we are the cause of the argument."

"No doubt. Wait. I understood that word. It translates to 'greed.' And I think that referred to a harlot. The conversation does not bode well."

"Am I the harlot?"

"I cannot tell. I do not think so, or the reference would have been made before now."

Henrie put his arm around Collette as Bertrand entered the hut. His dark face was covered with sweat, and the scowl made him appear murderous. He had a cell phone in his hand.

He pointed with the phone at Henrie. "You call this number." The number was already on the call screen. It was the telephone number for the KaliKo Inn.

He could only hope that George had been given prior warning by someone. Anyone.

19: Chelsea

Oscar McMurphy and Simon Finnegan strolled into the Inn as if they had all the time in the world. In fact, they did not.

Oscar McMurphy sat in the foyer, in between the large doors leading to the dining room and the library. She glanced around, apparently looking for no one in particular but in reality looking for Nancy.

If Nancy found out Honey Bear had left The Avenue, she would lock him up. She was still unsure of allowing him access to open cat doors, even had he stayed on this one street.

Simon Finnegan trotted up the steps to the second floor landing. He looked quickly into the hallway, then ran downstairs and toward the back guest room and the all-season porch. Nancy came out of the porch with her phone in her hand.

"Honestly, Sam, you have to get over here! Everything is going wrong! Henrie's in trouble, Annie is going to be arrested, and I can't find Honey Bear! I've been all through this house!"

Simon Finnegan darted in front of Nancy, through the foyer and out the door. Oscar McMurphy stayed rooted in place and heard, "For heaven's sake! Even the cats are crazy! One of those cats from DoubleGood almost tripped me!"

Outside, Simon Finnegan sat on the porch and whispered into the bushes, *"She's looking for you, and it sounds like she's been all over the house."*

"*Oh no,*" said Honey Bear. "*I'm in for it now. Do you have any ideas?*"

Simon Finnegan thought for a few seconds. "*Remember when we got saved? And Sis? The cats always took us in through the basement. Sometimes that cat door is locked, but maybe it isn't.*"

"*That's a good idea. Wait here. If I'm not back right away, I've gone in through that door.*"

Honey Bear ran through the bushes to the edge of the wall, then dashed around the corner and down the basement steps. Sure enough, the cat door was unlocked. He opened it an inch or two to look and listen. The coast was clear.

He got inside in time to hear Nancy, still on the phone, open the basement door. Quickly, he ran to the downstairs apartment – the room they used as safe space during tornados – and jumped onto the bed. JoJo was staying here this week, and the bed was still rumpled. Books and magazines were strewn around the bed and floor, and a half-full glass of water was on the bedside table.

Honey Bear marveled that someone so neat and clean upstairs could be so messy down here, but then he realized he had to look comfortable. He didn't have time to knead the bed into compliance and turn in a circle three times. He rolled into a ball and pretended to be asleep.

When Nancy looked into the door and cried, "Honey Bear!" he opened one lazy eye, then closed it, as if he didn't have time to wake up from his nap.

Nancy sat on the bed and pulled him to her with one arm, as she nearly shouted into the phone, "He's here! He was napping in JoJo's room. He must have been too tired to hear me!"

Honey Bear allowed himself to be roused. He licked his paws and cleaned his ears, something Nancy expected to see after a nap, then jumped to the floor. It was time to get together with those other cats.

Under the detective table, a morose group sat up or lay on the cushions, each in their private sorrow. Honey Bear brought the meeting to order. He opened it in the same manner Tiger Lily always did.

"It's time to report. Let's hear from those of you who stayed here, and start with Henrie and Annie."

Speckles looked at her two small companions and realized she would have to speak. Daryll would take too long and Moriah was not used to reporting. She said, *"Well, it sounds like Henrie has been kidnapped where he is in that far-away place. Probably his friend, too. And when they called Annie to tell her, some police officer said they were suspects in a murder."*

Moriah interjected, *"Not suspects. She said something else, but they can't leave until the murder is solved."*

Daryll said, *"So two problems? Far away? Can we help?"*

Oscar McMurphy said, *"We can't help them, but Tiger Lily and the other cats are with Annie."*

Daryll said, *"And Sis?"*

Simon Finnegan said, *"Yes. And Sis. They'll have to help Annie. I'm afraid Henrie is on his own."*

Moriah puffed up. *"That's not fair. He needs help, too."*

Honey Bear glared at her. *"There's nothing we can do for him. We have to focus."* He looked at the other cats. *"Did you hear anything else? Anything after Pete and Cyril left?"*

"No," said Speckles. *"When they left, the call to Annie was almost over. Those other people left, and they were going to find out how much money Annie could get together."*

Daryll said, *"I don't understand? Can't she just get it? Like Martha? She has a drawer? With an envelope? And her money is there?"*

Moriah liked Daryll and thought he would make a nice boyfriend. But she got tired of his tentative nature and the way he ended every sentence with a question mark. She closed her eyes, took a deep breath and said with finality, *"No, it's not like that. My mommy has a bank where her money goes. And what she calls investments. And stocks and bonds. Her money is in lots of places, and she can't just open a drawer and get to it right away."*

Daryll sniffled. *"You don't have to be mean?"*

Honey Bear stomped his foot. *"Stop it. Let's move on. We have information from the antique shop, and you probably have things to tell us, too."*

Oscar McMurphy hissed, *"Tiger Lily left me in charge."*

Simon Finnegan hissed, *"Us! She left us in charge!"*

Honey Bear bowed his head and shook it. He forced out the words. *"Then. Ask. For. Reports."*

Silence reigned for several seconds, until Simon Finnegan sat up. *"I'll give the first report. We watched everything at the shop. Claire helped. She knew things about inventory and...other things...and she helped. Anyway, the kids took a something-or-other..."*

Oscar McMurphy jumped in, *"...small, but too big for us to carry in our mouths, and expensive..."*

Simon Finnegan talked over her. *"...very expensive, and he was quick about it. They worked together."*

They stopped talking. Moriah, who had followed the conversation fairly well, asked, *"Who worked together?"*

Honey Bear took over. *"Very good question, Moriah."* Honey Bear was warming up to this being in charge stuff. No matter what the two hardware store cats said, he knew that everyone looked to him for direction. Today, at least.

"The two girls worked the jewelry counter – we'll get to that shortly – and the two boys worked the rest of the store. The boys had Frank hopping back and forth. Frank was good, but there came a time that the young one..."

Speckles inserted, *"Marty."*

"Yes, Marty, kept Frank's attention long enough for the older one..." he looked to Speckles.

"Clarke."

"Yes, Clarke, put a something-or-other in his pocket. They'll probably try to hide it somewhere."

Moriah said, *"Oh! That was what they were doing!"*

Everyone looked at Moriah. Surprised, she looked at each of them in turn. They seemed to be waiting for her to speak. She swallowed and said, *"They came in, kind of quick-like, and went right up to the landing on the second floor. Clarke gave Brooke something out of his pocket. She looked at it, said it was really pretty, then she put it on the shelf on the back wall."*

Silence.

Honey Bear finally said, *"Show us."*

One by one, the cats walked out from under the covered table. Honey Bear was the last to leave. He looked up at George, who sat at the dining table, and nodded a greeting.

On the second floor landing, Moriah sat. The others formed a semi-circle around her and followed her example. They looked up at the shelf on the back wall.

Simon Finnegan said, *"That's it."*

Several cats asked, *"Which one?"*

Simon Finnegan pointed with his chin and said, *"That heavy glass-looking thing with pink roses. It could be a paperweight, you know, something that doesn't do anything but sit on top of paper."*

"It could be a box," said Honey Bear. *"We have some of those at our house. It doesn't look like it, but you can open it and put small things inside."*

"It would have to be real small?" said Daryll. *"Smaller than me?"*

Still looking up, Oscar McMurphy said, *"So, okay, it looks like we solved our first case."*

They came to attention and looked around at one another. Oscar McMurphy continued, *"So now what? How do we let Pete know?"*

Honey Bear thought about all of the cases in which he had been involved. *"We have to wait for the right time. We need Cyril, and Cyril has to have an excuse to get Pete to look in the right direction. Let's go back to the office. We have to talk about the jewelry."*

One by one, Honey Bear in the lead, they walked down the stairs, into the dining room, and through the cloth to get underneath the detective table. Honey Bear nodded a greeting again, this time to both George and Ian.

Once settled in the office, Honey Bear asked, *"Who will report on the jewelry?"*

Oscar McMurphy straightened. *"I will. Someone took a ring, an expensive ring, and they think it was the kids. It probably was."*

Moriah said, *"But..."*

Speckles, excited, said, *"We can send in our new cat burglar! Moriah was in training today, and she can go into the rooms and look for it!"*

Moriah said, *"But..."*

Simon Finnegan asked, *"Are the kids gone? Can she go in now?"*

Daryll answered, *"They're gone?"*

"Let's all go." said Honey Bear. *"We can all get in on it."*

Moriah said, *"But…"*

"I like that idea," said Oscar McMurphy.

Moriah said, *"But…"*

Honey Bear stomped his foot. *"Enough! Let's go!"*

Moriah moved quickly to get in front of Honey Bear. She was almost trampled for her effort, but she held firm. Honey Bear stopped.

She glared at him, her head the only part of her body that wasn't underneath him. He hissed, staring, nose-to-nose. Moriah was too proud to wiggle out from underneath. She stayed where she was, glaring up, until he finally backed away.

She sat up, licking and fluffing her hair until it looked "just so" again.

Honey Bear hissed, *"What. Is. Your. Problem."*

Moriah took a deep breath and licked a front paw.

Speckles came up behind her and whispered, *"Talk to him. He can be really mean when he's mad."*

Moriah sniffed, shook out her mane of hair one more time, and said, *"We don't know it was them."*

Honey Bear growled, *"You weren't at the store. You didn't see them."*

"No," she answered. *"I was here. The kids put that something-or-other on the shelf, then they left. They didn't go into their rooms."*

Oscar McMurphy cut in, *"So that means...what?"*

Moriah turned her head and glared at Oscar McMurphy. *"Someone else did come in."*

Simon Finnegan asked, *"Who?"*

Moriah sniffed and rotated her head on her shoulders, stretching her neck muscles. Finally, she said, *"After I saw the kids, I still had one room to go into. The one that faces the winery. The one the girls are staying in."*

"And?" This from Honey Bear, who was still angry, impatient and a little embarrassed.

"Remember this morning? When it was confusing why the kids were going back to the antique store?"

Heads nodded, some in agreement, some in confusion.

"Well, it was those other two, the ones staying in the carriage house, that asked them to go back. And they went into their room after the kids came back."

"Did you see the ring?" asked Oscar McMurphy.

Moriah looked at her, incredulous. *"Do you think they would hold it up and wave it toward me through the window?"*

Speckles gave a forced, nervous laugh. *"Haha, yeah, that would have been funny. But come on, now. Let's settle down. Moriah's new at this. She just had her first training session today."*

Honey Bear sniffed, but he saw Moriah's point. *"You're right. It could be them. We need to investigate."*

Several cats spoke at once. *"What do we do next?" "When will Cyril be here?" "Should we send in our cat burglar?" "How do we figure it out?"*

Once again, Honey Bear found his footing. He wondered how often Tiger Lily had to regroup, and remembered all the times he had tried to sabotage her efforts. In the future, he would be more cooperative.

He called for silence. *"These are all good questions. Thank you, Moriah, for pointing out a potential error. We need to take steps."*

"What steps?" "How?" "What can I do?"

"Speckles and Daryll, you will go out to the carriage house and play on the lawn in front of it. While you do that, figure out if the two are still inside. One of you report back to me."

"To me," said Simon Finnegan.

Oscar McMurphy hissed, *"To us."*

Honey Bear rolled his eyes and began again. *"In the meantime, since we know the kids are gone, Moriah will continue her practice."* He looked at Moriah. *"Is there any room you haven't been in?"*

"Um…I haven't been in that back one. The one with the door to the beach."

"Does anyone know if the guest in that room is here?"

Speckles said, "He's on the big boat with Ray."

"Then you'll go into his room and practice. The rest of us will wait in the library to hear from the three of you."

The three little ones left. Speckles and Daryll were happy to be given responsibilities. Moriah huffed a bit under her breath. Who put that big galoot in charge, anyway? On her way down the hall, she dropped little fluffy pieces of hair.

Cheryl sat at the radio station in The Marina. She had just gotten off a telephone call, and she was stunned.

She tried to raise Ray without success. He and his client had probably docked somewhere. She tried his cell. No answer.

She paced the radio area, looked at the activity on the docks, just beginning to pick up for the season, then returned to the radio.

Once again, she tried that, then his cell. This time he picked up.

"What's up? You called just a few minutes ago."

"I did. Am I interrupting?"

"No. Jock and I are at the hot dog stand here in Marsh Haven. Louis is somewhere. I don't know where. He still doesn't want me tagging along."

Cheryl laughed. "Did Jock get the Spanish dog?"

"He did. He loves that Spanish. I got a slaw dog."

"As always."

"You know me. Things never change."

"Well…maybe they will now."

"Huh?"

"Things might change. I got a call. Have you ever considered a different career? Or the same career, just from another location?"

"Are we moving?"

"We might."

"What? What's up?

"I'll start from the beginning. Don't say anything. Just listen. A corporate realtor called. I got the feeling he was like a business head-hunter. He's from Boston, and he has a client, a woman. She was with him on the call. She comes from a long line of shippers in the Boston area, and she's used to the ocean, big boats. She's been involved in the tourist industry there, and she's ready to break away from the family. She has millions, and she's been looking for something similar but different."

Ray didn't say anything.

Cheryl asked, "Are you there?"

"Yeah. You told me not to say anything, just listen."

"Oh, I did. Okay. Well, she's been looking around, and she thought, 'what about the Great Lakes area?' So she asked this guy to look for places, and they found us. They've been through our website, and they've looked at the online maps and things, and, well, she wants to buy our place. And everything that goes with it."

"Everything?"

"Everything."

"The Escape?"

"Yes. The building, the docks, any equipment and out buildings, the marina business, The Escape, the charter business…"

"What about Jock? Are they gonna buy Jock, too?"

Cheryl realized this wasn't going as well as she had hoped.

"No, honey, of course not. Let me back up. They expressed an interest. I didn't say yes or no. I said you and I would have to discuss it."

"I can't tell you what to do, honey. The Marina is yours. The Escape is mine. I'm not interested in selling. And our house. Our house is on the back side of that property. Do they want that, too?"

"They didn't know about the house. I asked, and they looked it up. They could see that it's cozied into state park land, and they asked if it could be part of the deal."

"I can't believe this. Cheryl, are you unhappy?"

"No! Why would you ask that?"

"I mean, are you really considering this?"

"I haven't told you what they offered, and that's before they take a look at the house and add it to the deal."

"I don't know if I want to hear."

"I think you do. Are you sitting down? Have you finished your hot dog?"

"Yes, I'm on a bench on a sidewalk by the dock. And yes, I have finished my hot dog. And Jock is listening."

"Listening, listening, or just looking at you and listening to your part of it?"

"I think he's listening, listening. You know how you can tell that he is really interested in something?"

"Yeah."

"That kind of listening."

"Good. He has to be involved in this decision also."

Cheryl told him how much had been offered.

Ray disconnected and stared off into space, stunned. Jock lay on the sidewalk beside him, head on his paws, and sighed. This was not good. Not good at all.

George and Ian sat at the dining room table. The group had decided George had to stay by the telephone, but he couldn't be left alone. Someone needed to stay for support. Since Pete had other duties, Ian volunteered to stay.

"There's not much I can do for Annie at this point," he said, "and the bank is used to me being away from the office."

They drank coffee and tried to make small talk. Mostly, they drank coffee.

George had listened to Nancy on the phone to her husband, Sam, as she wandered around the house. Now, she was in the basement. Apparently, she found Honey Bear. George marveled at how those cats went everywhere in the house, but no one ever noticed them walking around.

Now, he did. Honey Bear appeared from the basement, and the two cats that belonged to Holly and Jolly walked in – George noted they appeared nonchalant – and joined

Honey Bear. They walked under the table cover to the detective agency.

The table was used on occasion if the number of guests called for expansion. Most of the time, it sat against the wall next to the door from the dining room into the kitchen. It was covered with a floor-length cloth. Underneath the table were a number of cushions placed there for the comfort of Annie's cats.

The sequestered area underneath the table was called the detective agency because Henrie had placed a sign to that effect. A decorative sign had been made up to say "Seven Cats Detective Agency." The "Seven" had been marked out, and the numeral "9" inserted. George counted cats in his head.

The seven were, of course, Annie's cats. The two additional could be Holly and Jolly's cats. But what about the extra ones? Honey Bear, Moriah, Speckles and Daryll?

A second, smaller sign said, "Tillie, A Hero With Paws." George thought about Tillie, the little Jack Russell terrier owned by Carlos and Isabel. He had not seen Tillie since Annie and the cats left. She was small enough to use the cat doors on The Avenue and was often seen keeping company with the cats of the neighborhood.

George mused that she must think nothing was going on at the Inn, otherwise, she would probably be here with everyone else.

George said to Ian, "Do you think it's alright that I let all the neighborhood cats hang out here during the day?"

Ian looked up from his cup of coffee. "What?"

"The cats. Do you think…oh, never mind."

Ian looked back at his cup and George stared aimlessly into the room. He shook himself to attention when the cats came out, one by one, led by Moriah. Honey Bear looked up at George and seemed to nod on his way by.

George watched as they moved in single file to the stairs, walked up, and sat in a semi-circle facing the back wall. They looked up. At something. What?

He leaned over in his chair to be able to see through the door and up the stairs. He stood and walked slowly and quietly into the foyer, moving his head and body to try to determine what they saw.

Ian joined him. He, too, was silent. He leaned in. "What are we lookin' at?"

"I dunno. Is anything up there worth seeing?"

"Um…no?"

As they watched, the cats stopped looking at whatever it was and moved into a circle to apparently converse among themselves.

"Whatdayaknow?" said George.

"Go figure," answered Ian.

After a while, the cats stood, and again, single file, this time with Honey Bear in the lead, they walked down the steps, into the dining room and under the table. Honey Bear appeared to nod on his way by. George and Ian watched until the last tail swished out of sight.

Still staring at the table, Ian asked, "Does this stuff happen all the time?"

George just shook his head. They returned to the table and their coffee, not taking their eyes off the cloth over the detective table.

Eventually, the three smaller cats came out from under the table. Georgia's cats, Speckles and Daryll, ran through the foyer and out the door. Clara's little princess of a cat, Moriah, walked down the hallway toward the all-season porch. George had always thought she was fluffy. Now he noted she was built low to the floor with a barrel of a belly. She had a sexy little sway to her back hips. In that regard, she took after her mother.

George turned in his chair to face Ian. "We have more important things to worry about than the cats."

Just then, the Inn's landline phone rang. George answered and heard Henrie's mellifluous voice. Slight French accent, perfect enunciation, absolutely no contractions.

Ian sat to attention and, pen poised above a notebook, prepared to write everything he heard.

George had been coached well, but until the call came, he wouldn't know if it would be a straight ransom call or a call from Henrie asking for money to be wired for no specific reason. And he had not been able to discuss the matter of the photograph with his coach.

As he answered, he betrayed nothing. It was as if Henrie were calling to ask the time of day.

"Henrie, hope you're enjoying your trip. I didn't think you would call. Can I do something for you?"

"Yes, if you would. You see, I have made new friends, and they are in need of funds. Perhaps you can arrange a transfer."

"Sure, buddy. How much do you need, and where should I send it?"

"I need…let me see…" George could imagine that Henrie now read from a script of some sort, or from hastily scribbled notes.

Henrie must have covered the mouthpiece. George could barely hear him talking to someone in the room.

He came back to the line. "I regret to say they are in need of five million dollars."

George coughed a little, then said, "Well, I have to tell you I was going through your books. I was curious, you know. Anyway, I found a little slush fund that had, oh, something around two million. There was another fund that had less. I think I can find – maybe – two and a half million. Three tops, but I'm not sure about that. Do you want me to transfer what I found?"

"Yes. That would be…one moment."

Again, George heard muffled voices. He dared not look up at Ian. He paced the dining room, phone to his ear, looking up to the ceiling or down to the floor. Never at Ian.

Henrie again. "It appears my new friends have seen a photograph of what they believe to be my home, and they believe I must have access to at least five million. I cannot convince them otherwise."

George had been thinking about this situation and was prepared. For effect, he pretended to be thinking about it for the first time.

"Gosh, I don't know, Henrie. A picture of your home? You live here at the Inn. Do you think they saw a picture of that? And they think it's your house?"

"Yes. I believe that is the situation."

"Uh...let me think...do they need to be convinced?"

"Yes. I believe they do."

"Well, ya know, there's a picture of the Inn on the website banner. It's a street view, shows the Inn, and the sign in front of it. Do you think you can show that to them? So they know this isn't your house? It's a hotel?"

"That is an excellent suggestion, George. I shall ask if that would suffice. There is one other issue."

"What's that?"

"Oh. I believe a resolution has come to mind."

George had gone through all of the photographs on the web. Enough pictures of Annie were on the site to prove she was Henrie's boss. George was grateful to hear Henrie thinking on his feet. He was healthy enough to do that, at least.

"So, what do you want me to do with those funds?"

"I shall call you back. You will be there for a while?"

"Yeah. I found it easier to just stay here, so I'm bunking in your apartment for now."

"Very well. Thank you, George. We will speak soon."

George disconnected, but held onto the wireless receiver. "I need some air."

He walked toward the all-season porch, thinking about the long, sandy beach on the other side of the door. Ian followed. George intended to take off his shoes, exercise his toes in the sand, and stretch every muscle he could without leaving telephone range.

In the hallway, he nearly tripped over Moriah. She struggled with a small spiral-bound notebook. She gripped one cover with her teeth and dragged the notebook behind her. She stopped and dropped it where she was.

George and Ian kept walking. George said, "They find the craziest things and make toys out of them."

As he rolled his feet into the sand, he handed the landline to Ian and took out his cell. He had to call Mr. Jones first, and then he would call Chris and Annie.

20: Lavender Lake

Annie sat at the table and fumed. "Why won't he let me go after them?"

Chris tried to calm her. "Don't worry, Annie. They'll be okay. Sis is capable of protecting both the girls…"

Annie interrupted, "…as long as they stick together! What if they split up? What are they doing?"

"I don't know. But just think, there's been a murder, and what do they always do?'

Annie didn't respond.

"Annie, what do they always do?"

"They investigate."

"Exactly. They started when we found the body. They are carrying on."

"And how are they going to tell us what they find? This woman, this Sheriff, doesn't like us. She suspects us. She can't talk to them like Pete can."

"Like you can. They'll talk to you. Maybe even to me. They'll let us know, one way or another, what happened."

Annie sniffed. "Or they'll come back smelling like skunk."

"That, too." Chris turned off the burner under the teapot and poured hot water into a carafe. Annie smelled cinnamon and apples.

Annie sat back and listened to the rain. Sis, Tiger Lily and Little Socks had gone out, to the woods, in the rain. At least the weather had calmed. Thunder and lightning were no longer part of the equation.

Chris poured tea and put a plate of scones on the table.

Annie said, "Something has been bothering me."

"About what?"

"I'm not sure, but I keep coming back to the mushrooms. And the Sheriff seemed interested in mushrooms. Talk me through it."

"Through the mushrooms?"

"Yes. From the time we saw Dennis and he told us…no. The further back we go, the better. Let's start with getting to the first cabin. We offered mushrooms to John and Lucy. How did that go?"

"Um…I knocked on the door…we invited them over, and he asked us to come in."

"Yes. She was in the kitchen. She wasn't sure she wanted to come."

"Then she changed her mind, and they were 'delighted.' What did we say to change their minds?"

Annie thought about it, then said, "We told them we were inviting the young couple."

"And Dennis. We told them about Dennis."

"Yes. And then they were delighted. And I asked her about mushrooms and gave her my basket, and she picked out the ones she wanted."

"You didn't hand them to her?"

"No. I didn't."

Chris was silent. Annie asked, "What?"

"I don't know. You say she picked out her own, and we watched Dennis go through the basket. There were bad ones all mixed in with the good. That night, Lucy, or maybe John, said they know good ones from bad."

"So she didn't pick out any bad ones."

"So it would seem. But why didn't she say anything?"

"What?"

"Why didn't she say anything? You handed over a basket of mushrooms, good and bad, and she knew several were bad, but she didn't say anything. We could have eaten them. We could have served them to our guests."

"That's it! That's what bothered me. It was floating in the back of my mind. I should probably tell the Sheriff."

"Probably. I wish we were in Chelsea."

"Yeah. Pete would be here."

"We wouldn't have picked mushrooms."

"There wouldn't have been a murder."

"There might have been a murder, but we wouldn't be under suspicion."

"Is it five o'clock yet?"

"Somewhere."

Sis didn't care for the rain. Neither did Tiger Lily or Little Socks. Little Socks had no extra fat under her skin. She shivered, but she was brave about it. She couldn't let Tiger Lily take all the limelight.

In the woods they walked carefully, trying to find their new friends without much luck. They had places to get out of the rain. Big leaves, holes, rotten tree stumps and such.

Sis finally found Ms. Bunny. She pushed her face out of a hole and said, *"Hello. Why are you out there in the rain?"*

Tiger Lily answered. *"We have to find out who murdered the man and then let the Sheriff know. We have to go home.*

There's an emergency there, but we can't leave until the Sheriff knows who killed the man."

Ms. Bunny asked, *"Where's your handsome friend?"*

Little Socks scoffed, *"He's staying inside out of the rain."*

Tiger Lily shushed her. *"That's not true. We were the first ones to get through the door, then Mommy wouldn't let anyone else through."* She looked at Ms. Bunny. *"He tried to come. He really did."*

Ms. Bunny considered Tiger Lily for a few seconds. Then she said, *"I wish he were here, but I guess I can talk to you. We all heard that terrible scream. We thought it was the wolf man, come to kill someone. But it wasn't him."*

"The wolf man is real? I thought he was made up."

"He's real. He comes every ten years. The stories about him come down from the generations."

Tiger Lily looked at Ms. Bunny closely. It appeared she was telling the truth. She pushed on. She had a mission. *"Back to the man, did you see who did it?"*

"I wasn't the one to see them, but the raccoon family four trees to the left did. They said that older couple did it. Brought him out here, made him eat something and left him."

"Did they see what they made him eat? Was it mushrooms?"

"I don't know. You'll have to ask them. They aren't very pleasant, but maybe they'll talk to you."

Tiger Lily wanted to make sure she knew where she was going. *"Four trees to the left?"*

"That's right. Good luck, and tell your handsome friend I said hello."

Ms. Bunny left after giving Tiger Lily a flirtatious glance, something Tiger Lily was not about to replicate when she passed the message to Mo.

Sis counted trees and walked four to the left. She called up, *"Raccoon family, yoo-hoo! Are you there?"*

A bandit face appeared. Not a pleasant one. It was Mr. Raccoon, and he had been sleeping.

"Don't you know we sleep this time of day? What do you want?"

Tiger Lily said, *"Please, Mr. Raccoon, sir, we want to find out about that couple, the man and woman that killed the other man. Did you see them do it?"*

"I did. What of it?"

"Could you please tell us about it? Anything would help. Anything at all. What they did, what they said…."

"Oh, alright." He turned back into the tree and said, *"Mother, wake up. You need to help me with these human pets."*

Little Socks said, *"We aren't pets! We're…"* but Tiger Lily shushed her by standing on her tail.

A second head filled the hole. *"What's this all about? The children are asleep."*

"We're sorry, ma'am, but we want to know about the man being killed. Anything you can tell us would help."

"Well…" Mrs. Raccoon looked at her husband. He nodded. *"Alright. They walked out here last night, making an awful racket. The older man held a gun on him and made him come almost to our tree. Well, he was probably twelve trees to the north. Then the woman said, 'you have to eat this,' and he said,*

'*no, I can't, it will kill me,*' and the woman said, '*that's the point of all this.*'"

"*And they made him eat it?*"

"*They did. The man eventually gave the gun to the woman, and he used his hands to force mushrooms into his mouth and make him swallow. He sure had an awful scream while they made him eat it.*"

"*Did they say anything else? Like why he had to die?*"

Mrs. Raccoon thought about it and looked to her husband. He finally said, "*They were talking on the way here, but I didn't hear the words. You might check with the opossums up the way. They may have heard something. Or the skunks.*"

Sis shuddered.

Little Socks hid a giggle.

Tiger Lily said, "*Thank you very much, and I'm sorry we woke you. Could you tell us, please, how to find the opossum and skunk families?*"

"*Don't you remember? You ran over the skunk nest just yesterday.*"

"*Sorry, ma'am. We don't. We're city folk.*"

Mr. Raccoon huffed. "*I knew there was somethin' wrong with ya. You go over yonder there,*" he pointed with his front paw, "*about six or eight trees thataway.*"

Tiger Lily moved in that direction, counting trees as she went. They were getting further into the woods. Sis hung back, afraid of getting sprayed again. Little Socks stayed behind Sis, hoping to be shielded from any wet stuff coming from a black and white creature.

Tiger Lily found the skunks first. She stopped before stepping into their nest. She called out, *"Excuse me, Mr. or Mrs. Skunk? Are you there?"*

Mrs. Skunk pushed her nose out where it could be seen. Tiger Lily was happy to see the nose and not the other end.

"We're trying to get information on the murder that took place here last night. Mr. Raccoon thought you might be able to tell us what they talked about on their way into the woods."

"I can, but first, I want to talk to your big friend there."

Tiger Lily turned. Sis was hanging a few yards back, Little Socks still behind her.

"Sis, come up here. She'd like to talk to you."

Sis whimpered.

Tiger Lily looked back at her. *"She's scared. I guess she scared you, too."*

"She did, but I got over it. It takes a while for people – or animals – to get over me. Anyway, tell her I'm sorry. I realized afterward that she was friendly, but, you know, she frightened me and I did what I do."

"I'll tell her. Did you hear the people talk?"

"I did. They said something about their daughter, and an accident, and she was killed."

"Did they think he did it?"

"I think they knew he did, and he knew it, too."

"He did? He didn't seem to know who they were."

"I don't know about that. You might go up further toward the cabin. One of the chipmunk families lives real close to that cabin. They may have heard something."

"Thank you. How close to the cabin do we need to go?"

"You can stay in the tree line. Just go up almost to the edge and call out for Chipper."

"Chipper?"

"Yes. He's the oldest boy, and he's real curious about people. He's always poking his head up near that cabin."

"Thank you." She turned to her companions. *"Come on. I can't do this by myself."*

"Oh, and by the way…" Tiger Lily turned back to listen to her, *"…that little Chipper's a talker."*

"Thanks again."

At the tree line to the cabin, they saw a string of evidence tape and that nasty sheriff. Several deputies walked around. They carried umbrellas and looked closely at the ground. Tiger Lily whispered, *"They're looking for clues! Maybe they already know who did it!"*

That thought was dispelled when the Sheriff's radio sparked to life. The voice said, "We don't have any hits yet, Sheriff. Both of those couples are just gone. They must have left hours before the body was found."

The Sheriff answered. "Have you talked to anyone in New York about John and Lucy Hunt?"

"I got a call from their home police department. They can't find a sign of anyone living there. It's like they cleared out and don't plan to come back."

"Well, that makes them look guilty, but it could be just a coincidence. Let's keep the BOLO out on both vehicles. And did that police chief return my call?"

"He did. I'll text his cell phone number to you. Do you think they could be the ones that did it?"

"Well, they didn't run, but they picked the mushrooms, they cooked for him, and they supposedly found the body. Coincidences are piling up all over the place."

Tiger Lily whispered, *"So they don't know for sure. Not like we do. They could spend a lot of time looking for the wrong people, including Mommy, and we may never get home."*

Sis said, *"Let's stay on track. Who are we supposed to look for?"*

"Someone named Chipper. Look, on that rock by the house. I'll bet that's him. He's listening to everything."

Little Socks said, *"I'll get him."*

"Wait!" but Little Socks was gone. She kept her belly low to the ground and used bushes and rocks to shield her body from view. Halfway to the rock, she stopped, behind a rock herself, and hissed, *"Hey! You! Are you Chipper?"*

The chipmunk turned to stare. He gave a quick nod.

"We need to talk to you. Follow me."

Little Socks, who had the ability to hide her black body in green grass in plain sight of humans, hurried back. Chipper was right behind.

Tiger Lily greeted him and said, *"Sorry to disturb you, but we need to know what happened here last night. There was a murder, and we're trying to figure out why it happened."*

"Oh, yeah." The little chipmunk hopped up and down, and his head moved up and down and side to side as he talked. *"The people here didn't like him. They've been talking*

about killing him the whole time they've been here, and yesterday they got excited. They said 'an opportunity presents.'"

Sis repeated the phrase as a question. *"An opportunity presents?"*

"Yep. That's exactly what they said. Something about mushrooms, and he was allergic, and those idiots over there gave them an idea and an opportunity."

Tiger Lily stiffened. *"Idiots? Over there?"* She pointed in the direction of their cabin with her chin.

"Yep! Idiots! Invited everybody over for dinner. Picked poison mushrooms. If the idiots didn't serve the mushrooms, they would find a way to do it. Hated him for what he did to their daughter."

"But he didn't know them. How could he know the daughter and not know them?"

The little chipmunk talked faster and faster. Tiger Lily realized she had to do what she did with Kali and Ko. The two of them would talk together, over and around one another, and every way but sideways. Tiger Lily dealt with it by backing up and listening to the edges of the conversation. That way, she seemed to catch the important parts. She did that now with little Chipper.

In one run-on sentence, Chipper said, *"They had a ceremony every night and they brought out a picture of a young couple kind of young not real young sort of young maybe a little over making baby age and they would make a fire in the pit and they would say words read stuff and then talk to one another about the man how he stole her life in her prime and something about a car accident and he was drunk and they hadn't met because he didn't know who they were or what they looked like and then yesterday the idiots brought the mushrooms and didn't they read a story about him nearly dying in prison because of mushrooms and yes it was right before he was released and maybe this would work and maybe the idiots would do it for them but if not they would do it themselves and then they left and then he brought them back and she said excuse me I wanted to give you something before we left and he said I didn't know you were leaving and they said we just decided we'll leave tonight after we do one last thing and then she went into the cabin and came out with the mushrooms and a gun and she gave the gun to the man and she said to the now dead man you have to walk into the woods and you'll get what you gave our daughter and he said who's your daughter and they said you know you killed her and he said oh no are you Josie's parents I was so sorry about what happened I tried to contact you I wrote you from prison every week for three years don't you know how sorry I am I was so young and we were both drinking and there's no excuse and they said you're right there's no excuse and then he said didn't you see how much that young woman looked like her can't you find her in other people and then the woman said shut up real loud and then he said they were just like me and Josie they have the world in front of them and then she yelled shut up again and then they walked him into the woods and then there was this awful scream and then they came back and they were already packed up mostly but she was so worried she couldn't find that picture the one of him and her and what were they going to do about that and he said it's alright we have our memories and she said it could be used by the police and he said if we can't find it they won't be able to and she said well I guess it's off to Canada and they left."*

Tiger Lily shook her head a couple of times to clear out the cobwebs. She turned to look at Little Socks. She was cross-eyed and weaving back and forth. Sis looked ready to throw up.

Tiger Lily took a deep breath. *"Thanks, Chipper. I think we have everything we need for now."* She walked over to Little Socks and bopped her on the nose. Little Socks snapped out of it.

"Do you remember the pictures you saw?"

"Yes."

"I think Chipper said something about a picture. And something about a picture they couldn't find before they left. Do you know anything about that?"

Little Socks looked at her feet and mumbled something.

"What?"

"I knocked it over."

"You? You're a burglar. How could you knock it over?"

"I don't know. It was an accident. It landed on the floor behind the dresser."

"Maybe that's the important one. Let's go look."

"Now? With all those police people there?"

"Let's wait just a while and see if they go."

Sis said, *"We have to get in before the door closes. They don't have cat doors here."*

"Darn! Let me think."

They sat in the grass, just inside the tree line, and thought. Thankfully, Chipper was called home to dinner.

Little Socks finally said, *"We have to trust that sheriff lady."*

"She doesn't like us."

"We don't have a choice."

And as it turned out, they didn't. Sheriff Tate walked in long strides toward her vehicle and all of the other officers did the same. Before the cats and Sis had time to react, the doors were closed and the cabin was deserted.

When the coast was clear, they investigated the exterior of the cabin. It was solid, well made, and had no access from outside. Unless you were a biped with a key.

Chris reached for his cell phone, realized it was George and put it on speaker. "Yes, George. We're both here."

"Great. I have a couple of things. I talked to the guy at the Embassy again, then Henrie called – I'll get to that – and I called the Embassy guy back, to fill him in."

"Mr. Jones?"

"Yeah, him. He seemed to think the kidnappers got hold of a photograph that could hamper our talks, and he was right."

Annie said, "What?"

"Somehow they got a picture of the Inn, and they thought it was his house, and worse, you were in the picture."

"So they think he's a rich man and he has relations with a white woman."

"Right. So, being grateful for the heads up, when Henrie called, I could play dumb and still let him know what he needed to know, how to get them to the website to see the house with the sign, you know, and pictures of you, Annie."

"Okay, I understand that. How did Henrie sound?"

"He sounded good. He was calm and clear-headed. It didn't sound as if he was injured. He was careful not to say the words 'ransom' or 'kidnapped.' The people that have him wanted five million, but I let him know, in my digging around, you know, being curious, I had already found a couple of slush funds that amounted to about two and a half million, three tops. He was going to get back with me after, you know, proving he's not rich."

"But Henrie sounded okay."

"He did. Chris, how are you coming with the money?"

"My banker sent four million to Annie's account about an hour ago."

"Wow," said George. How about ditching Annie and hooking up with me?"

Chris laughed. "I think you're hooked up with someone else."

"Trust me. For that kind of money, Candice won't care. But back to business. Ian is here with the landline in his hand, and as soon as we hear anything, I'll get back to you."

Chris watched Annie's face. It was alive with emotions, most of them not good. He reached over to clasp her hand and she smiled. It was a dim smile. Chris said, "Thanks, George. Stay in touch."

"I will. Oh, I take it, since you answered the phone, that you haven't been arrested yet?"

"Bye, George."

"George, before you go," Annie started, and she couldn't go on.

Chris finished her thought. "Thank you for being there, George. Thank you for everything."

"No problem."

The officer at the door knocked. "Hey, your pets came back."

Annie ran to the door. When she saw them, soaked and miserable-looking, she didn't know whether to laugh or cry. She opened the door, repaired after a fashion with duct tape, and let them in. Sis, ever polite, shook herself dry before crossing the threshold. She didn't seem to notice – or maybe she did – how wet the officer got in the process.

Annie used a towel on the two cats until they escaped to huddle with the others.

"What duz you find out?" asked Sassy Pants.

"Yeah," said Mr. Bean. *"We tried to follow you. Mommy wouldn't let us. And then she taped the door."*

"It's okay," said Tiger Lily. *"It was probably better that we didn't have a lot of cats running through the woods."*

"Trill?"

Kali interpreted. *"He wants to know if you saw the pretty bunny."*

Little Socks rolled her eyes. *"We did, and she sends her kindest regards, Mo."*

Mo purred and lay back.

Sassy Pants repeated her question, this time with a little sass. *"What duz you find out?"*

"We have lots of friends in the woods," said Tiger Lily.

"Yes," added Sis. *"Even that skunk was friendly."*

Kali and Ko said together, *"What did you learn?"* *"Who did it?"*

"It was the older couple, but the Sheriff doesn't know that yet. She's looking at everybody, even Mommy and Chris."

"Did you find clues?"

"We know where one should be. There should be a picture of Dennis and a girlfriend, the daughter of that couple, in the cabin. We couldn't get in to check."

"Why not?"

Sis said, *"The police were there, and when they left, they closed the doors."*

"Do we find out anyting else?" asked Sassy Pants.

Tiger Lily looked to Sis and Little Socks, then back to the others. *"They were headed for Canada. I might be able to figure out how to spell it if we could find something to write with."*

They stayed put but turned and looked all around the room. Nothing jumped out as pertinent to their needs.

Mr. Bean said, *"You need to learn how to type. You could send a text. Or an email."*

"I would have to have a phone or a computer for that."

"Yeah. Well, we'll keep our eyes open."

Tiger Lily looked at each one in the group. *"We'll have to keep our eyes open for something else, too. According to our new friends, the Lavender Lake Wolf Man is real."*

Sheriff Tate knocked on the door. Annie answered. "Sheriff, please come in."

"Please, call me Sondra."

Annie and Chris exchanged a glance. Perhaps Lavender Lake Campground had shifted a bit closer to Chelsea.

"Would you care for tea? Coffee? Are you off duty? We have wine as well."

Sondra sat at the table, looked at her watch and said, "I'm off duty now. And by the way, I sent your protection home."

"Our protection?" said Chris. "Is that what he was?"

"Well, no, not really. But I'm going to reframe it that way in my mind."

"Fine with me," said Chris, and he poured a glass of Traminette.

Sondra said, "I called your friend, the Chief of Police. He's a busy man."

Annie nodded. "He's got a lot on his plate, and now, he's got things on his plate that shouldn't be there."

"He mentioned something about that. Actually, I asked him. You know, since I heard your side of the conversation. How's that going?"

Annie had to turn away. Chris answered. "They've heard from Henrie. He's okay, for now. We're putting things together."

"Yes. I heard."

Annie said, "You can understand if we aren't pleased about being forced to stay. Have you made progress?"

"Yes and no. Both of the couples are gone. Both cleared out before this morning, apparently, or at least before you discovered the body. The young couple used a debit card at a gas station two hundred miles north of here, but we've had no hits since."

"They said something about Canada, but I thought that was planned for later, maybe next summer."

No one noticed that Tiger Lily perked up. Little Socks, too.

"That's interesting," said Sondra. Did they mention a location?"

Annie and Chris looked at one another. Annie said, "Quebec? No. Ontario?"

Chris, ever the man for big lakes, said, "Hudson Bay."

"Yes, by way of Sault Ste. Marie."

"That helps. Do you have a road map?"

"No," said Chris. "Even better, we have a computer."

Chris got his laptop and brought it to the table. He logged onto Google Maps and asked for directions from Lavender Lake to Sault Ste. Marie.

Sondra moved her finger over the map without touching the screen. "There," she said. "They got gas there. This appears to be their route. Excuse me."

She walked outside to call her office.

While she was gone, Tiger Lily jumped to the table and looked intently at the screen. When she saw a word that could possibly be "Canada," she touched the screen with her paw. She jumped back as the screen shifted. She didn't know her touch would pull that word closer.

Annie leaned in. "You touched Canada, big girl. That's right. That's where the young people are going."

Tiger Lily, frustrated, touched the screen, bringing the word into sharper view.

"Is that what you wanted to tell me?"

Tiger Lily looked at her without blinking.

"You wanted to tell me something else?"

One blink.

Sondra walked in and saw the exchange. Annie stood up; Tiger Lily looked at the sheriff and jumped off the table; Chris found a reason to walk to the sink.

"Hey, don't undo your conversation on my account."

"What?" asked Annie.

"I did some research on your police chief before calling him. People say he has a sixth sense about things, that he can solve cases that no one else can solve, that he sees things no one else sees. I asked him about that. Do you know what he said?"

Chris stayed at the sink. He leaned against it and appeared unconcerned. Softly, Annie said, "What did he say?"

"He said you can communicate with these cats. He can communicate with his dog. Together, the cats and his dog make an unbeatable team. He said not to knock it until I tried it. What was your cat trying to say?"

Annie took a deep breath. "I don't know. Something about Canada, but I don't think it was about the young couple."

"Can you ask her what it was about? Or, I don't know. How does this work?"

Annie sat at the table and locked eyes with Tiger Lily. She patted the top of the table. Tiger Lily looked at the Sheriff, then at Annie, then Chris. Chris shrugged his shoulders. She looked back to Annie and in one graceful leap landed on the table in front of her.

"Big girl, it might be easier to do the yes/no rather than the blinking thing." She moved and put both her fists in front of Tiger Lily.

"Were you trying to tell me about Canada?"

Tiger Lily shook her head before answering. Annie couldn't know that she was thinking, *"Cats don't do tricks. Dogs do tricks. Cats. Do. Not. Do. Tricks."* But she could see no other way around it. She put one paw on Annie's right fist. Yes.

"Were you telling me about the young couple?"

One paw on left fist. No.

"So, the older couple, John and Lucy, are going to Canada?"

Yes.

"Do you know where in Canada?"

No.

"Do you know who killed Dennis?"

Yes.

"Was it John and Lucy? The older couple?"

Yes.

"Did they make him eat something bad?"

Yes.

Here, Annie threw in a red herring. "Was it pie?"

Tiger Lily hissed, then touched Annie's left fist. No.

"Sorry. I had to show the Sheriff here we weren't making it up. Was it mushrooms?"

Yes.

"Do you know why they did it?"

Yes.

Annie looked at Tiger Lily, then up at the Sheriff. "I don't know where to go now. This was easy. It was one or the other, and she was interested in Canada. I threw in the mushrooms, because that seemed to be a really important piece of it, and by the way, I can clarify my statement in that regard. But now, I just don't know what to ask."

"Are there other ways she can communicate?"

Annie closed her eyes and shook her head. "You won't believe me."

"Try me."

With her eyes still closed, Annie said, "Sometimes she can find pictures in magazines that lead us in the right direction. Or write words."

"She writes words? Really?"

"Really. The words have to be simple. She must have heard the word Canada, and she was able to pick it out on the screen."

"You're right. I don't believe you."

"How else did I know to ask about Canada?"

Sondra was silent. "I don't know what else to do. Really, I don't."

Chris said, "Let me try." He sat at the table, two fists in front. Tiger Lily shifted to face him.

"Did you find a clue?"

Yes.

"Do you have it here?"

No.

"Can you get it?"

Tiger Lily thought for a minute, then touched the table in between his two fists.

"What does that mean?" asked Sondra.

Annie said, "There's a problem. It's possible she knows how to lead us to a clue, but she can't do it on her own."

Sis barked twice.

Chris looked up at Sis, and Sis moved to the door. She sat, expectant. Chris looked back at Tiger Lily. "Do we need to follow Sis?"

Yes.

Sondra sighed. "I have to tell you something. I hate to burden you, but your Chief of Police said I could trust you."

Annie wondered where this would lead, but she motioned Sondra to continue.

"I'm up for re-election this year, and my main rival is the chief deputy, Stan Graff. He's going to hang me on this murder, one way or another. First, Dennis was a friend of his, and if I can't solve it, or lead the department to solve it, he'll make it a point in the election. Second, if I do what

I'm getting ready to do, use your pets as guides, he'll hang me if the evidence is good or bad."

Annie nodded. "But you have a better chance of defending yourself if you solve the case, right?"

"Right."

"Then what do you have to lose?"

21: Cameroon

Mr. Jones disconnected a call to the Embassy from one phone and picked up another being held by Yannick. It was the man from the bed and breakfast, George.

Mr. Jones waited until Yannick left the room.

"Yes, George, tell me everything."

Mr. Jones listened on speaker while he and another Embassy staffer made notes. At times George consulted with someone else about a point or about an order in which things were said. Clearly, he had a support system in place so he could to do it right.

"It sounds good. Everything sounds good. Now, from your perspective, it appears they will have to find internet access to verify what Henrie said, and then they will get back to you about an amount. Correct?"

"Yes. Can you use that somehow? Track them?"

"My office already considered that possibility. Trackers are in place on the websites of both the bed and breakfast and the office of Henrie's friend, Collette. This is good news. Tell me about the money."

He whistled when George told him how high they could go. "But I shot two and a half, three tops. I figured we might be able to go up a little from there, but I didn't want to give them a figure higher. If they need more, maybe I can say I found another account."

"I think not. They will continue to push it if you do that. Perhaps if you say Henrie's employer had access to a modest amount and is willing to help, but only if necessary."

"Okay. That's a good idea. A better idea."

"At some point, you will need to sleep. Make sure you have a support system this evening that allows you to do that. Someone that can answer the telephone and wake you."

"No problem. The night shift is coming in now."

"This is all under the radar, correct? No media?"

"No media. Everyone involved is either an employee of or an associate of our network here in Chelsea."

"I'll have to visit one day."

"Yes. You will. Make sure you come to the blues bar up the street. That's where I'm supposed to be. I wish I were there tonight."

Mr. Jones disconnected and turned to his associate, Mr. Smith. Mr. Smith arrived earlier in the day, coming by car from Chad, a country to the east.

In answer to an unasked question, Mr. Smith said, "They will have to come to Maroua for internet access, unless someone out there has a satellite connection. I hate that we have to hide this from the local police. It's hard to get significant numbers into Maroua with transportation being what it is. I've got two men waiting upstairs, and Mr. Brown will be here soon with two more."

"How are they coming in?"

"They came across the Nigerian border with a group of day workers."

"Will six be enough?"

"Barely. There are two likely spots to find them. We will deploy to the local internet cafés and wait."

At that moment Yannick escorted Mr. Brown into the room. Mr. Brown gave the outward appearance of being native to any country in the region. His Harvard education was not at all apparent.

Before leaving, Yannick asked, "May I offer refreshment to anyone?"

Mr. Brown said, "Yes, please. Whatever you have that is easy to fix for a meal, for me and my associates, if that is possible."

"Certainly. For anyone else?"

Mr. Jones shook his head and Yannick departed.

Mr. Brown asked, "Why are we doing this? I thought we couldn't deploy for kidnappings anymore."

"This is a special circumstance."

"These people are that important?"

"No. They're lucky. We think this is one of the major groups, a new hub for activity in Cameroon. If we can get to these folks, we have a shot at taking out a kingpin."

Mr. Brown thought about that for a moment, then replied. "So this could be a real coup for the Embassy, and there are, what, six of us assigned? Plus you?"

Mr. Jones nodded. "Arguably our best seven, but yes."

Mr. Smith asked, "Are we all leaving on the chopper? Us and the hostages?"

"Yes. And I have a truck loaded with cargo to go on as well. It waits at the rendezvous point."

Mr. Smith said, "We need to pick up the pace. We've been here too long already. Folks at the airport are probably asking questions."

Mr. Jones said, "I paid the bribe and I have a cover story, for as long as it hangs together. They watched me unload drugs – or what they thought was drugs – and they'll watch me load butchered meat when I take off. We'll take the hostages and most of us out like halves of beef."

Mr. Smith nodded. "As soon as you and your crew eat, Brown, let's head out."

Henrie heard another vehicle pull into the complex. This one sounded newer, or at least, better maintained. Bertrand left the hut and joined the group. Henrie listened until he heard the group move away, possibly to another hut.

He leaned closer to Collette and said, "I have good news."

"What's that?"

"George was aware of our circumstance. He did not say it, and he did not act as if he knew. But he knew. Obviously, money has been gathered. He was also prepared to guide me about the photograph that angered Bertrand so much. There is hope."

"Praise be. Perhaps we will be home soon."

"Perhaps."

Henrie was not sure of the time, but he thought two to three hours had passed when he heard the taxi start up. Pop, pop. Then the other vehicle. They left the compound.

22: Chelsea

Moriah clutched the notebook in her teeth and started up the hallway again. George and Ian were nice guys, but apparently they didn't know a good clue when they saw it.

She found Honey Bear and the two large cats in the library, sitting in the windowsill. They stared toward the carriage house.

Moriah dropped the notebook and straightened. *"Hey! What am I supposed to do with this clue?"*

Three heads snapped around.

"What clue?" asked Honey Bear.

"This one. I got it from the back room."

"What is it?"

"How would I know? It looked like a clue, so I got it."

Honey Bear looked to Simon Finnegan and Oscar McMurphy. *"Was she supposed to bring it out?"*

"I don't know," answered Oscar McMurphy. *"I think she was supposed to leave it there, so we could...um..."*

Simon Finnegan finished the thought, *"So we could take Pete to it."*

"Oh. Right," said Moriah. *"Well, I can take it back."*

Just then, the front door opened and Louis walked in.

Honey Bear jumped to the floor and trotted to the notebook. He rolled into a ball, covering the book so it could only be seen by someone looking closely.

Louis stepped into the library, looked around, and saw only cats. He sat in a comfortable arm chair and turned on the television. When the volume was at the perfect level –

low enough he could hear but loud enough to mask his words – he pulled out a cell phone and made a call.

The cats looked at one another. Moriah said, *"I'm still in training. Let me do this."*

She walked sedately to Louis, wiggled her butt for take-off, and jumped to the arm of the chair. She rolled into a ball, curled her tail around his upper arm and sighed. With her eyes closed and a soft purr running, she could hear both sides of the conversation.

Suddenly, Speckles was in the room. Quickly, she took in the situation. Moriah appeared to nap by that guest. She must be spying. Honey Bear, now sitting up, was on top of something. Was he trying to hide it?

Simon Finnegan and Oscar McMurphy were on the windowsill, but facing into the room. What great look-outs they turned out to be.

Speckles trotted to Honey Bear. *"We believe they're gone. It's time to send in the cat burglar. Is she busy?"*

"Yes," answered Honey Bear. *"She's having a busy day. She found this clue, and now she's spying on a telephone call."*

"Huh. Well, we need her to do a little burgling."

Louis chose that moment to push the phone into his pocket and get up. He gave Moriah an affectionate pet on the head as he walked away from the chair and out of the library.

Moriah waited a beat, then looked around. He was gone. She sat up, shook her pretty hair into place, licked a paw, and jumped down. Trotting over to Honey Bear, she said, *"He's a bad man."*

"What?"

"He talks in a fake accent."

"How do you know it's fake?"

"Because he forgot to use it when he made that call. Some woman on the other end reminded him to 'speak Frenchie.'"

"What else did you hear?"

"They're working with fake people to buy up places around here. Some guy is coming tomorrow to look at the state park, and they made an offer on The Marina and The Escape. Once it looks like those are solid, they're going to try to buy all the places on The Avenue."

"I'll be darned," said Oscar McMurphy. *"This might be a real clue that Pete needs to see. What should we do with it?"*

Honey Bear climbed off carefully and considered the situation. *"We can't put it in the agency. They might find it."*

Simon Finnegan said, *"Let's put it under the sofa. No one will see it there."*

Oscar McMurphy said, *"No. Someone might accidently kick it, and we won't be able to reach it."*

Speckles said, *"How about under that chair that you were sitting in? It's high enough we can reach into the middle but low enough you'd have to be looking for stuff to see it."*

"That could work," started Honey Bear.

"No," said Moriah. *"Those kids sprawl all over the floor when they're in here. They'll see it."*

They considered their options, which were few.

"I know," said Speckles. *"We could put it on that porch in the back. The kids never go there."*

"We have to walk it all the way almost to that man's room to do that. He might see us."

Speckles was disappointed in herself. She had two spectacular ideas, and both of them were shot down.

"I know," said Honey Bear. *"We take it to the agency, but we put it underneath a couple of cushions."*

"Yeah!" "That will work!" "Let's do it!"

Speckles added, *"And then let's get over to the carriage house before those people come back."*

Pete and Cyril returned to the Inn. Pete was tired. Cyril was thirsty. They were both hungry.

Nancy heard them and came to the foyer. "Come on in, boys. You need to sit down and have some lunch. Cyril, I'll bet I can find Henrie's stash of dog food somewhere."

Cyril huffed. He hoped for a roast beef sandwich, or maybe ham and cheese. But if he had to have dog food, he could handle it. He was just that hungry.

Pete dropped heavily into a kitchen chair and put his feet onto a second one. "I'm sorry, Nancy. I'm just so tired. I'll take them down in a minute."

"Don't worry about it. You have so much going on. George is out in the back yard stretching his toes in the sand. Ian is with him, you know, just to make sure there are two people when a call comes in."

"What about tonight," asked Pete. "Will someone be able to stay here while he takes a break?"

"We don't know yet. We're trying to keep all of the chatter to a minimum, so we're not talking to anyone. Candice knows, of course, but she's just telling people George is busier at the Inn than he thought he would be."

"This is unusual, people not knowing. Usually, everyone knows, and everyone is helping."

"Something like this would get out, though."

"You're right. But that means George has to run twenty four seven."

"We'll get by."

Nancy put a plate filled with two avocado shrimp sandwiches and a cup of chicken, lime and rice soup in front of Pete. "I have ginger lime iced tea, plain black tea, coffee… what would you like?"

"The first one, please. I hate to ask, but do you have anything as mundane as a roast beef sandwich in the refrigerator?"

"Oh, sure. I'm sorry, Pete. I thought…"

"No, not for me. What I have is great. I was thinking of my friend, here. He's been working hard all day."

"Sure. I don't have a sandwich, but I saw leftover ham, bacon and sausage from breakfast."

Cyril bumped Pete's hip with his head in a gesture of thanks and sat, waiting for his late lunch.

Pete said, "I thought the neighborhood cats were here. Where'd they go?"

"I have no idea. I'm keeping the cat food dishes filled, because they do seem to spend a lot of time here, but I haven't seen them, well, not since shortly after you left this morning. And speaking of that, you said you'd be back to make an arrest. Or four. What's up with that?"

Hilly came into the kitchen. "Pete, do you want to look at this list of stolen items, or do you want George to look first?"

"Let me take a look. That might help me with my next thing. The arrest. Or four."

Pete took his feet off the chair and leaned over the list. "So if you marked it off, you got it back, right?"

"Right. You'll see that everything that came from the grocery store is gone, and, this is just my opinion, the box store probably lost a lot that we'll never know about."

"What's this handwritten stuff on the bottom?"

"George wrote in some things that were stolen yesterday. I checked off some of those, but look. One thing taken from DoubleGood yesterday wasn't returned. It's an expensive video game."

"Well, I'll add that game to the two things they got today. Are those kids here?"

Pete, Hilly and Nancy looked up when, almost on cue, the front door opened. Cyril rose and walked to the door between the dining room and foyer. He sat, expectant. The four kids came in, talking among themselves. They stopped when they saw Cyril. By that time, Pete stood behind him.

"Kids. So glad you could make it. Come on into the dining room."

The kids didn't move.

"That was not a request."

Silently, Brooke in the lead, they walked into the dining room and sat, the girls on one side of the table and the boys on the other. No one said a word.

Pete said, "Do you know where your parents are?"

They looked at one another and said nothing.

Nancy said, "I hear they go over to the winery and stay there until late afternoon or early evening. Do you want me to call over there, Pete?"

"Please. Ask them to come back here. I can't question juveniles without a parent or guardian in the room. Until they get here, you kids sit tight."

Brooke said, "We have rights."

"Yes, you do," said Pete. "Consider yourselves under arrest for now, and for now, your rights consist of one telephone call. To your parents."

Clarke stood as Pete spoke. "Under arrest for what?"

"Theft. Sit back down."

Clarke sat. "We returned all that stuff."

"No. No you didn't. And you took a couple of expensive items today."

"Prove it. We don't have anything."

Six cats trotted into the dining room. Honey Bear stopped next to Cyril and appeared to converse with him. Cyril nodded several times, looked toward the stairway once, and nodded again. Pete watched. When Cyril met his eyes, Pete gave a brief nod.

"We'll wait for your parents."

While they sat, Pete made a telephone call. He didn't care if the kids heard him. In fact, he hoped it made them take notice.

His second-in-command – the department was too small to have a deputy chief – answered the phone.

"Marco, I need you to get a search warrant for the KaliKo Inn, all rooms, including private and common areas. Also, I want a warrant for guest vehicles, luggage and belongings, including purses and clothing."

"Sure, boss. What are we looking for?"

"I want it to be somewhat open, but put three items on it specifically." Pete looked at the paper again. "A God of War, Stonecutters edition. That's a video game. A rare Kelva dresser box, painted pink roses on blue batik."

"How do you spell that?"

"Uh, Kelva, K-E-L-V-A and batik, B-A-T-I-K. You've got the rest, right?"

"Right, boss. You said three. What's the other?"

"An emerald ring, thirteen carats, set in white gold and surrounded by about two carats of diamonds."

"Wow."

"Yeah. Wow."

Pete looked at the kids. They stared at the table, stone-faced.

"Get that warrant to the Inn as soon as you can. I'm here now, waiting for the parents. When they get here, I'll question the suspects."

"I'm on it." Marco rang off and Pete gestured to Nancy, who stood in the kitchen door. "Would you and Hilly mind sitting with the kids? I'm going out back to get George."

Cyril stood to come with him. Pete said, "Stay." Cyril stayed. He sat in the doorway to the foyer. If any of the kids tried to leave, they would have to go through him.

George, as promised, was on the beach in the back. He was in a deck chair. His shoes were off, his toes were in the sand. He was asleep. Ian slept in another chair, his feet on a small table. The Inn's land line telephone receiver was in Ian's hand.

Pete walked to Ian quietly and put his hand on his shoulder. Ian woke quickly, nearly dropping the telephone.

Pete whispered, "It's okay. Just me. How tired is George?"

"Pretty tired, but if you need him, he'll be fine."

"Okay. I think I need him." Pete stepped to George while Ian stretched himself awake.

Like Ian, George woke quickly, saying, "What? Who?"

"It's okay. Nothing to do with Henrie. I need you in the dining room, though."

"What's up?"

"I'm back to make that arrest. Or four."

"Geez. I'm awake now. Let's go."

Back in the dining room, they waited another ten minutes for Jim and Connie.

Ian stayed in the kitchen, telephone in hand, while Nancy and Hilly busied themselves cleaning the kitchen. Not that it needed it, but they both saw an opportunity to "learn something."

George motioned Henrie into the foyer. "You know how the cats do strange things sometimes?"

"Yeah. And?"

"Well, they were doing something strange today. They went up there," George pointed to the second floor landing, "and just…looked."

"Looked? At what?"

"Nothing that I could tell, but maybe it has to do with this?"

Pete looked at Cyril. Cyril had joined them, and he tapped Pete's right foot one time. The three walked up the steps. Quietly, Pete said, "I can't really do anything until the search warrant gets here, but, you know, no harm in looking. It is a common area, right?"

"Right," said George.

Pete looked down. Moriah, Clara's rotund and fluffy cat, was leading the way. On the landing, she jumped to the top of the sofa and stared up at the bookshelf.

Pete and George looked, too. George said, "What are we looking at?"

Pete took out his phone, opened his text messages and found the photograph sent from Frank. "This. We're looking at this."

And they were.

Marco arrived with the search warrant at the same time the parents came. They were a little tipsy and under the supervision of Jesus.

Jesus looked at Pete as he said, "They wouldn't leave. I relayed the message, but they didn't want to come. I kicked them out and walked with them to make sure they didn't go to Mo's Tap."

Pete nodded his thanks and looked at the search warrant. "Marco, I want you to put on gloves and get an evidence bag. Upstairs on that shelf," he turned to point, "you'll find this."

Marco looked at the photograph and nodded. "So that's 'rare Kelva on blue batik.'"

"You got it," said Pete. "Then go into each of the kids' rooms – Hilly, can you help him? – and look for the video game."

"What about that ring?"

"We'll do these first. I imagine it'll be harder to find a ring."

Jesus escorted Jim and Connie to the dining room where they sat. Pete thanked Jesus as he left and sat at the head of the table. George pulled a chair to sit slightly behind and to the left of Pete.

"Here we are," said Pete. I'm ready to arrest your four children on three counts of theft."

"They gave all that schtuff back!" Connie had trouble with her esses.

"They gave most of it back, yes. I'll probably tack on all of the food that was eaten that could not be returned, a couple of damaged items, according to the notes on this list, and a few other things. By the way, I need to administer the Miranda rights."

While Pete did that, George took possession of the Kelva box. Marco gave it to him, ensconced in a plastic bag. Pete noticed that Clarke and Brooke masked looks of surprise as George held it up for examination.

"Do you understand these rights as they have been explained to you?"

No one spoke.

Pete cleared his throat. "Excuse me. May I have your attention, please? Do you understand your rights as they have been explained to you? Clarke? Brooke? Marty? Cassie? Jim? Connie?"

As he said each name, he looked into their faces and extracted a brief nod. After Connie nodded, she said, "Why are you giving ush our rightsh? We under arrescht too?"

"You might be."

Marco returned to the dining room with a brand new game of God of War. "Stonecutters edition," he said, handing it to Pete. It was safely wrapped in plastic.

"So, here are two of the items, one moderately expensive, and one very expensive. Do you want to make it easy on yourselves and tell us where we can find the ridiculously expensive thing? The ring?"

Brooke and Clarke looked at one another. Brooke spoke. "If we tell you about the ring, will you drop the charges?"

"Not hardly."

"Well, then, we won't tell. You'll never find it."

Pete looked down at Cyril. He seemed to have a ridiculously happy grin on his face. "Do you have something to say, Cyril?"

Paw to right foot. Yes.

Is it in the house?"

Paw to left foot. No.

Pete was startled. "No?"

Jim and Connie stared at one another. Connie leaned over and asked, "Ish he talking to a dog?"

"Yesh." Jim had trouble with his esses also.

Pete looked at the five cats, sitting in a semi-circle behind Cyril. He looked back at Cyril. "Does one of the cats know where it is?"

Right foot. Yes.

Moriah stepped forward, swishing her pretty mane in the process. Pete said, "Our newest detective, huh?"

Moriah preened.

Pete looked at Cyril. "Is it in the carriage house?"

Right foot. Yes.

Pete handed the search warrant to Marco. "Marco, would you take Hilly over to the carriage house and execute this search warrant?"

"Sure thing, boss."

"Take Clara's cat with you, please."

"Uh, okay?"

Marco reached down to pick her up, but the little cat scampered between his legs and out the front cat door. Pete walked to the door with Marco and watched as the cat ran through the grass toward the carriage house in front of them.

He went back to the table, sat, and said, "Okay. You may be off the hook for the ring, but you're on the hook for everything else. The things you stole and returned, the things you stole and didn't return, after being given a chance, and the one thing you stole today, knowing that we were on to you. You did a smart thing, hiding it in plain sight, but this is an intuitive house. We tend to find things that end up here."

23: Lavender Lake

Sondra used her radio to call for back up to meet her at the cabin, and she followed a dog, two cats and two humans through the woods.

As they walked, she said to Chris, "Tell me your secret to finding mushrooms."

"It's easy," he said. "You don't look for mushrooms. You look for trees."

"What trees?"

"Oak, elm, sycamore, ash."

"You're kidding."

"Nope. Know your trees, find your mushrooms. Just don't get the bad ones."

"Got it. And this dog of yours, Pete didn't mention her. He talked about his dog, these cats, and there might have been a water dog of some kind."

"Jock. He's a Portuguese water dog. Sis, my giant schnauzer, is new to the group. She was rescued this past winter, in that horrendous storm that buried most of us and the east coast last winter."

"That was a bad one. She was out in that?"

"We think she was either abandoned or she ran away from her owner. Either is possible. He was bad enough that she might have taken the opportunity, even in that storm."

"She seems to be a part of the, for lack of a better word, solution now. At least she acted like she knew what she was doing."

"We won't know. Frankly, I never know for sure, until they lead us to something we need or want. Annie, though, she's rock solid sure. And they do have special skills."

"Can that cat really spell?"

"Yes. 'That cat' is Tiger Lily. She's the grand dame of the group. The rest are as smart as she. They have different skills. The little black one, for example, Little Socks, she's what Annie refers to as a cat burglar."

"You're kidding!"

"No. I understand where she gets it. When something small is found, something important to an investigation, Little Socks is usually involved."

"What about the rest of them?"

"Let's see. Next in age are the three litter mates, Kali, Ko and Mo. Kali and Ko are big scaredy cats, but every now and then they do something brave. Mo, the boy, is a long-haired lover. His special skill is in getting everyone to fall head over heels in love with him. Sassy Pants is next in age. She's kind of spastic at times. Annie calls her eclectic. I'm not sure what her skill is, but I'll tell you. Once, she and Little Socks were kidnapped, and that spastic little girl seemed to me to be involved in her own rescue. She held it together and waltzed out of her prison with her head held high."

"Is that all of them?"

"No, the youngest is Mr. Bean. He's a lover, too, but a different sort than Mo. Mo sits and waits for love to come to him. Mr. Bean goes out there and asks for it. He's quick, and he's strong."

"And they all help in these, um, investigations?"

"As far as we can tell."

At the cabin, they waited only five minutes before two Sheriff's vehicles pulled in. Sondra greeted them and spoke with them privately, in low tones, then she returned to Chris, Annie and the kids.

"Okay. I need to ask you to stay outside, but I guess I'll need one search cat? Is that it?"

Annie said, "Probably." She looked at Tiger Lily and Little Socks. "Which one of you goes in?"

Little Socks stepped to the porch and sat, waiting for the door to be opened.

Sondra looked at her officers and shook her head. She pointed. "You stay here with them. You come with me. This is new territory. Let's go."

Chris waited in the yard for the Sheriff and Little Socks to come out. He reached into his pocket and pulled out the vibrating phone. "George. What's happening?"

"Nothing yet. We haven't heard a thing. I just wanted the two of you to know we… we haven't heard anything yet."

"Thanks for that. Annie and I are going crazy up here waiting to hear."

George cleared his throat. "I, um, need to get off the line, but I have one more question."

"Shoot."

"Have you been arrested yet?"

Chris laughed. "No. We have our detective cats and a dog-in-training on the case."

"No kidding? We have some of that going on here, too."

"Really? What's going on?"

"Uh…nothing. Nothing at all. It was just a joke. Tell Annie not to worry about a thing."

As he hung up, Chris vowed to himself to say nothing to Annie, but he figured something might be going on in Chelsea, too.

Tiger Lily heard chittering in the grass. She turned to see Chipper.

"Is everything okay? I mean, the black cat went inside with the police. Is she okay?"

"Everything is fine, Chipper. Thanks to you, we may be able to prove we didn't do it, and we might get to go home tonight."

"That's great I mean that's great really great but we would like to have a party and you come and all."

"Really?"

"Yeah. Mom sent me out here and said if you can get free tonight to come to the woods and we'll all get together can you come?"

"I don't know. If we stay over another night, we'll have to figure out how to get outside. Tell your mom we're grateful for the invitation, and if we can come, we will."

"Okay I'll tell her and guess what maybe we can all go to the edge of the woods by your cabin and you won't have to go very far not even into the woods if your mom won't let you."

Tiger Lily shook her head to clear it a bit. *"Thanks. I hope we can come."*

Annie stood on the porch, nervous. She had been told to stay out of the house and out of the way. That wasn't what made her nervous. Nor was it the deputy, lounging against the porch railing.

She was nervous because she didn't like sending Little Socks in by herself, even if this Sheriff turned out to be a good person.

She kept reaching for her phone. Chris had taken it and wouldn't let her have it. Why? Because she would answer any call from anywhere that might have anything to do with Henrie.

She was with the most important person in her life. Arguably the second most important person was on the other side of the world, in trouble, and there was nothing she could do.

And now her alpha cat, her little burglar, was in a cabin with a Sheriff from another jurisdiction who would just as soon arrest her as clear her. Maybe. At least she seemed open to the idea that the cats were special. Or was it an act? Could they really trust her?

Hopefully they could. She had practically given Little Socks to her on a silver platter. Without question. If she was of sound mind, would she have done that?

Why was it taking so long?

Little Socks jumped to the top of the dresser where she had knocked the picture down. She looked down, between the wall and the dresser. There it was. On the floor and behind the dresser.

She sat and looked up at the Sheriff. She expected the Sheriff to look. To move the dresser. To bend over and look under the dresser at the floor. Anything.

This Sheriff didn't do anything. She stood there and argued with a deputy.

"I'm not sure why we're doing this, but that guy in Chelsea said these cats can find what we need."

"Really? This really ties it for me. I may have lost the last election to you, but this time, I'm taking you down. This is the height of incompetence. Following a cat into a crime scene."

"Yes. And there she is, doing…well, she's doing something."

"She's sitting on the dresser, looking at you and me."

Little Socks got onto her stomach and reached down with one paw, to illustrate where the clue was hidden.

"Oh, now look. She's reaching for a dust bunny. This is ridiculous."

"Give her a minute. She has to do something soon."

Little Socks jumped down. She walked all the way around the dresser. The decorative trim went nearly to the floor. She could not get underneath. Someone would have to move it.

The Sheriff said, "See? Look. She's still looking for it."

Little Socks stood and slapped the dresser with her body. That worked for Tiger Lily. At least, when Tiger Lily wanted to go outside, she could body slam the door and someone would open it for her. Wouldn't these idiots realize they needed to move the dresser?

The Sheriff went to the dresser and opened the drawers that were hit by the little cat's body. "No, they're empty. I'm not sure what she's trying to say."

"She's trying to say you're an idiot and this idiot that works for you is getting campaign signs made this week."

Little Socks wanted to bite him, but she remembered what would happen. She would go to kitty jail and she might not be released alive.

Once again, she jumped to the top of the dresser, danced around the area over the picture, and pushed her paw into the narrow space between dresser and wall.

"Well," said the deputy, "you now have a spastic cat. I'm outa here."

"Wait one minute. Let me...."

The Sheriff finally went to the end of the dresser, picked it up a bit, and moved it away from the wall. The picture stood against the wall for just a second, then it fell against the dresser with a tiny "clack."

"Here's something," said the Sheriff. She took a photo with her phone. "So I'm not charged with planting evidence, will you do the honors?"

Grudgingly, the deputy walked behind the Sheriff and looked into the tiny space. "Well I'll be darned." He pulled on a glove, moved the Sheriff out of the way and pushed the dresser away a little more. He reached down, pulled out the picture and looked at it.

"I'll be darned. This is Dennis. A younger version, but it's Dennis. He's been a friend of mine for years now. Well, he was a friend. Don't know who this woman is, though."

"We'll find out. My guess is that she's a friend or relative of our missing couple. I'll want you to take charge of this part of the investigation. For starters, check the prints on that picture. I want to be sure that we can tie the picture to them, regardless of who that woman turns out to be."

Sharply, he said, "Yes, ma'am."

He walked out, carrying the photo carefully with two gloved fingers. The Sheriff stood next to the dresser, eye to eye with Little Socks. "I'm sorry, Little Socks. I'm new to this kind of thing. I didn't know what you were saying. I hope you forgive me, and I thank you for your service."

Little Socks, never one to linger over sentimentality, jumped to the floor and trotted out of the cabin.

24: Chelsea

Nancy and Sam wanted to do something to help George, but he didn't seem to want the help. At least, not as far as Henrie was concerned. He accepted everything they had to offer when it came to keeping the Inn going.

George had moved into Henrie's ground floor apartment. Nancy and Sam moved into Annie's third floor apartment. With JoJo in the basement, every room of the Inn was filled.

Because of the tense situation, Sam stayed close but out of sight in the kitchen while Nancy settled the bill with Jim and Connie. Nancy didn't think she would need him, but it was nice to know he was close by.

Settling the bill was easy enough to do. The shared computerized financial system captured all of the charges from the Café, Mo's Tap, the Confectionary and Sassy P's. It would have captured charges from the yoga studio as well, but this family didn't use the services of that business. The only items that had to be added were the unreturned or damaged goods from across The Avenue.

There was a significant charge from Babar Foods, the grocery store. The charge was for items picked up for meals with an airy, "just charge it, please" and stolen foods.

There were stolen goods – returned but damaged, so charged at full price – from DoubleGood and The Drug Store.

Drinks and food items were charged at or stolen from CyberHealth.

The antique dresser box was returned to Frank, but he charged a stocking fee of three hundred fifty dollars. Jim and Connie didn't argue.

As Nancy rang up the final charges, she said, "You're welcome to eat and drink at the Tap and Sassy P's, but you won't be able to charge it to your room. You'll have to make sure the kids have something. I see they've been used to getting take-out from the winery during their visit, but, again, they can't charge it to the room anymore.

Jim said, "I have to say, the management here has been less than hospitable. That woman that owns the place, Annie, we haven't seen her at all."

Connie said, "That's right. And she left George in charge. He is the rudest person I've ever met."

Sam walked in from the kitchen. "Rude, huh? If you think George is rude, then you're probably in for a rude awakening."

Jim's head snapped up. "What?"

Sam chuckled. "I didn't mean nothin'."

Jim continued to look at Sam, but he spoke to Nancy. "That young girl, JoJo? Is that her name? She just can't handle a kitchen that serves eight to ten people."

Sam settled back to watch the show. Nancy was never one to be a wallflower.

She said, "The notes say the children and you ate well, everyone having seconds, even thirds, and the notes mention the foods you said you liked. Let's see, the spring frittata, and the cinnamon French toast roll, the, um, yes, that's the strawberry cheesecake breakfast bar. Were you saying that just to make her feel better about herself?"

"Well, yes," said Connie. "We, um, well we never liked it. We ate to be polite."

"I see. Sam, you see that, don't you? That they ate double and triple portions in order to be polite?"

Sam shook his head and looked up at the ceiling.

"And who are the two of you?" asked Connie. "Are you covering for this vacationing owner? Or do you work here on a regular basis?"

"Oh, Sam and I don't work here, but we tend to spend a lot of time in and around the place. You see, Annie's our daughter."

Nancy rose and walked away. Sam continued to stare at the ceiling. Nancy turned to say, "Oh, I'm helping JoJo cook breakfast tomorrow. I told her we'll give your demon children hot dogs and cold grits. I hope they enjoy it. You, too."

Ray and Cheryl were on semi-speaking terms. Ray was scared and angry. He was afraid Cheryl would actually want to sell The Marina. And he had been bluffing when he said she could sell, but he wouldn't. The truth was, without The Marina, he would have to move to another deep harbor port to set up. He didn't want to consider that.

Given their current situation, Ray didn't want to spend the evening alone, nor did he want to go to one of their typical haunts on The Avenue. He suggested a light meal at Chateau Simon.

They sat at a table in a window overlooking the vineyard. The view was outstanding, but it didn't include water.

Ray sighed. Jock, under the table, sighed. Cheryl sighed.

Jock perked up. A friend was coming in. It was Tillie! And here came Simon to say hello.

Ray said, "Well, we wanted to get away from The Avenue, but The Avenue has come to us."

Cheryl waved Carlos and Isabelle over. "Join us, please."

Ray added, "Yes, and don't tell Jesus we were here."

"Jesus loves it that you're here. Remember, he and Minnie are partners."

"Oh, that's right."

As they sat down, the animals moved to a table that didn't have four feet underneath it.

After they ordered, Carlos said, "Change may be coming to Chelsea."

"Really?" asked Ray. "What do you mean?"

"The park manager came over today to order some things for breakfast and lunch tomorrow. Says several people are coming from the state capital to look at the place. They're bringing a buyer."

"A buyer? It's public," said Cheryl. "How can someone buy it?"

"If the pocketbook is deep enough, anyone will sell."

Ray and Cheryl looked at one another. Something sparked in Ray's mind. He looked at Carlos. "Who wants it?"

"I don't know. He didn't know. Well, he said, 'someone from Texas.' That's all he knew."

"Strange," said Cheryl. "I wonder how often that happens."

"Yeah," said Ray. "I wonder."

Ray took his phone from his pocket and sent a text to Pete. "Need to talk to you in the morning."

Tillie was so happy to see friends that she couldn't stay still. She jumped from Jock to Simon and back again. She was also excited because she had news. *"Guess what? Someone wants to buy the state park. I wonder who it is and if they people will be nice."*

"They won't be," said Jock. *"They'll be crooks and liars."*

"Why do you say that?" asked Tillie.

"Because it's being organized by one guy, and they're going to try to buy The Marina, The Escape, and everything on The Avenue, too."

"I knew it! I knew he was up to no good!" spat Simon. *"My mom and dad love him. They think he's going to bring lots of business here."*

"Who?" asked Tillie, completely confused.

"That Frenchie," said Simon.

"He's not French," said Jock. *"Sometimes he forgets to use his accent."*

"That's mean. Where's he from?"

"Somewhere here in the states. I don't know where. I think they make and take accents wherever they go. The guy buying the state park is pretending to be from Texas, and the one wanting to buy my place is pretending to be from Boston."

"Have they made an offer?"

"Yes, and Cheryl likes it. She thinks they're overpaying – they are – and she thinks it will be a great retirement income."

"Can you stop them?"

"I think we need to work together to stop it from happening all over town."

"How?"

Simon said, "I want to help, but I'm so far away. I wish there was a way I could talk to all of you, you know, whenever something like this comes up."

"We'll just have to come out here more often," said Tillie. "I wonder how we can make that happen."

"One thing at a time," said Jock. "One thing at a time. Right now, we have to concentrate on stopping these sales. How do we let everyone know?"

Tillie said, "I'm the only one of us on The Avenue on a regular basis, and this week, Tiger Lily and everyone is gone. But those other cats are around. I've seen them going in and out of the Inn. I almost went in once, but, you know, without the other cats being there, I didn't want to intrude."

"I think you have to. At least, you have to talk to those other cats, and to Cyril. Have you seen him this week?"

"He's been really busy this week, but something's happening at the Inn. I think there are thieves there or something. I'll try to catch him there, and the cats, and we'll talk about it."

Simon asked, *"What cats?"*

"Oh, Simon Finnegan and Oscar McMurphy, you know, Fat Cat and Scaredy Cat. And Honey Bear is there a lot this week."

"I don't like him," said Simon.

"He was mean to you when you moved here, but he's better now. He lives here now, too. Back then, both of you were guests. Now he's a regular."

"If you say so. Maybe I'll give him another chance. Are there others?"

"Yeah. Do you remember the nanny kitties? Their baby's daycare is broken, so she has to come to the Inn during the day. They've been coming over, too. Their names are Speckles and Daryll."

"I met them once."

"Good. And there's a new kitty in town. Her name's Moriah. She lives at the flower shop."

Jock said, *"It looks like I have to leave. Tillie, you'll have to coordinate things for us on The Avenue. If you need me, get Cyril to bark for me."*

Nancy poured a glass of wine for Sam and said, "You know what? I think we need a break."

"You and I were thinking along the same lines. I called Frank to see if he and Mem were free, but they aren't. Something about a rare box of some sort. Had him all upset."

"Oh, that. He'll feel better about it tomorrow."

"What? How do you know?"

"Never mind, dear. Why don't we go out to dinner? I was thinking about the winery that the nice young couple owns."

"Brian and Janet? I haven't seen them for a while. Let's do that. Should we take Honey Bear? He might like to see that cat of theirs."

"Oh, no. That's one cat that Honey Bear cannot abide."

"He can't abide most of them."

"Sam! You know that's not true. But this one was rude beyond all measure when we were all staying in the carriage house."

"Yep. It was that cat's fault alright. Certainly not the fault of your angel."

"Sam, what's gotten into you?"

"I don't know. It's like, well, everyone is all on pins and needles, and they're getting' into my brain. I'm sorry, sweetheart. Let's let bygones be bygones. Let's start over. Dear, may I have the pleasure of your company at Chateau Simon this evening?"

"It would be my pleasure."

At Chateau Simon, they greeted Ray and Cheryl and Carlos and Isabel on their way out. They sat at the same table in the window.

When Louis entered, he recognized Nancy as one of the women at the Inn during breakfast. He waved.

Nancy waved back and beckoned him to come.

"Please join us. We just arrived and haven't ordered yet."

"I would love the company." He turned to Sam, "Excuse. I am Louis. And you?"

"Sam. I'm the husband of the lovely Nancy here."

Louis held Sam's gaze. "Yes, lovely." He turned back to Nancy. "You work at the Inn, no?"

"That's right. I work at the Inn, no. I'm Annie's mother. But you haven't met her. She's on vacation this week."

"I have seen her on the, what you say, web, and I spoke to her when I reserved the room. Yes, that was the correct word."

"George tells me you're looking for property for a resort."

"Yes. I have not had the luck. I have been up and down the shore, in and out of many towns. I have seen many wonderful towns that would meet our needs, but so far, my offers have not yielded the fruit."

"What do you need? I mean, are you looking for vacant land or land that can be reclaimed?"

"The preference would be for the vacant land. That, I have not found."

Sam said, "Hey, you're not from here, are you?"

"No. I am French."

"You don't say. What part of France?"

"I am from a small town not far from Marseilles."

"I've traveled there a bit," said Sam. "What's the name of the town?"

"You would not know. It is off whatever path has been beaten." Louis changed the subject. "Nancy, may I be so familiar to call you this name?"

"Certainly. How can I help you?"

"I am missing something from my room. It is not much, and nothing of value to anyone but myself. It is, shall you say, my notes to myself about the places I have visited."

"Could you have misplaced them? Do you take them with you during the day?"

"No, I leave them in the room. I wonder, is there ever the problem with theft? At the Inn, I mean?"

Nancy shook her head. "Typically, I would say no, but those little demons have been stealing things from all over The Avenue. Thank goodness they're leaving tomorrow. Anyway, we weren't aware they had stolen from any of the rooms. Well, they have most of the rooms, I guess."

"Ah. Well, perhaps they are the culprits. I will say something to George in the morning."

"Don't wait too late. The family is leaving right after breakfast tomorrow. Oh, and if all you see is hot dogs and grits, come on into the kitchen. I'm making a special breakfast for the kids tomorrow, but you can have real food."

The plan – as much of a plan that they had – was to keep the number of people in the loop to a minimum. Within the loop, Candice had to keep Mo's Tap going, Ian was training youth in marathon swimming that evening, and Gwen had a conference out of town.

That left Jenny. Someone had to stay with George, to help him keep the phone calls straight, to keep notes, and to let him sleep for at least a few hours.

She packed a bag and threw it on the couch in Henrie's apartment.

"I'll bunk here. What do you have to eat?"

"Uh…we have breakfast stuff. JoJo was making something a while ago for tomorrow, but…"

"Never mind. I'll call Mo's and get take-out. What do you want?"

"Great! Get me a burger, medium, grilled on chopped onions, everything on the side. Get it with Provolone cheese and a toasted pretzel bun. Sweet potato fries. Oh, and a helping of that Asian slaw Georgia makes."

Jenny stared. "Is that all?"

"Think we can get a six pack of Dragon's Milk?"

"What's that?"

"A regional stout. We started carrying it a couple of weeks ago."

"No. No six packs. You're on duty until you're not."

"Nobody told me about this part of it. Bummer."

Jenny called the bar with her order. As she finished George's, the woman on the other end of the line said, "Say, who is this? This sounds like it's for George."

"This is Jenny. Candice? Is that you? I've got the night shift."

"Great! I'm glad he'll have company. Should I send a six pack of Dragon's Milk?"

"No, he has to stay clear. If it makes you feel any better, he asked for it, too."

"It doesn't. Do you want me to deliver?"

"No, I'll run up and get it. How long?"

"Ten minutes. Is there any news?"

"Nothing to report. Hey, how can I keep him relaxed and sharp this evening?"

"Seriously? If you're up to it, get him to play The Game Of Thrones."

"The television show?"

"It's a board game. Annie has one. It's probably in the library."

"I've never heard of it."

"It's addictive. If you play, you won't get to bed until sometime tomorrow morning."

"I don't need that much sleep."

"I'm not talking one or two o'clock. You'll be up until four or five. Oh, one more thing, you'll need to get JoJo to play with you. You have to have at least three players. I'll add a burger and fries for her."

"Tell me again why I want to do this?"

"You want George to be relaxed and sharp."

"Anything for the team."

25: Cameroon

Henrie and Collette huddled together. To Henrie, it seemed hours since the men left the compound.

Collette asked, "When do you think we'll hear from them?"

"I do not know. I assume they had to go to Maroua to an internet café. I doubt they have access on their own."

"Do you think they know how to search for the Inn?"

"Bertrand seemed comfortable with the web address. They must use modern technology on occasion. They have cell telephones."

Collette shivered. "I hope they finish this quickly. You know, they could have called my family, my law firm."

"No, they could not. You are a woman and totally unworthy of the price."

"Thanks."

Henrie was thankful for the brief moment of levity. "You well know that is not my opinion. I would pay at least two hundred dollars for you."

"Thanks a lot. Hey, do you think they will call on their own, without coming back here, I mean?"

"I doubt that. If they want to continue the façade that I am not under duress, they need me."

"And what then? George sends money to some bank and they just let us go? And let's think about that sentence for a minute. Do they do business with banks?"

"I do not know. They must have some mechanism for receiving funds, particularly if this – kidnapping westerners – is an ongoing source of funding. Perhaps someone with a legitimate business is prepared to accept and turn over funds."

"That makes sense. But if banking here is anything like banking in the States, certainly they will be caught at some point."

"Not if they are smart. They can mask a large inflow of cash as a large sale, and funnel the money back to Boko Haram through semi-legitimate means. Bertrand drives a taxi. Other members must have jobs, or must own businesses of their own. There would be many avenues through which the funds could be dispersed."

"Catching them at the source, where the money comes in, would be important."

"Yes. I am certain they know that we know this. My guess is that they have accounts with several layers of ownership to somehow mask everyone's identity."

Collette sighed. "Assuming they have a mechanism to move the money, I am drawn to the second part of my question. Will they just let us go?"

"I do not know. If arrangements can be made to get us to the airport in time for our scheduled departure, possibly. If not, they would have to decide what to do with us until another flight can be scheduled. I doubt they would wait long."

"Do you think George and the others can move quickly?"

"I have no doubt."

Mr. Jones remained at the hotel in his informal headquarters. Mr. Smith, Mr. Brown and their agents were sequestered behind dumpsters and inside abandoned vehicles near the two internet cafés. Vehicles that could have been abandoned – or that could be top notch transportation in Cameroon – waited for them, up and down the street and on either side.

Mr. Jones would maintain radio silence until he received word from the Embassy that web contact had occurred. Or until he was hailed, like now.

"Brown."

"Jones. Go ahead."

"Likely suspects at site one, repeat, site one. Three. Arrived in yellow cab."

Mr. Jones listened to another radio for several minutes. It finally came to life. Through his earpiece, he heard, "Someone at site one logged onto victim website."

Mr. Jones smiled grimly and spoke into his radio. "We have contact. Team Smith, proceed to site one."

"Ten four."

Silence overtook the room.

Yannick knocked one time and entered, carrying a tray of Jollof rice and hot tea. "You must eat while you can."

"You're right Thank you, Yannick. Are you certain you will face no repercussions from this?"

"I will not. I am a necessary evil. Someone to cater to the western devils, thereby providing potential income."

"And you are comfortable in this role?"

"I am not. This is my home. This is my business. Until the last four or five years, I enjoyed my life. Now, I hang on, waiting for our government to step in. I hope – before I die – to love my life again."

"What do you think will happen to Mrs. Masilla?"

"She will suffer nothing. Boko Haram would not bother with an old woman who has no resources. I do not know why they approached her in her home. That was unusual."

"That was my thought."

Mr. Jones finished his rice and motioned to Yannick. "Thank you for the food. Now, I must ask that you leave. The less you know, the better for all of us."

26: Lavender Lake

Annie and Chris sat in the gazebo looking toward the woods. The moon was still new, and the sky had cleared. Hundreds of twinkling stars were turning into millions.

All of the cats and Sis seemed to be having a great time at the edge of the tree line, meowing, huffing and trilling into the trees and weeds, just like they were talking to someone.

As long as there were no foxes, Annie could live with it.

They sat without talking, thinking their own thoughts about Henrie, the murder, and life in general.

They were interrupted by the arrival of Sheriff Tate. Annie moved to make room for her and pulled out a glass from the small bar. "Have a glass of Merlot," she said as she poured.

"Thanks. Wine and starlight, always a good combination."

"It is. Do you know who was in the picture? Do you have a case yet?"

"We're closing in. We sent a copy of that photo to the sheriff's department up there, and it's interesting."

"It's confusing," said Annie. "Chris and I were both sure Dennis didn't know those people."

"He probably didn't. Since this started, the Sheriff was already looking into his record. The file was on his desk when I called. Seems our friend Dennis had one arrest. He was driving while intoxicated, and it resulted in the death of his passenger. They had photos, and they matched the one we sent. The passenger was a young woman named Josie Hunt."

"That's the name of the couple, isn't it?"

"It is. They were her parents."

"In the picture, Dennis and this woman – Josie? – looked like a couple? But he didn't know them?"

"I asked the Sheriff about that. He found one notation in the file that said the parents refused to confront the driver and they never wanted to see him alive."

"Well, I guess they changed their minds. It looks like they hunted him down."

"Looks like."

"Does that mean we can leave?"

"Not just yet. We need to dot our i's and cross our t's. We need formal statements from both of you. We need to get it on tape, too, so you'll have to come down to my office tomorrow morning."

"How much do you want us to say about the cats?"

"You have to tell the truth. Just try, please, to not come off as a couple of crazies."

"Yeah, right. We'll try. How long will this take?"

"Probably a couple of hours."

"Maybe we can still be on the road by noon...."

Tiger Lily and Sis talked to Chipper, now on this side of the woods, and several of his friends.

Tiger Lily said, *"Thank you for having a party for us."*

Sis asked, *"Did you invite the meat eaters?"*

"*We invited everybody,*" said Chipper. "*Nobody will eat you. Not tonight. We're happy you found out who murdered that man. We don't like mean people.*"

Sis cowered behind Tiger Lily.

A little bit to the right of them, Mo trilled.

Ms. Bunny said, "*Oh, stop it, handsome!*"

Tiger Lily asked, "*You understood that?*"

Sis, gaining a little confidence, chided her friend. "*Everyone can understand him except most of you cats. You just have to listen better.*"

Little Socks snapped, "*He needs to speak English!*"

Mo trilled. Sassy Pants interpreted. "*He say you needs to shuts up.*"

Little Socks stomped to the edge of the woods and came nose to nose with a young skunk. She stopped short, then leaned in to touch noses. She liked the little fellow. He had a chunky black body and white stripes that made an interesting design on his back and tail.

Tentatively, she asked, "*Do you have a smeller? Like your mom?*"

"*I do. I just got it. It was a little spitter until yesterday, now I have full spray. Look!*"

The little skunk turned, and Little Socks ran, yelling, "*No! Not now!*"

The little skunk, stopped before the spray came out, was hurt. "*I was just gonna show you.*"

Momma skunk joined them. "*Orville, stop that now. You went around all day yesterday stinking up these woods, and now you're going to mess with your new friends.*"

"I wasn't messing, Ma. I was just gonna show her."

"You need it when you're in danger. You don't play with your sprayer when nice folks are around."

Orville hung his head. *"Oh, all right."* He sighed. Without looking up, he whispered to his mother, *"Is she coming back?"*

"Yes. Here she is." She turned to Little Socks. *"You'll have to forgive little Orville. He's so proud of himself. He won't spray you now."*

"Thanks," said Little Socks. It was unlike her to be forgiving, but she was drawn to the stripes. *"I'll be sure not to get him excited or anything."*

Kali and Ko hung back several feet from the edge of the woods. Kali spotted a squirrel. It appeared to be a mother.

She approached slowly, Ko following in her wake. *"Hi. I'm Kali. This is my sister Ko. We're a little shy."*

"I can tell," said the squirrel. *"I'm just here to see if you're the right sort of cat to bring my children around. They're waiting in the woods."*

Together, Kali and Ko said, *"We're the right sort." "We are."*

The squirrel seemed to make a decision. *"Then wait here. I'll bring the kids. They're excited to meet city cats."*

The little squirrels were so excited, they forgot to stay in the tree line. Kali had to chase one and herd him back to the woods.

Mr. Bean got a little too close to the woods and Tiger Lily bopped him on the nose. *"Don't get close! Mommy will make us go in!"*

"But I see those cute things in there…"

Tiger Lily looked, and her mouth went wide open. *"Foxes! Those are foxes! Come out of there right now!"*

Mr. Bean did a one eighty in the air and ran to hover behind Sis. Tiger Lily acted with more bravery. She turned without jumping and ran in the same direction. She heard one of the baby foxes say, *"Mom, they look just like pork chops. Can we have one?"*

Annie couldn't sleep. She rose quietly, not waking Chris. She picked up his cell phone and went to the door, planning to go to the gazebo. Tiger Lily touched her leg at the door.

"Okay, big girl. Come out with me, but let's be quiet."

At the gazebo, the door safely latched and Tiger Lily inside, she called George's cell phone. While it rang, Tiger Lily climbed onto her lap and stretched up on her chest. When she put her front legs around Annie's neck, Annie hugged her close and started to rock back and forth.

George answered and sounded wide awake.

"You're awake?"

"Yeah. You wanted to wake me up in the middle of the night?"

"No, this is just when I… oh, forget it. Why are you up? Is something happening?"

"No. We're waiting for the next call. Jenny and JoJo are with me. We're playing Game Of Thrones."

"You're a wicked player. Did you tell them that?"

"No, but they're figuring it out."

Annie heard Jenny say, "We're gonna get food. Tell Annie hey."

Annie waffled between a laugh and a cry. "Is there anything I can do, George?"

"No. Ian let me know the money transferred in. We just have to wait for them to call."

"We could lose the window, you know, for when they have tickets."

"I know, but there's nothing we can do. Not tonight. How is your situation?"

"We have to go in to give statements tomorrow morning. We should be on the road by noon."

"Jenny isn't going to like that."

Annie heard Jenny say, "I'm not going to like what?"

"Annie and Chris are giving statements tomorrow."

Jenny grabbed the phone from George. "You. Are. Not. Giving. Statements."

"It's just a formality, Jenny. They know who did it. They just have to find them."

"Anything can happen. You aren't in the clear until the other people are found and charged. And let's face it, convicted. Who is it, anyway?"

"An older couple. Apparently, several years ago, Dennis was driving drunk and killed their daughter. They're on the run, probably in Canada by now."

"Well, I don't like it. I'll cancel my hearing and go up there."

"No. That's silly. We'll be fine."

"Then I'll call in a favor. I'll have someone meet you there."

"Really, we'll be fine."

"What time are you going?"

"Um, I think nine."

"Do. Not. Talk. Without. An. Attorney. Present."

"Good grief. Jenny…"

George took the phone back. "Annie, if you have to give a statement, you need to go to bed."

"If you have to be sharp for Henrie, you have to go to bed."

"Yeah. Too keyed up."

"Me, too. I'll let you go, though. Thanks for everything, George."

"No problem. This will be a story to tell my grandchildren."

"You're going to have…"

"Forget I said it! Bye!"

Annie sat in the gazebo for nearly an hour, holding Tiger Lily and rocking back and forth…back and forth.

27: Chelsea

George awoke with a start Wednesday morning. He sat up in bed, confused. It took thirty seconds to remember he was in Henrie's bed, in Henrie's apartment. He remembered Jenny would be on the couch.

It was time to make the donuts.

George stuck his head into the living room. "Jenny, time to wake up."

"Uh???"

"Wake up."

"Nuhhh…."

"Hey, you were supposed to be my helper, my rock, my support. Wake up!"

"Mmph."

George shook his head and went to the bathroom. A shower would help him. If Jenny was still comatose when he got out, he would throw her in.

By the time he was out of the shower, Jenny was moving. When George got to the efficiency kitchen, he saw her sucking on a cup of coffee.

"Couldn't keep up with me, could ya."

"I coulda kept up. Just never played before. We shoulda stopped three hours before we did."

"You need to wake up. Don't you have court this morning?"

"Yeah. I'll be okay."

"Take a shower. I laid out fresh towels. Then come out for breakfast. I can hear JoJo in the kitchen already."

I curse both of you with wildling attacks."

"Hey, what was that you said about calling an attorney for Annie?"

"Oh, gosh! I need to do that now! Where's my cellphone?"

The Inn's landline rang. George stared at it. He had almost forgotten why he was here.

Jennie said, "My call can wait."

Louis looked for his notebook one more time. In his drawers, in his luggage, under the bed, under the furniture. His blood pressure spiked again.

It wasn't that he needed the notes so badly. Anything he couldn't remember was a telephone call away.

No. He couldn't risk anyone here finding it. If they started to put two and two together, he would lose the whole deal.

This game they played wasn't for fun.

It was for the mob.

They didn't joke around.

He put his jacket on and looked once again through all the pockets. Nothing.

He had to go. He had one more morning of obfuscation, and then he would leave Chelsea. Other pieces were coming together.

Today, state officials would accompany a man from "Texas" to negotiate the purchase of state land. They thought they knew who the buyer was, but they had no idea.

The fake shipping heiress from Boston would be in town this afternoon.

Today, he would spend more time in the company of Ray. If he mentioned the possibility of selling, Louis would be a most accommodating listener.

Nancy heard the phone ring. George did not come out of the apartment. This had to be Henrie, or about Henrie. She watched Honey Bear go under the detective table.

"I swear. He loves napping in there," said Nancy. "JoJo, tell me what you need. I'll help with breakfast this morning."

"Sure. Um, can you do the bacon?"

"Certainly." Nancy did what George had done every other morning. She took out the meats, mostly pre-cooked, and added them to the griddle.

"Why do you always call it 'bacon' when there are several meats here?"

"Because it's mostly bacon. People can't get enough of it, and if there are left-overs – that's rare – it's gone before dinner. At least, it is when Annie's here."

"I take it the bacon makes it a little longer when she's not?"

"Yeah. Like last night. There were a few pieces left in the fridge, until Jenny and George and I got to it."

"You had it with supper?"

"No. We were playing a board game, and about three o'clock, we got hungry. I made grilled cheese with bacon and sautéed onions."

"At three o'clock."

"Yeah. I think it was three. We had a break in the game when Annie called George, then we played until nearly five."

"Annie called at three o'clock? In the morning?"

"I guess she couldn't sleep. Anyway, she wanted to know what was going on, if George had talked to Henrie, you know. She wanted to know how everyone was doing."

"Well, I suppose that makes sense. But back to you and this game. George is supposed to stay sharp. What were you all thinking?"

"He's the one that made us keep playing. He wasn't going to rest until he took the iron throne."

"I know about 'go fish,' 'don't pass go,' and gingerbread houses. I would have been lost."

"I generally am, too. But he's good. It was pretty energizing, but I think I'll take a nap when Little Fred goes down today."

"Where are those hot dogs?"

"Drawer on the right in the fridge. You're serious about that?"

"I surely am. I bought a box of quick grits from Laila yesterday. I'd better get that started, too. I'm just going to boil the hot dogs. No sense giving them a sense of adventure with grilled dogs."

"How will you fix the grits?"

"Plain. Boiled in water. No cream, no butter, salt or pepper, no seasoning of any kind. And I hope it's cold by the time they get down. It will be like they woke up to a prison mess. And remember, I don't care if they smell the bacon. The breakfast meats stay here in the kitchen for our other guests."

Georgia ran in with two cats and a two-year-old. "Gotta run! You got it, JoJo?"

"Got it. Here Little Fred. Let's get you some breakfast."

Two small cats trotted into the dining room and under the detective table. JoJo helped the chubby girl get into the high chair and spread a buffet of bacon, scrambled eggs, French toast with cinnamon, baked apples and milk on the tray.

Nancy had just plated the grits into an unheated serving dish in the dining room when six polite people entered, two adults and four youth. She saw Jim put down what looked to be a piece of luggage on the foyer side of the door. She assumed everyone was packed and that all the bags were now in the foyer.

"Good morning," chirped Nancy. "How is everyone today?"

"Fine, thank you," answered Brooke. She stared at the buffet. Boiled hot dogs, buns, condiments, something that looked like cream of wheat, individual boxes of breakfast cereal, milk, orange juice, coffee and water.

"This is it?"

"Yes. It's probably similar to what you get at any hotel breakfast bar, but the selections today are not as extensive as they usually are at the KaliKo Inn."

Marty sniffed and said, "Hot dogs? I can smell bacon."

Together, Jim and Connie said, "Say thank you, Marty."

Marty huffed, looked at his shoes and whispered, "Thank you."

"You're very welcome," said Nancy.

She looked up to see Louis come through the door. "Louis, go on into the kitchen. JoJo will help you fix a plate in there."

Quietly, the family made their breakfast selections. Nancy glanced up to see the honeymooners come in. Mitch looked pale. "Mitch, Livia, please go on into the kitchen. JoJo has plates for you in there. Are you feeling alright, Mitch?"

"Just a little under the weather, is all."

Nancy reached into an apron pocket and pulled out her phone. As she sent a quick text message, Livia stopped and said, "He's going to buy me the most beautiful ring today! I can't wait!"

"Well, how nice. You'll have to show it to me."

Mitch went on into the kitchen while Livia stayed behind. She whispered to Nancy, "He told me he was going to get it late yesterday afternoon, but something happened and he wasn't able to get to the store before it closed. I hope it hasn't been sold to someone else."

"I'm sure it hasn't been. Gema – I assume you're getting it from Gema's Creations – anyway, she makes lovely items, but they're a little pricy. I doubt anyone in town would buy it. If it is as lovely as you say, I mean."

Livia turned to go but stopped. Brooke and Clarke stared at her as if they had something to say. Nancy glared at them and they looked back at their plates.

When Livia was out of the room, Nancy whispered, "You keep your thoughts to yourself. I'll just stay right here with you so you don't get too talkative."

Connie said, "Don't bother. We're leaving. Kids, finish your breakfast now. Jim, go pack the car."

Jim left to do her bidding. Four youth glared. Nancy sighed and put on her most angelic smile.

As Marty and Clarke gulped down a third hot dog each, Pete and Cyril arrived. That was enough to cause them to bolt from the table. Nancy thought she heard them actually help Jim by carrying bags as they went.

"Good morning, Pete. Cyril, how about a hot dog?"

Cyril grinned and sat, waiting for Nancy to pop one into his mouth whole.

"Pour yourself a cup of coffee and have a seat, Pete. I'll bring your next victim to you."

She nearly ran into Louis on his way out. "Oh, do you want me to ask George..."

"No, please, I do not need to ask anything. All is well. I will see you before leaving this afternoon."

"Alright. Let me introduce you to..."

But he was gone.

"Friendly guy," said Pete. "Not."

"He must be late. He's going out one last time with Ray today."

"He's the guy?"

"The guy?"

"The Frenchie that wants to build a resort?"

"I believe he's scouting properties, yes. Speaking of which, did you know someone is buying the state park?"

"What?"

"I'll tell you later. Oh, and I think George is on the phone with Henrie, and maybe doing other things. That light on line one has been going off and on. He and Jenny are in the apartment. We'll check with him when you're finished."

Pete looked at his phone. He had just received a third text message from Ray. He quickly replied, "Busy now. Catch you later."

Nancy nearly tripped on Oscar McMurphy. "What?"

She and Simon Finnegan were under the table almost before she could register they had come into the house. And here came Tillie.

"Tillie! I haven't seen you all week."

Tillie stopped to give a polite hello, then ducked under the table. By now, Cyril lay at the corner of the detective table with his head under the cover.

Nancy shook her head, and went to the kitchen doorway. "Mitch, could you come with me for a minute, please? I need a little help, and you're just the guy to give it to me."

When he neared the door, she turned and motioned with her arm to be seated next to Pete.

Ray tucked his phone into his pocket. Pete was busy. He saw Louis walk across the parking lot from the Inn. "Well, fella, he's here. Looks like we get to skedaddle while Cheryl handles that lady from Boston."

Jock gave a happy bark. At least, Ray thought it was a happy bark.

When Louis got to the boat, Ray said, "Morning, Louis. This is your last day. Let's spend it wisely. Are we going north or south?"

"Today, south," said Louis. I think I look one more time at town down there. We might be making the decision today."

Moriah was the last cat to arrive. She waddled in – she thought of it as a sexy sashay – and realized this was her guy. This was her moment.

Instead of going under the detective table, she jumped to the dining table. In the process, she rearranged a half-filled water glass and a salt shaker. Unperturbed, she licked salt from her paw and shook her tail to dry it out.

Pete stared at her.

She stared back.

"You're going to be a pistol, aren't you," said Pete.

Moriah blinked once.

Mitch, more than a little nervous, said, "You wanted to talk to me?"

"I did." Pete reached into his pocket and pulled out a plastic bag. In it was the glittering emerald ring.

Mitch couldn't stifle a gasp, but face composed, he asked, "What's this?"

"This, Mitch, is the ring you took from Gema's Creations yesterday."

"Excuse me?"

"There is no excuse. I have statements from Gema and Frank. Better than that, I have statements from one girl, Brooke, I think you know her, that puts this ring in your hand while you all stood at the jewelry counter."

"You're going to trust that little thief? She must have taken it."

"And put it in your room?"

"In my room? You were in my room? One, I didn't put it there. Two, you didn't have a right to be there."

"Oh, but I did. I had what we in the legal profession like to call a search warrant. That warrant was legally executed with a staff member of the KaliKo Inn and an interested third party."

"What? Who? A third party?"

"The party that found the ring. In your room."

"What?"

"Let me put it to you in terms you can understand. I had a search warrant for all rooms, all personal belongings, all luggage, because I thought one of those teenagers stole this ring. I was wrong. We didn't find the ring in their rooms, on their persons, or in their belongings. We kept looking, though, and when we went into your room, with a staff member, one of the cats was in there. You noticed the cat doors, right?"

Mitch had a glazed look. "A cat?"

"Yes. A cat was sitting in the middle of the floor, and the staff person asked her to 'scoot.' She scooted right over to a luggage rack and on top of a suitcase. Do you know what she did next?"

Mitch slowly shook his head, eyes unfocused.

"She kind of unzipped a little compartment on top of that suitcase and reached in with her paw. When the staff person went to her to get her off – you know, it was rude that she was depositing hair all over your luggage – she saw something green and sparkly. Guess what it was?"

Mitch hung his head.

"And guess what else? I did a little background search on you last night. Want to know what I found?"

Mitch didn't respond. By now, Livia was in the room. She stood behind Mitch and listened in horror.

"I found a general equivalency degree issued by the state of Nebraska. Now that typically means the degree came from a juvenile facility."

Mitch said nothing.

"Those records are sealed. They're private. I couldn't get to them if I had to. But I was able to dig a little bit more and come up with the names of your parents. I talked to them."

Livia gasped. "They're alive?"

Pete looked at her. "He didn't kill 'em or anything, if that's what you're asking."

"No, I mean, he said…I thought they were dead."

"Oh, no ma'am. Alive and kicking, and wondering if they were ever going to hear from their boy again. And you know what, Mitch?"

Mitch said nothing.

"They weren't surprised that you stole this ring. They said, 'It's a wonder that's all he got.' Now why do you think they said that?"

Mitch said nothing.

Pete went on. "I understand you had an issue with a card the other day, up in Marsh Haven."

Mitch looked up now, a question in his eyes.

"Yes, I did a search on your credit, too. You're maxed out on several cards; a lot of people want money from you. I'm surprised you haven't gone to a loan shark. But, hey, I haven't investigated that avenue. I did make a call to your employer. Turns out he's your father-in-law? Anyway, he mentioned he might look into your client accounts."

Mitch looked at his feet.

Pete went on. "Being a good community member, I thought to give the Inn a heads up on your credit card issues."

Mitch looked over at Nancy, standing behind and to the left of Livia.

"You probably didn't know the contract you signed allows them to pre-charge your card to cover any expenses you might have on The Avenue during your stay. These kind folks at the Inn were a little behind on you. They were focused on the kids. But then, that kind of played into your hands, didn't it?"

Mitch said nothing. Livia, by now, had moved to the far side of the room. She was as far as she could be from Mitch and still watch and listen.

"Given what you have charged to the card – meals, drinks, incidentals – and the room, you're over your limit on this stay. Looks like you'll owe about five hundred more than you have. And I've checked all your cards. This is the only one with anything. How do you plan to pay that, Mitch?"

"I'll pay it," said Livia. "I'll pay what he can't afford to pay, and I'll leave him a couple hundred on the card. He's going to have to figure out how to get home. Well, he doesn't have a home anymore. I doubt he has a job. I'm going to go pack right now. Don't let him out of your sight until I get back here with my credit card."

Livia nearly ran from the room while Mitch looked after her.

"What, cat got your tongue? You didn't even say good-bye. Anyway, Nancy, can you figure out how much to take to leave him a couple hundred? He'll need it to get out of town when he gets out of jail."

"What?"

"Jail. We're going to walk down to the jail now, and I'm charging you with theft. You haven't said anything yet, so while we walk that way, I'm going to read the Miranda to you, make sure you understand your rights. Come on."

Mitch got up slowly, head still down.

Pete said, "Cyril, come!" and he gave Moriah a long, slow pet from the top of her head to the tip of her fluffy tail. "Welcome to the team."

Tillie was excited to find nearly everyone there. And here came Moriah. Oops. She stopped. Tillie, who had a habit of thinking everyone could read her mind, started in the middle of her thought, which was the beginning of a sentence for everyone else. *"We'll have to go ahead without her because it's too important."*

She looked around at the group, expectant. They looked back, confused.

Simon Finnegan said, *"What?"*

Cyril, the wise one of the group, said, *"I think you did it again, Tillie. I think you started thinking what you were going to say and you thought we heard you. Start from the beginning."*

"Oh, sure. I do that sometimes. Well, it's like this. I saw Jock and Simon last night, and we started putting things together. This French guy, Louis, is up to no good."

Oscar McMurphy said, *"That's what Moriah said."*

"It's like this. According to Jock, he only pretends to have a French accent."

"That's what Moriah said," exclaimed Simon Finnegan.

Tillie nodded. *"He has people helping him, people he calls on the phone, and they're trying to buy all kinds of things. One guy is going to buy the park, and a woman is going to buy The Marina and The Escape…"*

"That's what Moriah said!" yelled Speckles.

"Hold on, let me finish. And then, they're going to buy everything on The Avenue."

"Moriah said that, too?" said Daryll.

Tillie looked around at the group. *"What are we going to do?"*

"I need to tell Pete somehow," said Cyril.

Honey Bear said, *"We have a clue. It's right here."* He lifted the corner of a cushion where the notebook had been secreted.

"It's a clue, alright," said Cyril. *"What is it?"*

The cats looked at one another until Daryll finally said, *"We don't know?"*

Honey Bear added, *"It came out of his room, and I think he's been looking for it."*

"Why do you think that?"

"My mom, Nancy, said something this morning, before we came downstairs. She said she had to say something to George about an important notebook that is missing, and then my dad, Sam, said he didn't want to say anything about it and if you ask me – this is Sam talking – that's pretty strange."

Simon Finnegan said, *"It has to be important."*

Speckles asked, *"How can we get this to Pete?"*

"Well," said Cyril, thinking his way around the problem, *"getting it to him isn't the problem. It's getting it to him at the right time, so he knows what to do with it. I'll have to think about that."*

Cyril heard Pete call for him. He said, *"I have to go now. We'll be busy for a while getting this bozo into jail."*

George hung up the phone and looked at his watch. Ian should be at the bank. This had to happen fast. He called Ian's cell. "I need you to transfer three million as soon as humanly possible. I have account and routing numbers."

"Did they give you a transfer location?"

"Yes, an Express Exchange in Maroua."

"Are there other rules?"

"Yes. You have to reference a purchase order – I'll give you the number – and it's for farm equipment. I have a list of items."

With Jenny feeding him numbers and items, George passed everything to Ian. After what appeared to be three hours of silence – it was two minutes – Ian finally said, "It's done."

George opened the apartment door and said into the kitchen, "Nancy, there's a woman that wants to make a reservation. I told her this phone line is going to be cutting in and out until they repair it, so she gave me her number. Could you call her, please?"

"Sure. Do the two of you need anything in there?"

"Yeah. Breakfast. Coffee. Lots of both."

"I'll send JoJo."

Nancy was tired. Very tired. She couldn't understand how Henrie did this every day. How Annie did this every day. But, hey, she was older than both of them. Heck, she was almost as old as the two of them put together. Right? No. But she still had a right to be tired. Right? Right.

She looked through the reservation calendar on the computer. Thank goodness Annie got her started on computer things and thank goodness Henrie showed her the reservation and billing programs. And should she say it? Thank goodness she was better at this than she let on. With a passing familiarity of openings, she called the number George gave her.

She heard an east coast accent say, "Boston Harbor Shipping. How can I help you?"

"Hello. I'm returning a call from the KaliKo Inn in Chelsea. I'm sorry we're having trouble with our lines today. I guess the question is not how you can help me, but how can I help you?"

"Thank you for returning my call. I need a room, and I understand you have the best facility in town. I'm flying in on private charter in a couple of hours, so I have need of a room this evening. I'm staying two or three nights. Is that a possibility?"

"Yes. As it happens, a few rooms vacated today. I would be happy to put you into one of those rooms for...you say two or three nights? Should I make it for three? You could leave early, if necessary."

"That would be wonderful."

Nancy took care of the details of the reservation and closed the call. She looked up as Little Fred ran through the kitchen. "Hey there, darlin'. Where are you going?"

"Me go cat!"

"You're following a cat? This is the perfect house for that!"

Nancy took a second look and grabbed the darling before she followed a cat tail out the cat door.

The cats went into overdrive. Honey Bear decided Simon Finnegan and Oscar McMurphy were the best ones to handle the task. They ran out the door and over to the bakery, barreled through the door and rushed around until they found Tillie.

"She's coming! That lady from Boston is coming today!"

"A buyer and people from the state office are here, too. Isabel delivered breakfast over to the state park."

"What do we do now?"

"Can you go to the police department and tell Cyril?"

"Okay. We'll go now. Maybe he can get Pete over to look at the clue."

Tillie thought about it. *"I don't think he has a reason to go to the Inn now, not since everyone is arrested or gone. I'll go over and get it, bring it over here. Tell Cyril to get him here."*

"Okay."

They left, the cats going up to the police department and Tillie going to the Inn. She walked through the door slowly, looking in both directions The coast seemed to be clear.

Underneath the detective table, she found Honey Bear, Speckles, Daryll and Moriah. "We have to get the clue to Mr. Bean's. We think we can get Pete there, but not necessarily here.

Honey Bear dug until the notebook was in his mouth. He mumbled, "Let's go," and the cats followed Tillie out the door.

George looked at Jenny. "I know you have to leave for court. Don't worry about me."

"I'm not. I called Candice. She's on her way over. Georgia will open the bar."

"That's not…"

"That's our only option. We're not leaving you alone. And what's that look on your face?"

"Huh? Well, I'm wondering, you know, with everything going on, if we haven't lost track of the time. It has to be, what, sometime in the afternoon in Cameroon? I think we missed the take-off time for their plane."

28: Cameroon

Mr. Brown whispered into his headset, "One subject leaving, others staying. Orders?"

Mr. Jones said, "Team Brown follow. Team Smith remain in place."

"Ten four."

Mr. Brown walked from behind the building and got into a car headed in the opposite direction. He started it and drove ahead. His team watched as the subject got into his car, executed a u-turn, and drove in the same direction.

"Pull over, let him get ahead. We're on our way."

Two men got into another car and followed.

Team Smith held their positions, one man leaning against a car, smoking a cigarette. Soon, he whispered into his wrist, "Others leaving. Transportation unknown."

The method of transportation soon became apparent. A late model SUV stopped in front of the café and allowed them to enter. They left, driving in the same direction as everyone else.

Mr. Smith whispered, "Problem. SUV heading in same direction. You could be pinned."

Mr. Brown made a quick decision. "Team Brown, head to rendezvous point and ready our escape. I will continue to follow yellow cab."

Mr. Jones swore under his breath.

Mr. Smith said, "Team Smith, let's follow SUV."

If Mr. Jones had a satellite visual connection, he would have seen six vehicles winding their way from the center of Maroua. Two went southwest, past the edge of town to a native village. Three turned east and toward another business district. One worked its way through a residential district on the west side.

Team Smith radioed in. "We're not going in the same direction as Brown. His GPS went southwest. We're going east."

Mr. Jones said, "You must be going to the bank, or wherever the money is headed. Mr. Brown, did you copy?"

"Yes. Suggestions?"

"Get the hostages, take the middle man, and get out. Make sure he cannot make contact. Make the leaving look as natural as possible. Proceed to the rendezvous."

Henrie heard the taxi pull into the village. Pop pop. He and Collette moved closer together, to hold hands.

Bertrand entered the hut. "We see you not rich man like we thought. You call. You get three million. Do now. Send here, to this place."

Bertrand pushed a paper in front of Henrie, who recognized account and routing numbers. The name of the bank – or whatever it was – was on the paper as well.

"You tell get purchase order for farm equipment."

"Yes." Henrie dialed the phone he was given and breathed deeply. He thought the time had passed for getting a regular flight out, but he had to hope another means of escape was at hand. The Boko Haram would not risk having to hide them until the next time they could get a flight, and they would not risk letting them go.

Henrie took a deep breath again as George answered. "George, so good to hear your voice. I am ready to proceed with the funds transfer for my new friends. Do you have a pen and paper?"

"Yeah. Shoot."

Henrie passed on the information and listened as George repeated the numbers and instructions.

"Yes, that is correct. George, this must be done very quickly. Do you understand?"

"Got it. On it. See you soon, buddy."

Henrie held the phone out to Bertrand, who looked sadly into his face. "You know you not make flight, right?"

"Right," answered Henrie. He put his arm around Collette and waited for whatever would come next.

What came next was a man Henrie had never seen. He could have been native to Cameroon, or he could have been from Cambridge. What he wasn't was pleasant. He entered the hut, held a gun on Bertrand and said, in a perfectly mid-American accent, "We're taking the cab out of here."

29: Chelsea

Nancy went upstairs and found Hilly in the room facing The Avenue. "How are you doing, Hilly?"

"I'm almost finished with this room. I thought this one would be easier than the kids' rooms."

"You're probably right. I think this would be the best room for our new guest, anyway."

"Someone new is coming in?"

"Yes, a woman from Boston. She just called, and she'll be here this afternoon for two or three days. I put her in the schedule for three."

"It will be ready in an hour. Do you need me to do anything special?"

"No. I'm going to talk to JoJo to make sure, but I think I'll have to run up to the bakery to get some breads. Do you want me to pick anything up for you?"

"No, not today. I've been too upset to eat."

"Me, too. Well, I'll get going. I want to be here in case George needs anything."

She met Candice on her way out. "Do you need anything, dear?"

"No, Nancy. Thanks. Is he in the apartment?"

"Yes. I'm going to Mr. Bean's. I'll be back soon."

Nancy looked around the downstairs before leaving and didn't see Honey Bear or any of the other cats. Strange, she thought. They had been underfoot all morning.

Nancy was the fifth person in line for the bakery counter, so she sat at one of the tables to wait. She noticed several of the cats slinking behind a display. Let's see, there were Speckles and Daryll, and that cute new cat of Clara's, Moriah, the one that took an interest in Pete's conversation yesterday.

For a fleeting moment, she thought of Honey Bear, but she didn't see him.

A harried-looking woman came in with a small computer in her hands. She looked around for an empty table. Nancy noticed there wasn't one, so she motioned with her hand and said, "Please, sit here. As soon as the line works its way down, I'm going to order and go."

"Thanks. I really need a table for just a minute."

The woman opened her computer with one hand and took out a cell phone with the other. She punched in a number and talked while she booted her computer.

Nancy couldn't help but listen. First, the woman was close. B., Nancy was the classic gossip. She had to know everything.

"I swear," the woman said. "This isn't right. This is public property, and we can't sell to a private investor. I don't care how much the guy wants to spend."

She stopped to listen, then continued. "Do you know a reporter? Maybe that's the way we need to go."

Nancy could hear the voice on the other end, but she couldn't make out the words. The woman spoke again. "He's buying everything. The park, the campground, the piece of property on the other side of the street, all the beachfront attached to state property…they can't just sell it like that!"

The line at the counter was gone, but Nancy hated to leave. This was too rich. And sad. This must be one of the staff persons Carlos and Isabel mentioned the night before, and she wasn't happy. Not one little bit.

Nancy staked her place and announced her imminent return by putting her handbag on the table in front of her chair. She mouthed the words, "I'll be back," to the woman.

At the counter, she talked to Isabel about the bread she wanted. "I think I want to cater to our Boston guest. She's coming in today."

"We have a great recipe for Boston brown bread. We use whole wheat, rye flour and cornmeal."

"That sounds substantial. Is it bitter?"

"No. We put molasses, brown sugar and walnuts in it, and we serve it with cream cheese."

"I'll have to stop at Laila's to get that. What else do you suggest?"

"Henrie's not back yet, right? Have JoJo look up recipes for a traditional Boston breakfast. I seem to recall something about Johnny cakes." Isabel turned to the kitchen. Jerry was on his way to the counter with a tray of truffles. "Jerry, what do you remember about traditional breakfast on the east coast?"

"Johnny cakes, Boston baked beans, corned beef hash, and, um…oh, yeah, fish cakes. I think they use cod."

"Good ideas. I'll pick up some things. So you'll make a couple of loaves of bread, and I'll take a half dozen Boston creams, too. Is it possible I can get them this afternoon with the bread?"

"We'll make them fresh. I'll deliver them in the morning."

"Great! How about candy, Jerry? What's typical for the east coast?"

"Salt water taffy comes to mind. I could 'invent' something for you. Let's see…dark chocolate with a milk chocolate center, cranberries, maybe some cinnamon…how does that sound?"

"That sounds wonderful. She's going to think she never left Boston."

Cheryl had entered the store. "Boston? Are you hosting our Boston guest?"

Nancy turned. "She's your guest?"

"Yes." Cheryl sighed. "She's a double-edged sword, promising ultimate riches on the one hand and driving a wedge between Ray and me on the other."

"How so?"

"She wants to buy everything. The Marina, The Escape, the charter business, even our house over against the state park."

Nancy and Isabel stared at Cheryl, then they turned to stare at the state employee, who was now staring back.

At that moment, Pete and Cyril came through the door, preceded by Simon Finnegan and Oscar McMurphy.

30: Lavender Lake

At the police station, Chris and Annie were separated. Sondra wasn't worried about the bulk of their statements. She knew there would be slight discrepancies. Their differing points of view and vantage points would account for them.

The only problem might be when they talked about their suspicions of the older couple. Her job might depend on how these people held up in a formal interview setting.

She watched the interviews from a viewing room, going back and forth from one monitor to the other. Stan Graff – her rival and the man most likely to do something to tank the investigation – managed Chris's interview.

Sheriff Tate wasn't worried he would tank it on purpose. He would tank it because he couldn't help himself. But she had no choice. She had to involve him.

Chris went through the first part of the interview, telling again his recollections of Dennis, the Hunts, the mushrooms, and his discovery of the body.

Every now and then, she looked toward the other monitor and placed an earphone to her head. Annie's interview was the same, but from her perspective.

Now, we get down to it, she thought.

Looking again at the monitor for Chris, she heard the exchange. "At some point, you decided the couple had gone to Canada. Why did you think that?"

Chris didn't flinch. "One of the cats told us."

"How?"

"She came to the computer – we had a map up – and she pointed to Canada."

"The cat pointed to Canada."

"Yes."

"And it wasn't a bug on the screen? A flashing spot?"

"No. It was Canada."

The chief deputy shook his head and continued. "And you knew she was 'pointing to Canada' because of the Hunts?"

"No, not right away."

"You're really going to make me ask all of the questions, aren't you? You can't just tell me the story?"

"I don't know what you want to know. I don't mind-read."

"Okay. Where was I...oh, right. At what point did you decide she – the cat – was talking about the Hunts?"

"After we played the yes/no game. We ask yes or no questions, and she taps either a right hand or a left hand."

"She answers your questions by tapping your hand."

"Right."

"And you don't think that's crazy?"

"I think a lot of people think it's crazy, but she has never led us down the wrong path."

"So she led you down the right path this time?"

"It led to a photograph of Dennis with the Hunt's daughter, didn't it?"

"Well, I'm not sure of that at all. I'm not sure that evidence wasn't planted.'

"What?"

"When did you plant the evidence, Chris?"

Chris sat back in the chair, stared at Stan, and said, "I guess I want to talk to my lawyer."

"You aren't being charged with anything. Yet. You don't get a lawyer."

Chris sat mute.

"I asked a question."

Chris sat mute.

"I asked…" the door opened and Sheriff Tate came in.

"He's asked for an attorney. We're done here."

"He's not being charged with anything. He doesn't get to ask for an attorney."

"Outside."

Stan pushed back from the table and got up. He stormed out of the door in front of Sondra. Once the door was closed, he turned on her. "He doesn't get an attorney!"

"You accused him of planting evidence. He gets an attorney."

"You've gone soft."

"Stand down and I won't remove you from the case. Take fifteen then meet me in the viewing room."

Stan turned on his heel and stormed out.

Sondra sighed and returned to the viewing room. She checked on the status of Annie's interview. This one was handled by one of Sondra's supporters, a female deputy with fifteen years' experience as a detective. The detective, Christine Himes, was no longer in the room.

She ran the video back ten minutes until she reached the critical point. Christine Himes asked, "Why did you think the couple, the Hunts, went to Canada?"

"Tiger Lily told me."

"And that would be, um, your cat?"

"Yes."

"I see. And how did she tell you this?"

"She pointed to Canada – we had a map up on the computer – do I need to explain that?"

"Yes, please do."

"Sheriff Tate was asking about the young couple, Kyle and Dani, and we were trying to figure out the route they might have taken to Canada."

"And you knew they were going to Canada because…"

"I thought we covered that. Oh, well, okay. They said they were going to go to Canada next year, and they mentioned Sault Ste. Marie and Hudson Bay. Then the Sheriff said they had gotten gas two hundred miles north. So, we got out the map, to see if that would be on the route."

"Okay. You had the map open on the computer. Then what happened?"

"Tiger Lily got on the table and looked at the computer, then she touched Canada on the map."

"And you thought that meant something?"

"Yes. I knew it did. Tiger Lily never…well, it meant something."

"So she touched Canada. Does she know geography? Know how to read a map?"

"No. She can spell."

Christine's head snapped up. "She can spell?"

"Yes. She was looking for Canada. And then I asked if she meant the young couple, or something, maybe I said the young couple was going there, and she let me know I was on the wrong track."

"Wrong track."

"Yes. So I asked questions, then Chris asked questions, and it came out she was talking about the Hunts. And then she said we would find a clue."

"You would find a clue."

"Yes. And we followed them…"

"Define 'them.'"

"Tiger Lily, Little Socks, and Sis, Chris's dog."

Christine looked at Annie and asked, "Did you plant that evidence?"

"What?"

"Did you…"

"You have got to be kidding me! I want to speak to my attorney!"

"Okay. I'm going to take a break now. You're going to stay right here."

Christine walked out of the room and left Annie on camera. Annie appeared calm, but Sondra noticed the wringing of her hands underneath the table. She caught a motion as Annie wiped away a tear. Well, she had a lot on her plate right now.

Sheriff Tate looked out the window of the room into the hallway. She saw a reflection in another window. It was Christine and Stan talking in low tones, heads close together.

So much for the alliance she thought she had with Christine.

She walked into the hallway. Christine and Stan turned to her. Christine said, "Sondra, you have to listen to Stan. If you don't, you'll be in big trouble."

"What do you mean, Christine? Is this a threat?"

Stan answered. "I've already called one of the Commissioners. I told him you were headed for a mental breakdown, and he's putting an emergency personnel order in place."

"A what?"

"He's going to have me appointed temporary Sheriff while you take a leave of absence."

"You can't be serious."

"I am, he is, and this ends now. Until that order goes through, these people sit in holding, and then we treat them like the murderers they are."

Tiger Lily napped in the sunshine while Mr. Bean played with a doohickey. Unfortunately, the doohickey landed on Tiger Lily's nose. She woke up with a hiss.

Then she looked at the sun's placement across the cabin floor. A sunbeam lay fully across the bags that Annie and Chris left by the door. The plan was to pack the car and leave as soon as their statements were given.

It was late. Too late. Something was wrong.

Tiger Lily bopped noses until all the cats and Sis were awake.

"Hey! Wake up! Mommy isn't back! They should have been here two sunbeams ago!"

Stretching stopped and shock began. There was a chorus of, *"Where are they?" "Did they leave food?" "What if they're lost?" "Did dey leave wittout us?" "Trill!"*

Sis paced from the door to the bed, bed to kitchen table, kitchen table to door, and over again. A whine escaped and grew in intensity. Finally, she stopped. *"What can we do?"*

Tiger Lily had begun to look around the room. The only thing she saw was Chris's computer. He had left it open and plugged in. She jumped to the table to investigate.

The screen was dark. She touched the keyboard and it came to life. *"Hey, someone come up here and help me look."*

Little Socks and Mo jumped to the table. Little Socks said, *"What are we looking for?"*

"I don't know. They sometimes talk to other people with this. They talk about email and text messages. I'm not sure what this does."

"Trill!"

From the floor, Kali said, *"He said to let him look. He helps George do email stuff."*

Tiger Lily moved aside and let Mo stand in front of the computer. Mo gazed at the icons on the screen and used his paw to touch one that looked like an envelope. The program opened, and a blank email opened.

Mo trilled for several seconds, pausing on occasion to let Kali translate. *"You have to type in someone's name on the top line." "Then on the next line you say what it's about." "In the big box, you say what you want."*

"Okay," said Tiger Lily. *"Who do we want to send it to?"*

"Whose name do you know how to type?" asked Little Socks.

Tiger Lily thought about all of the people in Chelsea. She wasn't sure she could do any of them.

Mo trilled again. Kali said, *"He said that when George emails, he only has to put in one or two letters, and the name comes up."*

"That makes it easier. But I still don't know who to send it to. Last night Mommy talked to George and Jenny. Jenny told her not to talk to those police people without an attorney."

Several cats – from the floor – yelled helpful comments. *"Can you spell Jenny?" "Does Jenny have email?" "Do you know what to say to her?" "Can you spell what you need to say?" "Can she bring food?"*

"First things first," said Tiger Lily. *"Mo, what does that blinky think mean?"*

"Trill."

"That's where you start typing."

"Trill, trill."

"It's on the line to write the name."

Tiger Lily thought about the name Jenny. Ja. Ja. That was a J sound. She looked at the keyboard and found the J. She typed it. Darn. Chris knew a lot of people whose names started with J. She looked at the names that came up and settled on one that looked promising. She touched that name, and the "to" box was filled.

"How do we move the blinky thing?" she asked Mo.

He walked to the side of the computer and looked at the keys. He touched one, and the blinky thing moved to the next line.

"Sweet," said Tiger Lily. *"It's good you pay attention to these things. What should I say next? This is the what's-it-about line."*

"Help!" "Mommy's in jail!" "Need food!"

Little Socks said, *"Help. Do you know how to spell help?"*

"Yes. That's one of the practice words Mommy and Henrie put up in the basement."

She looked again at the keyboard and concentrated. With her paws, she typed, "hhhhheeeeellll..ppppp,,mm."

She sat back to look at the line. *"Well, that will just have to do. Mo, do you use the same key to move on?"*

Mo trilled. She took that for a yes and hit the same key. The blinky thing was now in the big box.

"What do I say now?"

Mr. Bean said, *"I don't think you have to use a full sentence. Can you spell 'mommy arrested'?"*

Tiger Lily looked at the keyboard. *"I'll have to punch lighter. I put too many letters in the other line. I'll try."*

Carefully, she hit m-o-mmmmmmm-y, then she sat back. *"I don't know how to spell arrested. I'll try this."*

She hit r-e-s-t-u-d and sat back. *"What do you think, Mo? Is this good enough?"*

Mo trilled.

Kali said, *"Mo said it will work."*

"Okay. How do we send it?"

Mo peered closely at the screen. He pointed to a button near the top and looked to Tiger Lily for permission. She nodded. He pushed it, and the email seemed to float through the air and out of the computer.

"Now what?" asked Little Socks.

"I guess we wait to see if it worked. I don't know how we'll tell."

Annie was escorted back to her room following a restroom break. She asked, again, "Why can't I see Chris? And why can't I call my attorney?"

Christine replied, "You haven't been arrested, so you aren't allowed an attorney just now. It's the same for your boyfriend. Just sit here and relax. I'll get lunch for you. You aren't vegetarian or that other thing, are you?"

"What? Vegan? No. What time is it?"

"Nearly noon."

Annie dropped her head to her hands. She tried to think what she had left out for the cats and Sis. Food, water, the litter pan. Sis must be desperate to get out.

What would Chris think when he heard she had put Jenny off during the early morning phone call? Maybe Jenny would check on them. Probably not. She had court today. She was busy.

Sondra came in to deliver lunch. It was a fast food hamburger, fries and, ick, a cola. "Do you have water?"

"No, sorry. The water here in town is filled with chemicals, and there's a rule about sharing the water cooler with prisoners."

"Prisoners? I'm a prisoner?"

"Sorry. No, you're still a person of interest."

"But you won't let me go, you won't let me call an attorney. What happened?"

"What happened is that a county commissioner is kicking me out of office and appointing my chief deputy interim sheriff. I have to stay here until all of that is in place, then I'll do what I can to get hold of your attorney. But I can't talk about that." She motioned with her head toward what Annie assumed was a camera.

Annie heard a commotion in the hall, and so did Sondra. Sondra stood and opened the door. She put her head outside to look and listen. That allowed Annie to listen.

A loud, deep male voice was nearly shouting. "You will let me see them now. Right now. They've been here for three hours, and they have a right to an attorney!"

Annie couldn't hear the response, but she next heard, "You're playing with words now. I want to speak to both of them, together, and if you don't make that happen in one minute, I'm calling the District Attorney to file a complaint."

Quiet voices, then, "Thirty seconds."

Quiet voices, then Christine came to the door. "You need to step out, Sondra. I'll get her accomplice, then I'll let the attorney step in."

Sondra said, "Watch your tone, and watch your words, Christine."

"You watch yours, and for the last time, step out."

As Sondra stepped out, Stan escorted Chris to Annie's room. They barely had time to acknowledge one another before the door was slammed and Stan began to speak.

"This is a special circumstance. We have not finished questioning you, and it is highly unusual for us to put suspects together before we're done. There will be an officer in the room at all times until you are finished with the attorney."

"Uh," said Chris, "I don't think so."

Stan didn't have a chance to respond. Sondra opened the door and showed the attorney in. "This is Jay Kranski. He's one of the more successful defense attorneys in town. He said your attorney in Chelsea made a call. She still represents you; he's standing in. Stan, you need to leave the room."

"You don't call the shots here, Sondra."

"Until I see it in writing, I still do. Leave. Now."

Mr. Kranski had not taken a seat. "I don't like what I see and hear, and I don't trust you to turn the camera off. I want to see my clients in the attorney's conference room."

"Not a chance…"

"Stan, shut up," said Sondra. "Come on, folks. I'll take you there."

Sondra waited in her office for the axe to fall. When it did, it came in the form of one of the County Commissioners. He held a letter in his hand and was accompanied by Stan.

She stood and faced them both. "So you think I'm not doing my job? Think I've gone 'round the bend? Tell me, something, Stan. Do you think these two folks killed Dennis? Then called the police to report it?"

"They're the most likely suspects."

"Even after finding a picture of Dennis with the Hunt's daughter? The dead one? And not being able to find the Hunts?"

"They could have altered that picture, then planted it. Convinced the Hunts to leave early, somehow."

"And they somehow got to Dennis's closed file in New York State and altered that, too?"

The Commissioner said, "A file? In New York?"

Stan said, "This is all a smoke screen, Commissioner. The real problem is that she believes the suspects talk to their cats."

"That was the mental, uh, breakdown to which you referred?"

"Yes. You have to watch the interviews. They're nuts and she's buying into it."

Sondra's telephone rang. She answered it. "Sheriff Tate."

"Uh, wait just a second. I'm going to put you on speaker."

As she hit the speaker button, the voice on the other end said, "I don't care about that! You have to make them arrest this couple!"

"Slow down now. We'll take care of it. You're Kyle, right? You were staying at Lavender Lake Campground?"

"Yes. Me and Dani. We left the night they killed the man."

"You saw that happen, or know something about it?"

"I'll tell you all about that when we're safe! They're following us. That older couple. We've seen them seven times since we left, at gas stations, diners…just now we saw them again on the highway. They're gonna kill us just like they killed that man!"

"Where are you now, Kyle?"

"We're at a police station in Timmins. That's in Ontario."

"You're in a police station. You're safe."

"No, we're not! They're gonna make us leave, because they don't believe us that those people are following us!"

Sondra took a deep breath. "Kyle, I need to talk to you about what you know about that night. First, I have to make sure you're safe. Is an officer with you?"

"Yes."

"Okay. I want you to put him or her on the line, but then you need to come back and tell me what you know. Do you understand?"

"Yes."

"Put the officer on."

"Officer Jones. Who's this?"

"This is Sheriff Sondra Tate of Lavender Lake. This young man is talking about an older couple, John and Lucy Hunt, who are under suspicion of murder. It's possible Kyle and Dani witnessed the murder. It's also possible they are being followed. I need to make sure you'll keep them safe until we work this out."

"If that's the case, certainly. We'll need more information."

"Of course you do." Sondra motioned to Christine to come in. "I'm going to take your number and have one of my detectives call you right back. I need to speak to Kyle again. I need more information."

"Certainly." The officer gave a telephone number and Sondra handed a slip of paper to Christine. "Follow up with him, please. Tell him everything we know about the Hunts and about the murder to date. The murder as committed by the Hunts. Do you understand?"

"Yes, ma'am."

Christine left, but not without looking at the Commissioner and Stan. They stood mute.

"Okay, Jones. My detective is calling now. Please put Kyle back on the line."

When Kyle came on, she said, "They're going to let you stay until we work this out. You're safe now. I need you to take a deep breath and start from the beginning."

"OK." Sondra heard him take a deep breath. Another. "We were walking back from dinner. That nice couple, Chris and Annie, they made dinner, and then, well, after dinner we walked back to our cabin, and we heard them in the woods."

"Heard who in the woods, Kyle?"

"That older couple, and the man, Dennis. He took them home in his ATV, so we were going a lot slower. We were almost past their cabin – well, you know how it is, if you walk along the lake? There's a cabin, then woods, then a cabin, then woods?"

"Yes, I know the layout."

"Well, we were almost past their cabin, and we heard them talking in the woods. He was getting loud, and they were saying weird things, like they were going to kill him, something about their daughter, and then we heard this gosh-awful scream. It was like an animal."

"What did you do?"

"Like idiots, we ran into the woods to check it out, and he was lying down, and they were standing there. The old man, he had a gun, and they just stared down at him."

"What did you do then, Kyle?"

"We waited until they were back inside their cabin, then we ran for ours. We packed and left. We didn't wait for anything."

"And you went toward Canada?"

"Yes. And we keep seeing them."

"Alright, Kyle. You need to know that Mr. and Mrs. Hunt are already suspects in this case, so we need to get a formal statement from you. Will you be able to stay there? I'm hoping that department will take the statement for us."

"Yeah. We can stay. If we're really safe, I mean."

"You are. I'll have to work on getting a warrant up there, and work out extradition for the Hunts, but let's just take this one step at a time. Stay on the line while I check with my detective."

Sondra stepped out and went to Christine's office. "Ask if they can take a formal statement from Kyle and Dani, and let them know a warrant is coming for the Hunts, just in case they are still in that jurisdiction."

"Yes, ma'am."

Sondra, irked at the sudden use of the term "ma'am" from a woman she – until this day – counted a friend, turned without a word.

Back in her office, she said, "Kyle, I'm going to close this call for now. They'll take a statement. You call me if you have any concerns, okay?"

"Yes. Thank you."

"No, thank you."

She looked at Stan and the Commissioner as she spoke. "Stan, bring Mr. Kranski in here, and let those folks know they're free to go."

"I..."

"Stan, do it."

The Commissioner had long since dropped the hand holding the letter to his side. When Stan left, he said, "There is still the matter of..."

"I know. The cats. Let me do my job here for a minute, okay?"

Jay came into the office, followed by Stan. "They're free to go? What happened?"

"Young man who was in another cabin called in to say he heard the murder and visually witnessed the aftermath and the perpetrators. Your clients are free to go."

"That's good to know. I'll let you know if we're going to press charges."

"I understand. Tell me, Jay, how did you know to come? No one here let them have a phone call."

"This is odd. I've known their attorney for several years. Always seemed to be a level-headed sort of person. Today she called, said she was sorry to call on such short notice, that she was in court, and she didn't get the email until just about eleven thirty."

"An email? From whom?"

"This is where I wonder about her sanity. She was babbling, and I could have sworn she said she got an email from a cat."

Stan, from behind Jay, looked stunned. The Commissioner folder the letter in his hand and tucked it into his jacket pocket. "Sheriff, we're finished here." He turned to go, looked at Stan and said, "You've used your last marker."

Sondra held out her hand for Stan and Jay to remain. When the Commissioner was gone, she said, "Jay, did you tell them that? Chris and Annie? That a cat sent an email?"

"I told them that's what Jenny said."

"What was their reaction?"

"They just looked at one another and said something like, "Tiger Lily learned a new trick."

Sondra motioned through the window for Christine to come in. When she entered and closed the door, Sondra said, "For the sake of everyone involved, let's not mention anything about cats. Erase the tapes; destroy your interview notes and any other notes you have mentioning feline detectives. If you want to file charges against me for ordering this, so be it. I'll hire Mr. Kranski here to represent me."

31: Cameroon

Mr. Jones left the hotel for the rendezvous point. Now, timing would be critical. They had to get the hostages and as many team members to the airport – under wraps, so to speak – before anyone from Boko Haram could raise an alarm.

At the rendezvous, a safe house on the west end of Maroua, Brown and his team waited with the hostages and the taxi driver. The driver, Mr. Jones knew his name to be Bertrand, was safely secured with duct tape. His mouth was trussed to his neck and shoulders. His upper and lower arms and hands were held to the sides of his body. His legs were taped from hips to ankles.

Mr. Jones didn't waste time. He turned to Henrie and Collette. "Do you see how he is trussed? Yes? When you go into the bags, assume you are trussed the same way. Do not move. You will leave as sides of beef. Do you understand?"

They nodded, and Jones turned to Brown. "Are your men ready?"

"Yes. They're with the bags in the van. Let's move."

Jones and Brown picked up the taxi driver. Jones said, "Follow us."

In the van, they made short work of bagging Bertrand, Henrie and Collette. As they finished, Smith and his team arrived with another man.

Brown said, "Here's the tape. Get him ready."

Smith and his men did, while Jones readied bags for the men. "We're set for everyone except me, Brown and one other man. They'll slip in right before take-off. Get yourselves inside a bag. Let's go. Who's driving the reefer with the real beef?"

Brown answered, "I am. Follow me to the airport."

Henrie wished he had said "I love you" to Grand-mère. He wished he had said "I love you" to Collette. He wished he had listened to the State Department.

He wasn't positive he knew what was happening, but it appeared these men worked for the State Department or some other United States agency. The man they called Jones appeared to be in charge.

He understood the premise without asking questions. He, Collette, Bertrand, several agents and perhaps another prisoner were to be smuggled into a helicopter, then possibly out to Yaoundé. He dared say nothing. He had to hope Collette was managing well.

The van stopped. Henrie heard Jones – it sounded like Jones but his manner was completely different – talk to a group of different men. He heard, "… sides of beef… payment… told me to take care of you… ready to go… want to help?... we'll handle it… next time."

Henrie listened as a large truck seemed to move into place. He heard sounds of mechanical loading or unloading. The doors to the back of the van opened, and Henrie listened as bags from this vehicle were unloaded by hand.

Soon, it was his turn. He forced his body to go stiff and didn't make a sound as his bag was thrown into a pile. Was it into another vehicle? Into the helicopter? He did not know.

He heard the van start up again and drive a short distance away, then stop. The helicopter powered up, and two people jumped in.

No one spoke until they were in the air and moving in what Henrie could only hope was a southerly direction.

Eventually, he heard voices. The two men who had jumped on before take-off opened the bags, one at a time, and helped people to their feet. He heard Collette say, "Thank you, bless you, thank you. Where's Henrie?"

Eventually, Henrie was free as well. He said, "Sincere thanks, sir, for your help," and he pulled Collette into his arms.

He saw Bertrand, now sitting up but still trussed. He could not bring himself to say a word. Not a kind word, not an unpleasant one. He looked away and vowed not to look back.

32: Chelsea

Honey Bear crouched behind a display at Mr. Bean's Confectionary. He hated to hide from Nancy, but he wasn't sure what she would do if he came out. He wanted to be a hero when Pete arrived, but maybe he was a scaredy cat after all.

Moriah seemed to understand. She moved behind the display and whispered, *"I think this is going to be good. You can't hide in here. You brought the clue all the way from the Inn. No one else could have done that."*

Honey Bear looked at her.

"It's big and heavy. No one else – well, maybe Simon Finnegan could have – but he's busy getting Pete. So it was up to you."

Honey Bear started to feel a little better. He sat up. *"You're right. Anyone else would have to drag it to Pete. When he gets here, I can carry it and put it in his hand."*

"That's right. Your mom will understand. Come on out."

He did as she said. He stood, and leaving the clue behind the display, he walked out. Nancy was busy. She talked to Isabel about bread and breakfast and candy.

Then Cheryl came in, and everyone looked at a woman the cats didn't know. And then Simon Finnegan, Oscar McMurphy and Cyril led Pete into Mr. Bean's. Now it would begin.

Pete took in the situation. Nancy, Cheryl, some woman with a computer, Isabel behind the counter, and several cats with little Tillie. "Does someone want to tell me why Cyril thought it so important to drag me here?"

Nancy said, "Well, Pete, we think we just uncovered a little something. Have a seat." She turned to Isabelle. "Do you think we can have coffee and maybe some of those chocolate macaroons all around?"

Nancy decided to continue with introductions. "This is the Chief of Police, Pete. And this," pointing to Cheryl, who pulled up a chair, "is Cheryl, the owner of The Marina, right down there." She pointed. "My name's Nancy, I'm connected to the KaliKo Inn at the end of the street, and your name is?"

"Sally…"

"Sally. You have concerns about a land deal happening at the State Park. Right?"

Sally nodded.

Nancy turned to Pete, "So what we have, Pete, is a situation. All of a sudden, the state is down here discussing selling every inch of park property in Chelsea to an investor from – where's he from, Sally?"

"Texas."

"Texas. And at the same time, an investor from Boston is coming to discuss the purchase of The Marina, The Escape and Cheryl's house, conveniently located at the edge of the south side of the state park."

"And you want me to do what, exactly?"

Honey Bear jumped to the top of the table, a notebook in his mouth.

"I declare," said Nancy. "My baby is here with a notebook. And isn't it strange that one of our guests was concerned about a notebook that had been stolen?"

Pete took the notebook from Honey Bear. He opened it and read, slowly, page by page.

Finally, unable to wait any longer, Nancy said, "Pete? What does it say?"

"It says," said Pete, turning another page, "your guest is a shill for someone, and they're looking to buy up everything. Everything. The park, The Marina, everything on The Avenue, that historic lighthouse museum, city park property… you name it."

"Who is he fronting for?"

"I don't know, but I imagine some of these names and telephone numbers will lead me to someone."

Sally said, "So the man – this Texan that wants to buy the park – isn't really the buyer? He's buying for someone else? Isn't all of this illegal?"

"I don't know," said Pete, "but now that we know the overall plan, we may be able to stop them. Do you have any influence with the state?"

"I'm getting ready to have influence with my boss. I'm gonna tell him…"

"Wait, now," said Pete. "We need to stop the sale but not necessarily alert anyone that we're on to them. Can you get him over here for a chat?"

"I can."

Sally reached for her cell phone and made a call. "Joe? Can you meet me over here at the bakery? … It's important. … Don't tell that Texan you're coming, just excuse yourself. … I'm saving your sad political behind, that's what I'm doing."

She closed her phone and said, "He's on his way."

Honey Bear accepted the love of his mother and jumped down to join the other cats. Moriah was the first to greet him. *"See? No one else could have done that, and your mom was pretty great about it."*

"You're right. Maybe I don't have to worry about getting locked up any more."

Simon Finnegan said, *"You did pretty good, but remember, Tiger Lily left me in charge."*

Oscar McMurphy hissed, *"Us! She left US in charge!"*

Honey Bear shook his head. *"I learned this week how hard it is to coordinate an investigation. I'm going to be kinder to Tiger Lily."*

Tillie said, *"It's hard. It really is. Especially when everybody has ideas. She has to decide which are good ones and which are stinko."*

Cyril added, *"We all help, and we all have our skills. Right now, one of my skills is that I can bark loud and get Jock over here. If The Escape is back, I'll try to get him. He needs to know what's happening."*

"How are you going to get out?" asked Speckles. The cat doors fit everyone in the room except Cyril.

"I'll pretend I have to refresh myself."

Cyril knocked Pete on the knee and walked to the door, looking back. That always worked. He trotted down the street to the farthest corner of the KaliKo Inn, the point closest to The Marina. He barked three times. Jock answered with one sharp bark, and in a couple of minutes, he arrived at the Inn. Cyril said, *"Come with me to Mr. Bean's. We've got important news."*

As they trotted to Mr. Bean's, Cyril said, *"Your mom is there."*

"That's okay," said Jock. *"They know I come to town by myself every now and then."*

Cheryl rose to let the dogs in. "Jock, what are you doing here? Is Ray…"

The dogs went to the corner while she looked down the street. No Ray.

Quickly, and talking over one another, the cats and Tillie filled Jock in.

"That's great. It's nice to know I won't lose my home. I know Ray will be happy, too. What are the humans doing about it?"

Oscar McMurphy joined the group. She had been sitting at Pete's feet, listening in. *"They're going to play a game. Those state people, they're going to pretend that they're putting the sale through, but they have to draw up some paperwork. And Cheryl said she and Ray will pretend to be real excited about selling."*

"Then what?" asked Daryll.

"I'm not sure. I think they're still working on that. The guy from Texas is staying in a hotel in Marsh Haven, and the Boston lady is staying at the Inn. The fake Frenchie is leaving the Inn this afternoon. So whatever they do, it won't be all at one time to all three of them."

Nancy and Cheryl walked to the Inn with some of the cats and Jock. Oscar McMurphy and Simon Finnegan went home for supper, and Moriah went to the flower shop. She had been missing her mother, Clara.

Nancy said, "I'm certain our children have been working together on this, even though we didn't know it."

"I never know what Jock is up to. And Honey Bear! Wow! He came up with the book that tied it all together!"

Nancy saw an urban taxi pull into the driveway. "Oh, look! It's our Boston friend."

A man with a Texas accent called the number in New York. "The talks are goin' good here. State folks seem mighty anxious to make a deal."

"Did you close it?"

"Not today. They told me they had the paperwork together and ready, but a sharp-eyed woman caught an error. They're going to fix it and I'll sign things tomorrow morning."

"What kind of an error?"

"She said the survey was wrong and didn't include some of the beachfront and that acreage on the south side."

"Well, I guess it's good they caught it. I would have preferred getting it signed today."

"We want it to be correct. Anyway, I have an appointment for ten o'clock."

"Get it signed."

"Yes, ma'am."

Nancy and Cheryl got to the door at the same time as the woman. "Hello. Welcome to the KaliKo Inn. I'm Nancy. Are you Stella?"

"I am. I'm so happy you had a room for me. I want to get settled, then I need to go to The Marina. I see it's just across the way, here."

"It is, but better than that, this is Cheryl, the owner. She can walk you over after you settle in."

Stella turned to greet Cheryl. "I'm so pleased to meet you. I didn't realize you knew I was staying here."

"Purely an accident, I assure you," said Cheryl. "We happened to be at the bakery at the same time." She held up a bag and continued, "We'll have some of the best cookies Chelsea has to offer."

Nancy said, "And I went to the bakery to order breads and other foods in your honor. Tomorrow at breakfast, you'll think you're still in Boston."

"How nice."

The taxi driver came to the porch with Stella's luggage. "Say, I'm supposed to pick someone up. Some guy named Lewis?"

Nancy laughed. "That's Loo-ee. It's French."

"Oh, Okay. Do you know if he's ready to go?"

"Come on in. We'll find out," said Nancy, and she opened the door for everyone to go in.

Louis waited in the foyer. He stood as they entered and noticed the driver carrying luggage. "Yes. You are the taxi? You take me now?"

"Yes. I'll just take your luggage. Come on out when you're ready."

Nancy asked, "Did you get checked out, Louis?"

"I did, yes. George handled it for me. Thank you for your hospitality."

"Don't mention it. We enjoyed listening to your accent. Tell me, were you successful? Did you find a location?"

"There are possibilities. Nothing came to fruit with this visit. Hopefully fruit next time."

"You're coming back? Will we have the pleasure of your company?"

"I believe so, yes. I will make the call. Thank you again." Louis nodded to each woman in turn and left.

Nancy turned to Stella. "Why don't we get you checked in, and I'll show you to your room. Then you can spend your afternoon with Cheryl."

Candice and George were in the kitchen when Nancy was finally free. George wondered why Nancy looked so impossibly happy while he felt such despair. To her credit, Nancy noticed.

"George, what's happening with Henrie?"

"I don't have a clue. We got the call this morning, Ian transferred three million, and we have heard nothing."

Candice said, "I tried to make him go to bed for a while, but he wouldn't…"

"…couldn't…"

"…he couldn't go to sleep. So here we are, drinking coffee. Well, he's drinking coffee. I've had enough to keep me awake for a week."

"I'm so sorry, George. And I'm sorry I wasn't here to check Louis out."

"That's okay. It was just a signature and keys. He didn't charge anything else."

Nancy shook her head. "I just don't know what to say about Henrie. I can't help but think it will turn out alright. It has to turn out alright."

"I wish I shared your optimism," said George. "Maybe I'm just too tired."

"You are. Maybe this will make you feel better. You may wonder why I'm so, um, happy?"

"I was wondering."

"Well, by luck, we had a gathering of crows. Oh, don't look at me like that, George. I'll explain everything. But first of all, you'll be happy to know there will be no resort. At least, not one anywhere near Chelsea."

"That's good, but why not?"

"Let me start at the beginning."

"That would be good."

"First of all, the woman you asked me to call for booking is already here. She's from Boston, supposedly…"

"Supposedly?"

"Yes. She has the accent, but her reason for being here is suspect. She didn't say this when she called, but I ran into Cheryl at Mr. Bean's, and the reason she is here is to purchase The Marina, The Escape, their businesses and even their house."

Candice cried, "They're selling?"

"No, they aren't. Just hang on a minute. It's confusing. Just before Cheryl came in, a woman who works for some agency with the state came in, and we learned that a man from Texas is here to buy the state park. All of it, including all lake-front access."

Nancy stopped, George thought, to make sure they were tracking. He looked at Candice. "That's everything surrounding The Avenue, hundreds of acres inland north and south, and all of the lake-front except the town park."

Nancy nodded. "And there's more. My Honey Bear found a notebook that…"

George cut in, "A notebook? About yay big?" He motioned with his hands.

"Yes. Louis said something to me about it. He wondered if it could have been stolen from his room."

"It was. It was stolen by Clara's cat."

"What? Honey Bear didn't take it?"

"No. I saw – what's her name? Moriah? – in the back hallway. She was dragging it down the hall, but it was almost as big as she was. I thought it was a toy of some sort."

"Never assume when it comes to those cats. Like me. Honey Bear handed it over to Pete, and I assumed he took it. It must have been a team effort."

"He gave it to Pete?"

"Yes. According to Pete, the notes detail a plan that has various people coming in to buy up everything. The city park, Annie's businesses, well, everything on The Avenue. The real buyer is unknown."

"But we have one of them here now?"

"We do, and she's going to get a proper Boston breakfast tomorrow, even though she probably doesn't know what that is."

"And this is making you happy?"

"Yes. The state has been informed, so they won't sell. Cheryl and Ray have been informed, so they won't sell. There will be no reason for any of them to come back."

"Just like that?"

"Just like that. Well, the state, Cheryl and Ray are going to play along, but eventually there will be legitimate reasons they can't go through with the sale. For example, the state is going to come up with a survey problem that can't be solved. And Cheryl said they can discover a clause in her parents' will. Maybe they can't sell unless it's to a public entity, and that it must remain public into perpetuity."

"So they won't know why…"

"Right. They'll just have to look somewhere else."

George stared at Nancy. Then he said, "Tell me about these cats, Nancy. How did they get to be so…magical?"

"They are magical, all right. And you can't say anything about it. Do you understand?"

33: Lavender Lake

Tiger Lily had planted herself at the window closest to the door and was not about to move. From time to time, she heard plaintive pleas for food or water. Every now and then, she turned to look at the cat food dishes. They were still nearly full. Big babies.

Suddenly, she sat straight up. *"They're here! Mommy and Chris are here!"*

Cats and Sis crowded around to look out the window, then they crowded around the door, clamoring to be the first to be recognized.

Annie and Chris paid attention to every cat and Sis as they came in, with pets, hugs, kisses and exclamations. Tiger Lily watched from the windowsill.

When each "child" had received attention, Annie and Chris stood. They looked at Tiger Lily, still on the windowsill. Tiger Lily anticipated a lecture. She mind-read a tongue-lashing – which would be totally out of character – for touching a piece of electronic equipment.

What she got was the opposite. Annie walked over slowly and held out her arms. Tiger Lily backed up a little, unsure, but she allowed herself to be picked up and hugged tightly.

"Big girl, when did you learn how to use the computer?"

Tiger Lily couldn't answer; Annie held her too tightly. Annie moved to the table, where Chris touched the screen to bring the computer to life. It was still set to email.

Chris pulled up the last message in the sent folder. It was addressed to Jenny. "The message line clearly says 'help.' If Jenny stood back and looked at this for a minute, she could see 'mommy arrested.'"

Annie pulled back and looked Tiger Lily in the face. "Did your siblings help?"

Tiger Lily blinked once.

"Several of them?"

One blink.

"You knew how to spell. Who knew how to send email?"

Mo jumped to the top of the table.

Chris asked, "Was that you, Mo?"

Mo blinked once. His blink had 'sexy' written all over it.

"And did others help, too?"

Tiger Lily and Mo both blinked once. One blink was still sexy.

Annie took a minute to hug each of her children individually, then said, "I have to make a call. Then let's have one last bathroom break, and we're getting on the road. We need to get out of here!"

Rather than dirty up the litter, the cats followed Sis out the door to refresh themselves in the grass. And to say a last good-bye to their new friends.

Chipper came to the edge of the tree line and chattered for everyone. *"Good-bye good luck have a great trip come back and see us sometime Ms. Bunny wants that Mo to come here for a little hug can he do that oh here he comes get out here so he can hug you don't let anybody else get murdered near you we won't* be there to help oh the mice want you to say hello to their cousin Brown Mousie has to be their cousin oh you have to go good-bye!"*

In the car, cats settled around Sis and prepared to be on the road for several hours. As Chris backed out, he stopped, said "Wait! I forgot something!"

He ran into the cabin and came back with a plastic bag in his hand.

He opened the back end. From across the seat, Tiger Lily watched him open the cooler and put the bag inside. When he got into the car, he said, "We almost forgot the morels."

34: Chelsea

Sam rocked back and forth, back and forth. The big rocker on the front porch had not seen much use this year, but the warm spring day drew him out.

He was tired of spending all day every day at the Inn, but he didn't want to go anywhere. He might slip, and word about Henrie would get out.

Today was Thursday. Henrie was due home late tonight, and they had heard nothing since early morning. Chances were that he was not able to get on the plane, he would not be home as scheduled, and it would get out anyway.

That would be a nightmare.

The State Department would take over and all activity would come to a standstill. Perhaps all activity had already done that.

Money was sent, then nothing. Sam fought back the urge to think that Henrie and Collette were already dead. Going to the negative was not like him, but he had no incentive at this moment to think about the positive.

The cellphone in his pocket rang. Startled out of his reverie, he answered.

"Sam? Why do you have Mom's phone?"

"Oh, hello, Annie-girl. Your mom needed a rest. I took her phone away from her. Is everything okay up there?"

"We're on our way home. It's a long story, so I'll wait until we get there to tell it. Hopefully one time. How's everything there? What's happening with Henrie?"

"We don't know anything." Sam struggled to keep the despair out of his voice. "George talked to him early this morning, had the money sent from the bank – tell Chris it was three million – and we haven't heard a thing. Ian said the money went to the right place, if George had the numbers right, that is. At least it was a legitimate account. We've heard nothing since."

"He was supposed to be on his way back today."

"We know, honey. We just have to hope that everything is going to be alright."

"I hate I wasn't there."

"There was nothing you could have done. George handled everything. No one could have done it better. You know George."

"Yeah. How is everyone doing there? You said Mom is sleeping?"

"Everyone has taken on a little more than they thought they would have to. We have a few stories to tell, too. Anyway, I'm making your mother sleep, and Candice is supposed to be making sure George gets a nap. Or something."

"Maybe the or something. At least he's relaxing. But he has the phone with him, right?"

"Right. And yours is still off, right?"

"Yes, Sam. Chris keeps it in his pocket. It probably doesn't have any battery left now anyway."

"That's my girl. How are all the cats? And that big dog?"

"Sleeping now. They've been busy. They had to solve a murder and help Chris and I get out of jail."

"I guess we're going to have a nice, long story hour when you get home. What time will it be, do you think?"

"Maybe close to midnight. I don't want to wake anyone. George is probably in Henrie's apartment. Are you and Mom staying there?"

"Yep. We're in your apartment, but we can…"

Annie cut him off. "No! Don't go. When we get back we can sleep in one of the rooms. Oh, are any of the rooms empty?"

"Let me see…we just sent that family packin'. They had all of the rooms on the second floor, and we filled one of those today. We have reservations for, oh, well, those other rooms will be filled tomorrow. Best not use them. That Frenchie guy left; he was in the back room. No one is going in there for a few days."

"Perfect. Don't wait up for us. We'll just take all our luggage into the back room."

"Okay. Tell Chris to drive safe."

"I will. And Sam? Thank you. Call me if you hear from Henrie."

"Okay, honey."

George had finally fallen asleep. He didn't hear Georgia load up Little Fred and the cats. He didn't hear Hilly leave. He didn't hear the woman "from Boston" come back from The Marina. He didn't hear Candice leave and Jenny arrive. He didn't hear JoJo's television on the floor below. He didn't hear Annie, Chris and the kids come in.

He did hear the telephone ring.

Before Jenny could get to it, he rolled over, picked up the receiver and answered. "George, um, KaliKo Inn."

Henrie's voice came over loud and clear. "I hope I have not awakened you, George. Henrie here. We are in New York and will be home tomorrow."

"Thank God!" cried George, wide awake now. Jenny ran into the bedroom, the other receiver to her ear. She didn't speak, though, leaving that to George.

"I have so many questions, Henrie, but first, are you alright? Is Collette?"

"We are fine. We suffered nothing but lack of personal care."

"Don't tell me more than I need to know."

Henrie laughed softly. "I will not. I cannot stay on the line; we must board. Please let Chris know – I assume he supplied the funds – that all will be returned. Full funds are in the hands of Embassy personnel. Also assure everyone, including the felines, that I will be home soon."

"I can't wait."

"I am sure you cannot. And now, may I ask you about taking over for me while I take a vacation to recover from my vacation?"

"No. Never. Not ever. I'm done."

35: Chelsea

Annie saw dollar bills fly through the air, out of her pocket and into a deep black hole.

It had finally happened.

The cat, so to speak, was out of the bag.

She now had round-the-clock protection for the cats. A security guard escorted each of them to "work" every day. That was the only solution. She couldn't lock them in the Inn for doing good work.

Local, regional and national media crowded the streets and pushed into all of her businesses. The cats were a sensation! They could spell! They could write! Send emails!

Not long ago, two of the cats were kidnapped and a relatively modest amount requested in ransom. Now, if she weren't careful, they would be kidnapped and held as novelties or ransomed for millions.

Tiger Lily's life was a nightmare. She was continually asked to "do tricks," like read, write, or send email from a cellphone. She had moved from her hostess stand to the barista's bar. She nodded hello from that distance and jumped to the floor behind the bar when reporters and well-wishers crowded Trudie's area.

Little Socks was hounded to perform her signature yoga pose. She had done it so often, her behind was always squeaky clean. She could no longer nap on the windowsill and had to make do with a yoga mat behind the front desk.

Guests reserved rooms at the KaliKo Inn just to get selfies with the big girls. They chased them all over, and when a hiding place was discovered, it was posted on the web's comment section. They were running out of places to get away.

Mo actually hid from men and women wanting to give him affection. George moved bottles around to allow him space behind the vodka. His tail drooped, he hung his head. He lost his "sexy," perhaps never to be found again.

Sassy Pants had given up requesting rubs on her tummy. Too many of the inquisitive people were rough, probably without meaning to be. She didn't chase bottle corks, and she spent as much of her day as possible hiding in Minnie's office. Brown Mousie joined her, so she didn't have to be alone.

Mr. Bean no longer danced in the window. He left that to Tillie. He didn't care if customers came into the bakery and probably wouldn't for the rest of his life. He hid behind the bakery counter, and Carlos, Jerry and Isabel stepped on his toes or his tail several times a day.

Even Sis suffered. She had been shy and hesitant before. Now, she was reclusive. Chris couldn't get her to leave the condominium except for a morning and evening run to refresh herself.

Annie and Chris fended off reporters and publicity hounds. Her businesses suffered financially. With the exception of the Inn, they were full, always full, of non-paying customers.

Everyone's life was a nightmare. She would have to sell, to move. Life would never be the same.

Chris shook her gently by the shoulder. "Annie? Annie, wake up. They're waiting for us."

"What? What day is it?"

"It's Monday. We're having the block party tonight."

"Oh. Right. Everything is back to normal."

"Yeah. Were you having a nightmare?"

"I think so. I can't remember it, but it had something to do with the cats. And money."

"Money?"

"Flying through the air, I think."

"What was the nightmare? You couldn't catch it?"

"I don't know. The bad news is that I don't remember my good dreams. The good news is that I don't remember the bad ones, either."

"Well, get up and get moving. I think you're helping to set up the temporary tattoo parlor."

To Annie, it didn't seem as if ten days had passed. So much had happened in the space of a few days that time now passed like a rocket.

At the tattoo parlor – a tent with tables, several chairs and an impressive array of tattoos from which to choose – she stocked three easels with tattoos. Teenagers took care of the furniture. She worked alone, listened to their chatter, and mused on the past two weeks.

The biggest news to Annie was that Henrie and Collette made it home safely. To most people in town, the biggest news was that there had been a problem in the first place.

Thank goodness the cats were not a news item. Annie's first telephone call out of jail was to Jenny. She replayed the conversation now.

"Jenny, thank you for Mr. Kranski. You were right; I was wrong. We were in trouble."

"I'm glad I could help, really, but Annie, what's up with those cats?"

"That's my real reason for calling, Jenny. Have you said anything to anyone? Besides Mr. Kranski, I mean?"

"No. I've been in court all day."

"Thank goodness. Listen, I promise to tell you everything, but you cannot say anything about this to anyone. Do you understand?"

"Seriously? You could make a lot of money…"

Annie had cut her off at that point. "Jenny! Please, tell no one. Let's get together tomorrow or the day after. I'll tell you everything."

Annie and the kids were safe, wrapped in the cloak of attorney-client privilege.

Ian marshalled his considerable resources once again to help with the block party. Teens continually clamored to be part of his after-school-hours training sessions, but he had stipulations. First, report cards had to be presented as proof their grades were in order. Second, he required fifty community volunteer hours per year.

An easy way to fit in his volunteer requirements – with everything else required of high schoolers – was to help at each community block party. If they helped at each one, six times a year, they could easily meet the fifty-hour requirement. Especially if they helped with set up or clean up. They were allowed to work any booth that was not alcohol-related.

Every other month, on the last day of the month, Chelsea held a community block party. Each one was different, depending on the time of year, and they were held in the semi-private park behind Annie's businesses, on the beach, on the second floor of Tiger Lily's Café, which was a catering venue, or at the KaliKo Inn.

The party on the last day of April was generally planned for the semi-private park, with plans to downsize and move to the catering venue in the event of rain.

Several features were sacrosanct. They were free to everyone. Children's food and games were provided. Each was dedicated to a specific charity; the charity this month was Autism Research.

Alena, a sharp-witted teen who once acquitted herself admirably with a bike-riding would-be murderer, preferred to work at the fund-raising booth. She planned it, produced design elements and worked the day of the party.

This year, she took over the management of community donation jars as well. Every business on The Avenue and most others around town had a donation jar on the month preceding every block party. This year, Alena involved children and youth from each class of Chelsea Public Schools. From Kindergarten to Seniors, each class designed a container to accept donations.

To make it meaningful for the children, she gained teacher support to help the students deliver, monitor and pick up the donations. This allowed them to keep track of the amounts received in their own jars.

Tiger Lily particularly liked the jar at the Café. Designed by the third grade, they used a large coffee can covered with photographs of a local child living with autism.

Every day, Tiger Lily watched the donations grow. As guests left, she could often be seen with a paw on the jar, an admonition for everyone to make an appropriate contribution.

Annie, the unofficial chairperson of the event, watched Tiger Lily one day and turned to Felicity. "We need to ask Ian to encourage this every year. I think the kids' jars are gathering more money than ever before."

"You're right. We had to ask the teachers to step up the collections. They were picking up once a week, like we always did. This month, they have to pick up two times. Most of the classes come now on Tuesday and Friday."

While the coins added up, Alena worked on her booth. She decided on temporary tattoos. She found an inexpensive vendor, gathered necessary supplies and made signs. She worked with Ian and Annie on the budget.

At their meeting, Annie said, "We can afford this. What we'll do is ask for contributions, because we never ask for money. Particularly from a child."

Alena handed Ian and Annie a list. "These are the kids that will help at the booth. We practiced on ourselves." She turned her forearm toward Annie and Ian to reveal a blue, pink and yellow butterfly, perfectly edged.

"That's lovely! When did you do it?"

"Two days ago. The company recommended a lotion to use as soon as the tattoo dries, and that helps it to stay. The most important things are to clean the skin, take your time putting it on, take your time removing the paper, and make sure the kids sit still for ten minutes."

"That will be the hardest thing."

"We're going to have an incentive. We'll put a timer by each resting chair, and when it goes off, we'll put on the lotion and let them pick out something free. If they don't wait, they don't get the freebie. And their tattoo will dissolve pretty quickly."

"What are the freebies?"

"Depends on the age. Bubbles, stuffed animals, school supplies, dolls, matchbox vehicles, board games... stuff like that. Adults are just going to have to suck it up and wait without an incentive. Unless they want bubbles."

"Where did you find the stuff?"

"The box store promised them. We used the manager's son as a poster child for one of the donation jars."

"Good work, Alena," said Ian. "I need to use you to train future fundraisers. I might add that to my list of activities."

Henrie and Felicity worked together at the food and drinks tent. As they set up hot and cold areas, condiments, plates, glasses and straws, Felicity pressed for information.

"Come on, Henrie. What happened? No one knew a thing. Well, in the middle of the week, we started asking about George, why he wasn't at the bar, but Candice just put it off to the guests from perdition."

"I heard about them. I believe George was on trial by fire. He did as well or better than I could have done."

"And you didn't answer my question."

Henrie was not able to bring humor into a conversation about his ordeal, nor had he spoken to anyone about it, with the exception of Annie and Chris. Except for George. He owed George that much. Now, ten days later, he sighed. He would have to broach the subject at some point.

Starting with Felicity made sense. Not too long ago, he and Felicity shared rides to and from the city, both going to meet lovers. He became a friend to hers, and Felicity became a friend to Collette.

Henrie took a deep breath and began. "I believe I made a dreadful mistake, and in deciding upon a reckless course of action, I involved someone very dear to me. The mistake, of course, was to travel to a region of the world that is declared by the State Department to be dangerous. I shudder to think what would have happened if they had not become involved."

"What did they do, exactly? What happened?"

"You are aware I intended to visit Grand-mère."

"Yes. Your mother's mother."

"Yes."

"Was she well? Did your visit go as planned?"

"Yes. We saw her every day. One day, she accompanied Collette and I to the village of my childhood. I barely remembered it; I was so young when we left Cameroon. She introduced us to my relatives, to friends of the family. I was pleasantly surprised to find Grand-mère in reasonably good health. She has lived fifteen to twenty years beyond her peers."

"How has she done that? Good genes?"

"Partially, and partially due to an easier lifestyle as she aged. Distressing, however, was the state of her wheelchair. I confess I did not think to ask after the state of the chair. I recall the conversation in which she told me of the acquisition. She was so happy to have it, I did not question the condition."

"How bad was it?"

"Deplorable. No other word can describe the monstrosity. While in New York, waiting to board the plane home, I ordered a better chair to be delivered."

"Electronic?"

"No. Nothing so fancy. She would be flummoxed with a chair with power. I ordered a simple chair with basic equipment. One that will not stand out in the environment."

"You don't want it to stand out? Would a delivery of that nature stand out?"

"Yes. I took the precaution of having the chair delivered to our hotel. Yannick, the manager, will see to the delivery in a more private manner."

"You have yet to address my question."

"I believe the question was about the State Department. You asked what they did. They went against their prohibition of dealing with kidnapped citizens. They did not do so for me or for Collette. They did so because an opportunity presented to reach into a new terrorist cell. I believe that is their term."

"And you are safe because of it."

"Yes. On the one hand, I could be angry with myself for causing them the time, trouble and expense. On the other hand, the hand I choose to select, I presented an opportunity they desired to accept."

"And you, Henrie. Are you alright?"

Henrie sighed. "Let me say this, Felicity. While no physical harm came to Collette or to me, we were damaged emotionally. The damage may be permanent. To look at us, to talk to us, one would notice nothing amiss. To live inside our skins, however, is another thing. For my part, I may never be able to forgive myself for making what was an atrociously ill-thought decision."

Felicity was silent for several minutes. Finally, she said, "How are the two of you? I mean, together? How is the relationship?"

"For the moment, we are on a break."

"I'm sorry to hear that Henrie."

"As am I."

Ramon and his jazz fusion band, Bergamasco, set up at the far end of the park, the end abutting the outdoor dining section of Sassy P's. They had help from Ramon's dog, a Bergamasco named Fiamma. And Cyril. And Jock. They vied for the attention of the flirty dreadlocked and matted canine. Today, however, Fiamma seemed to prefer the company of Sis.

Clara mentioned the issue as she brought bottled water to the band members. "Why is it those boys look so sad? And why is it the girls are over there, behind the drums?"

Ramon laughed. "I think she is playing with their heart strings. Either that, or she is weary of the game. She likes that giant schnauzer. You couldn't find two big dogs that looked less alike."

"Kind of like me and Moriah. Oh, look. Moriah's over there with them. She's so small I didn't see her."

"Small? Well, I guess that's a matter of perception. She is short, I'll give you that. I'm glad they get along, though. I'd hate to be kicked out from my one week a month home because my dog and your cat didn't play nice together."

"I think my cat has special skills."

"Say what?"

"We haven't had time to talk yet. Well, not about the pets."

Ramon's schedule kept him on the road three weeks of the month. He and the band arrived this morning for their break. While Ramon settled in with Clara, his "empress" – she referred to him as her kòkòt, Haitian for sweetheart – the rest of the band filled the carriage house of the KaliKo Inn.

"We'll make up for that tonight. But tell me, why do you think she has skills?"

"While Annie and the cats were gone, we had a crime or two in town, and the cats that remained – including Moriah – seemed to help out. Not that he'll say anything, but Pete seems to have a sudden affinity for my baby girl."

"It could be he likes fluffy things."

"That could be, but I think it's more than that. Look at those dogs. I do believe Fiamma is teaching Sis how to toss her head."

Ramon looked. Fiamma tossed her head over her right shoulder, mats and dreadlocks swaying in the wind. Sis did the same. The hair on her jowls jiggled a little. He noticed Moriah did the same. She tossed her head, and the wind caught her mane in a fetching manner.

Ramon sighed. "Well, I guess, for the boys, it will all be a matter of perception."

Chris and Ray painted circles on the grass for lawn twister.

Chris said, "I'm past the days of playing Twister."

"No way. You're an officer in the Coast Guard. You have to be supple."

"Nah. You said it. I'm an officer. I require my minions to be supple. So tell me. How did that conversation go?"

"Which one?"

"The one where Cheryl tried to convince you to sell."

"Well, she didn't really do that. Not really. She was intrigued, and she thought we would never want for anything, even if we live past one hundred. But, no, she didn't try to convince me."

"She wanted you to, what, think about it?"

"Yeah. That."

"Do you think you would have done it?"

"No, I really don't. Even if it had just been a woman from Boston wanting our place, not some nameless person or thing wanting everything, I don't think we would have done it. She was raised at The Marina."

"Things change."

"Yes, they do."

The town cats and dogs were in a frenzy. They loved block parties. So many people, and so many of them were children! It was heaven.

When the party began to fill up, Jock and Cyril helped with the lawn twister. To define the term "help," one has to visualize the field of play. Chris and Ray painted more circles than could be found on a regular game of Twister, allowing for additional space at the end.

As body parts and circle colors were called, the two big dogs did their best to follow instructions. They were close. Sometimes.

Fiamma and Sis worked the wine bottle bowling game. Fiamma stopped to watch the boys for a minute. *"They have flexibility."*

Sis turned to look. *"Is that what it's called?"*

"Well, let's just say they bend up nicely."

Sis grabbed a tennis ball and trotted to a young girl ready for her second toss. To the girl, she said, *"That was a good one. You'll get all of them with the next toss."* The girl heard, "Yip! Bark, bark!"

Kali and Ko, who had not left Henrie's side except to eat and sleep, and eat, and sleep, and eat some more, sat under the drinks serving table. Henrie served coffee, tea and Muggles' Butterbeer, a heated drink made with ginger ale, butter, brown sugar and cinnamon. Children loved it.

Kali stretched on occasion. To the casual observer, it appeared she stretched one front paw or another. Ko knew what she was up to, though. She said, *"One of these times you're going to reach for his foot and he's going to step on you."*

"I don't care. I just want to make sure he's still here."

Mo and Simon helped at the adult beverage tent. Mo assured all the cocktail glasses were clean and the straws stocked. Simon worked with his humans at the other end of the bar. Free tastes of the latest offerings from Chateau Simon were available, and Simon's picture was on every bottle.

Mo wasn't jealous, though. He figured he still had Simon beat on the popularity scale. Well... maybe. He guessed there might be room for another boy kitty. Just one more.

Tiger Lily and Little Socks made sure the napkins didn't blow away at the food table. Unfortunately, the napkins were white.

Tiger Lily said, "You're leaving all your spring hair droppings on the napkins."

"So?"

"So, so... they're black. Everybody can see them."

"They'll be happy to have them."

"No they won't."

"Well, you stay here and sit on them, then. I'm going for a cocktail wienie."

Moriah wanted to help at the food table. White wisps of hair kept floating into the bacon and cheese wrapped dates. She moved to the adult beverages. A clump of hair landed in a town councilman's beer.

At the tattoo parlor, Alena had to ask her to stay downwind, please, your hair is getting into the wet ink.

Finally, she sat underneath the balcony of the second floor of the Café. Chris, who ceded his position at lawn twister to Pete, sold his paintings and sketches here, with all proceeds going to the autism charity.

He watched the little cat for a while and decided she looked sad. He pulled a chair close to her, bent down and picked her up. She curled into his lap, grateful that someone would show her attention.

"Have all the other cats found something to do?"

She purred.

"Are you looking for something special? Something that only you can do?"

She looked into his eyes and purred louder.

"I have just the thing. I need a model to sit for a painting. Sometimes that helps art sales. Not that everyone would want a picture of you... well, everyone should want a picture of you... but they can see how much something I paint looks like the model. Are you willing?"

Moriah looked around, spied the easel, and hopped to a table nearby.

"That's it. Strike a pose for me."

Moriah fluffed her pretty mane, licked a front paw, fluffed her main again and posed. She gazed up and to the right, front feet planted on either side of her chubby little self, wind picking up the hair of her mane ever so slightly. Still in a seated position, she raised her tail and curled it just a touch over her back. The wind picked that up as well.

Chris smiled, chose a brush and a color palette, and painted. He was only halfway through when the number of people gathered around blocked the light from his work. He stopped, turned and talked to the admirers about the things he could do to memorialize their cats, dogs, gerbils, gold fish, turtles and lizards. Even children.

While Chris talked to the crowd, Daryll pushed through and shouted, *"Moriah? Moriah? Come with me?"*

Moriah jumped down and followed. Daryll led her to the nursery tent. *"Come in here? Speckles and I will teach you how to be a nanny kitty? You might like it?"*

Moriah watched as Speckles and Daryll moved slowly and deliberately around the tent, brushing their tails against the little balled fists of young ones crying or unhappy. They allowed their tails to be held until the young one was quiet, then slipped away to another. Moriah marveled at their talent and thought, *"I can do this."*

She added her voluminous tail to the mix and helped calm the babies.

Chris carried a cooler into the kitchen of the Inn. As he walked through the dining room he paused. "Annie, what happened here?"

He was looking at the detective table. Instead of the large sign and the smaller one that sat on top of the table, one framed sign hung on the wall. A header proclaimed, "Detective Agency." The text beneath said, "Felines & Canines On Duty 24/7. Inquire Within."

"Oh, that. Henrie decided he couldn't keep changing the number on the signs as more cats and dogs joined the agency. He made it all-inclusive."

"Huh. I guess that includes Sis?"

"It does."

Sis seemed to emphasize the point. She lay at the foot of the table, stuck her head beneath the cloth, sighed, and took a nap.

Chris turned on the news as they got ready for bed. Their least favorite roving reporter, Dan Tapper, was on the air. He reported from a campground up north.

"Annie, look. Dan Tapper's at Lavender Lake."

Annie looked up from her lapful of cats and stared. "Is it about the murder?"

"No, I don't think so."

Chris turned up the volume. They heard, "…and here at the Lavender Lake Campground, a legend has come to life. It's long been rumored the Lavender Lake Wolf Man makes an appearance every ten years. The last reported appearance was ten years ago. Until last night, that is. He was seen, live and close-up, by two campers. We will have first-hand reports from those campers, coming up after this message."

Chris hit the mute button as a commercial came on.

"What do you think? Is it true?"

Tiger Lily jumped from Annie to Chris. She put her paws on his shoulders and nodded as she blinked furiously.

Thank You For Reading!

The family of cats and the author hope you enjoyed reading this book as much as we enjoyed writing it!

About The Author

Kathleen Thompson was raised on a small family farm in Indiana. She has an undergraduate degree in Sociology from Manchester College (now Manchester University) and an MBA from Indiana University South Bend.

In a variety of towns and circumstances, she served as a probation officer, parole agent and juvenile residential counselor before moving into administrative, marketing and fund raising positions in human service organizations. Ms. Thompson took a break from human services for seven years to own and operate a bar and restaurant. Let's be honest; that's another type of human service.

While making plans to return to her rural roots, Kathi and her mother discovered an injured kitten at the family farm. The kitten, whose face was a mass of injuries, decided to make Kathi her guardian. She wrapped herself around an ankle, purred like a V8 engine, and wouldn't let go.

Against the advice of her mother, Kathi took the kitten home and to a veterinarian. The vet diagnosed road burn serious enough to take all the fur from the left side of her face, and the kitten – Tiger Lily – eventually healed and took a huge piece of Kathi's heart.

Tiger Lily was joined by the rest, rescue kitties, all: Little Socks (thank you, Aunt Mary); Kali, Ko and Mo (thank you, Connie); Sassy Pants (thank you, Ant Sherwy); and Mr. Bean (thank you, Pulaski Animal Center). Recent arrivals Speckles (thank you, Tennille) and Moriah (thank you again, Pulaski Animal Center) have joined the cast but will not live at the Inn.

Tiger Lily's Café rattled around in Kathi's brain – there isn't much else up there – for all of the years since, sometimes as an actual café and sometimes as a book. It was less expensive to write the book.

Connect with Kathi and her family of cats at their website: www.tigerlilyscafe.com, or find them on Facebook: www.facebook.com/tigerlilyscafemysteries.

Find us on the web: www.tigerlilyscafe.com

Find us on Facebook: Tiger Lily's Café, A Mystery Series by Kathleen Thompson

Text to join: Emails are sent every two weeks. You can opt out at any time. LILYSCAFE to 22828 (You may also sign up for the emails from the website.)

www.ingramcontent.com/pod-product-compliance
Lightning Source LLC
Chambersburg PA
CBHW062015170626
46813CB00001B/175